M000158944

Stephanie Looked At Her For A Moment Before Speaking.

"Really? I babysat the bride when she was little." She paused. "I've never set eyes on him. But then, I was surprised when I got the invitation. I haven't talked to any of the Johnsons for quite a few years. Not since Jennifer was in middle school. I was planning on coming to this conference anyway, though, so I figured why not?"

Harriet wasn't sure what to say about that, and was glad when she was saved by their hostess.

"Okay, campers, time to add up the score for your table. The winning table will be awarded our first door prizes."

Harriet had her head bent adding up her points on the calculator function of her phone, or she might have seen what was coming. As it was, she was defenseless when the bride strode into the room from the lobby and slapped her cheek so hard she almost fell off her chair.

"Stay away from my fiancé," the woman screamed.

Lauren leaped to a protective stance over Harriet, but the woman stormed out, across the lobby and out the front doors.

Mavis stood up. "Someone call nine-one-one."

Also By Arlene Sachitano

The Harriet Truman/Loose Threads Mysteries

Quilt As Desired
Quilter's Knot
Quilt As You Go
Quilt by Association
The Quilt Before the Storm
Make Quilts Not War
A Quilt in Time
Crazy as a Quilt
Disappearing Nine Patch

The Harley Spring Mysteries

Chip and Die
Widowmaker

DOUBLE WEDDING DEATH

A Harriet Truman/Loose Threads Mystery

ARLENE SACHITANO

ZUMAYA ENIGMA   AUSTIN TX

2017

DOUBLE WEDDING DEATH

© 2017 by Arlene Sachitano

ISBN 978-1-61271-326-7

Cover art and design © April Martinez

"Zumaya Enigma" and the raven logo are trademarks of Zumaya Publications LLC, Austin TX, http://www.zumayapublications.-com/enigma.php

Library of Congress Cataloging-in-Publication Data

Names: Sachitano, Arlene, 1951- author.
Title: Double wedding death / Arlene Sachitano.
Description: Austin TX : Zumaya Enigma, 2017. | Series: A Harriet
     Truman/loose threads mystery |
Identifiers: LCCN 2017009432 (print) | LCCN 2017013223 (ebook) |
ISBN
     9781612713274 (Electronic/Kindle) | ISBN 9781612713281 (Elec-
tronic/EPUB) |
     SBN 9781612713267 (trade pbk. : alk. paper)
Subjects: LCSH: Quiltmakers--Fiction. | GSAFD: Mystery fiction.
Classification: LCC PS3619.A277 (ebook) | LCC PS3619.A277 D68
2017 (print) |
     DDC 813/.6--dc23
LC record available at https://lccn.loc.gov/2017009432

This is for Bonnie, Amy, Judy, and Sally

Acknowledgments

This book takes place at an actual appliqué conference held in Galveston, Texas. Thank you to conference organizer Sally Coble and her three friends Bonnie, Amy, and Judy for answering my many questions about the detailed workings of this endeavor. Deviations from their wonderful event were created by me for story purposes and responsibility for these are mine alone.

Thank you to the Tremont Hotel for hosting the event and providing a primary setting for my story. Thanks also to Tina's on the Strand and especially store manager Boyce for putting on an event in real life that I was able to fictionalize in my story.

I would also like to thank my family and friends for all their support and understanding when I'm off doing 'book things'. I'd especially like to thank my granddaughter Claire who along with her sister Amelia provides endless inspiration for my writing and who pointed out to me that everyone in the family but her have been mentioned in past acknowledgements.

As always I greatly appreciate the support of Linne and Jack of The Craftsman's Touch Books, as well as Deon Stonehouse of Sunriver Books and Music and Diana Portwood of Bob's Beach Books. I would also like to thank everyone at Latimer Quilt and Textile Center in Tillamook for selling my books and giving me multiple opportunities to promote them at their events.

Last but not least, thank you to Liz and Zumaya for making this all happen.

Chapter 1

Beth Carlson winced as she settled into the upholstered chair in her niece Harriet Truman's bedroom and swung her swollen foot up onto the ottoman. The five pounds and counting she'd added to her petite frame since her car accident earlier in the month were not helping her foot heal.

"Don't forget to pack a light sweater. It'll be hot outside, but the hotel will likely keep it air-conditioned where your workshop classrooms are. I know air conditioning is air conditioning, but somehow, when you're on the hot, humid Gulf Coast it seems like it's stronger or colder or something."

Harriet laughed. "I already have a cotton cardigan and a lightweight zip-front hoodie in my bag." She pointed to her open suitcase on her bed. "They have a pajama party every night in a common room so we can do our stitching homework. They told us people really do wear pajamas, but I'm not about be seen in my holey sleepshirt, so I have to come up with something to wear for that, but I think everything else is packed."

Beth glanced at her watch.

"It's barely noon. If you haven't done anything about your pajama dilemma in the next hour and a half, I may have a solution. I packed up my sewing patterns in a box and put them in the attic, back when it was my attic, before you took over the stitching business. Mavis and I made lounge pants and shorts a few years ago for a church bazaar. You could drop me at my physical therapy appointment then go to Pins and Needles and get some fabric while I do my exercises. It won't take any time at all to make you a couple of pairs of shorts or pants. You can wear them with a teeshirt and be good to go."

1

"Do you think we'll have time to make some for Lauren, too? When we talked yesterday, she didn't have anything, either, and was just planning on wearing jeans."

Beth rubbed her chin with her hand.

"Well, if Mavis is done with her own packing, and she's willing to help, we should be able to do that. You need to get hold of Lauren and make sure it's what she wants. And she'll need to pick her fabric. And we'll need to take her measurements."

Harriet pulled her phone from her pocket and began dialing Lauren while Beth grabbed the landline receiver from the nightstand and rang her friend Mavis.

✂ --- ✂ --- ✂

Lauren Sawyer came through the door of the Pins and Needles quilt store in downtown Foggy Point and joined Harriet in front of the purple fabric rack.

"Okay, if we have to use clown fabric, count me out."

Harriet rolled her eyes.

"I was on my way to the flannel shelf, but I saw you coming through the window. I'm going to do the drawstring shorts out of quilt fabric, but I think I want flannel for the long pants so I can use them when we get back."

"Good idea. Teeshirt material would have been nice, but I'm thinking Marjorie doesn't have any, and there isn't time to go anywhere else."

"Since this is the only fabric store in Foggy Point, you're probably right." Harriet said, and headed toward the flannel section at the back of the showroom.

Lauren smirked as she followed.

"I'm quick like that."

"I'm really looking forward to some time away," Harriet said as she tilted a bolt of flower-print flannel out from the rack, studied it, then slid it back in place.

Lauren ran her hands across several bolts, stopping on a brown-and-green pine-tree print.

"I just hope the other stitchers aren't too intense." She unrolled a few folds of the fabric so she could see the full repeat of the print. "I like this. It will remind me of home."

Harriet chose a green-and-brown tartan plaid.

"This won't remind me of anything, but I like it."

They walked two rows over and began the process again, this time looking at cotton fabrics.

"Did you get into the needle-turn class?" Harriet asked.

Lauren nodded as she pulled a bolt of brown with geometric patterns in black, white and green from the shelf.

"I'm not sure I know exactly what needle turn is, but I guess I'll know by the end of the week."

"I'm assuming needle turn involves turning under the edge of an appliqué piece with your needle before you stitch it to the background fabric. I chose it because it had the shortest list of supplies required."

Lauren shifted the bolt into a two-handed grasp.

"I hear you. That factored into my decision process, too, but the main thing I was looking for was the word *beginner*. I got into both of my first choices. I'll be doing the wool felt pillow for my second class. How about you?"

Harriet considered an owl print in browns and grays.

"Same."

"Do you know what Mavis and Connie are taking?"

"Given they've been quilting about a hundred more years than we have, I'm pretty sure they're taking the two classes that weren't labeled 'beginner'."

Lauren laughed. "You're probably right."

"James is excited about his cooking classes."

"We're lucky your favorite chef decided he needed to learn to cook Cajun. I'm not sure why, since he already has the most popular restaurant in my neighborhood, if not all of Foggy Point. Harriet picked up her two bolts and headed for the cutting counter at the front of the store.

"We better get moving if we're going to get these made before we go."

"Do we need elastic?"

"I have all your notions all ready up by the register," Marjorie Swain called from three rows over. She was tall and stout and had a voice that could reach all four corners of her store. "Mavis called before you got here and told me which elastics you need. She likes the one we have that has a drawstring built in. It works well for shorts and pants."

"Well, that was thoughtful of her," Lauren said.

"Yes, it was," Marjorie agreed, and took her fabric. She stopped before she set the bolt down. "You two look after the other two while you're down south. I know Mavis and Connie think they can take care of themselves, but neither one of them is a spring chicken and as worldly as they think they are, neither one of them has traveled beyond Seattle without a family member in tow for at least twenty years."

Harriet looked at Lauren.

"With what's happened in Foggy Point in the last year or two, we'll probably be safer in Galveston."

Lauren laughed.

"Or practically anywhere else."

✂ --- ✂ --- ✂

Harriet walked through the door connecting her kitchen with her long-arm quilt studio and twirled around in a pirouette.

"What do you think?" She was wearing her new long sleep pants.

Connie Escorcia stood up and circled her.

"They look great." She turned to Lauren, who was taking the plastic wrap off a tray of cut vegetables set on Harriet's large cutting table. "Are you going to model yours?"

"Harriet wasn't really doing a fashion show. You just happened to arrive during her final fitting. I did mine already, and both pairs fit fine, so no need to repeat it. And mine look great, too."

"Where are the rest of the Loose Threads?" Connie asked.

Lauren ticked off names on her fingers.

"Robin is meeting with a support group for part-time lawyers who are moms, but she's bringing rotisserie chickens from the grocery store. DeAnn had to wait for her husband to get home from baseball practice with the boys so he could watch Kissa, and then she'll be coming and bringing fruit salad. Jenny is on her way as of five minutes ago and bringing dessert. Who am I forgetting?"

"Carla?"

"She's picking up Wendy from a play date then heading over, and I can't remember what she's bringing."

Aunt Beth repositioned her foot on an ottoman Harriet had brought in from the living room.

"Be sure you transfer some of the old pictures off your phone so you'll have room to take pictures of everything in your classes and anything they'll let you photograph at the keynote speech."

Connie left the food table and came to sit beside Beth.

"Don't worry. I'm bringing my digital camera, and I already asked the organizers if the people showing their vintage quilts were allowing pictures, and they are."

Mavis Willis came in from the kitchen.

"So, what time are we leaving for Seattle tomorrow?" She glanced at Lauren and Harriet before turning to Connie.

Harriet walked over and sat down on a rolling work chair she pulled over from the cutting table.

"We probably can't check into the airport hotel until after lunch."

Lauren joined her travel companions.

4

"How about we leave at eleven-ish and then stop and eat lunch halfway?"

"Works for me," Harriet said, and Connie nodded agreement.

"Lucky for us I have a software security contract with Sea-Tac," Lauren said, referring to the computer programming work she did for the Seattle airport. "We can leave our car in the employee parking lot for free."

Connie got up and headed toward the kitchen. "That's a nice perk."

"Yeah, well, it's the least they can do after what I did for them."

Harriet looked interested.

"Do tell."

Lauren laughed. "Not a chance. It's completely classified."

"Will you two stop?" Aunt Beth scolded. "You." She looked at Harriet. "Go get out of your new pajama pants before you spill something on them. And you, missy..." She turned to Lauren. "...go into the garage and get the box of plastic cutlery and the stack of paper plates."

"Yes, ma'am," Lauren said with a salute and went to do her task.

"Are you sure you and Jorge are going to be able to take care of Scooter and Carter?" Harriet asked her aunt. Scooter, hearing his name, came over and jumped into her lap.

Beth smiled at the little dog.

"He'll be fine as long as he has Fred here with him." She stroked Harriet's fuzzy gray cat, who was currently curled up on *her* lap. "Carter is another story. I think he spends a lot of time sitting in Lauren's lap while she's working on her computer."

"I'm sure Carla or Jenny or even Rod would take him if it gets to be too much."

Aunt Beth reached over and scratched Scooter's ear.

"I'm sure Jorge and I can handle all three of them. Don't you worry."

✂ --- ✂ --- ✂

Connie groaned.

"I shouldn't have eaten that last mini lemon tart, but it was so delicious."

Jenny smiled.

"That's why I brought them here. I made them and the pecan tarts for a historical society meeting, and there were too many leftovers to tempt my husband and I."

Harriet set her empty plate on the cutting table.

"I'm counting on you guys to keep an eye on Aunt Beth while I'm gone."

"I'll be fine," Beth protested.

5

"Try to make sure she doesn't overdo in my absence," Harriet continued, as if she hadn't heard her aunt. "She's supposed to use her cane for at least another week."

Jenny grinned at Beth.

"Don't worry. We've made a schedule and are going to drive her to her PT and various groups and meetings while you're gone. She'll be fine."

"I'm not a child, you know!" Beth complained.

Harriet laughed. "No, you're not, but you have been known to overdo on occasion."

Beth rolled her eyes but couldn't disagree.

Lauren stood up.

"I better get going. I need to get gas on the way home and pack my new jammies."

Carla scooped up her toddler, who had been playing on the floor with the dogs.

"I better take this one home and put her to bed. Take lots of pictures." She blushed as she usually did when she said something assertive.

Connie picked up her purse.

"As I said, I've got my camera *and* my new phone. Between the two, I should be able to take pictures of everything we do." She patted Carla's arm. "If it's a good workshop, maybe next year I'll stay home, and Rod and I will take care of Wendy so you can go."

"Hopefully, Aiden will be back by then so I can leave the house," Carla said. She was employed as the young veterinarian's as his housekeeper and was total in charge of his affairs while he was out of the country on an indefinite assignment in Uganda. Then, her face flamed red when she looked at Harriet.

"Carla, it's okay. You don't have to cringe every time Aiden's name comes up. We were dating, and now we're not and I'm okay with that." Even she could hear the lack of conviction in her voice.

Carla ducked her head, and the rest of the women exchanged looks. Mavis got up and moved over to pat Harriet's shoulder.

"Let's not spoil our send-off with talk of past troubles," she said in a quiet voice.

"Never." Harriet gave her a forced smile. "Thank you everyone," she said, standing and straightening her back. "I'll see my fellow travelers in the morning, and the rest of you in a little over a week."

The group said their good-byes, and one-by-one, they headed home.

Chapter 2

Harriet and Lauren arrived downstairs in the lobby atrium of the Tremont House Hotel first; Connie and Mavis were taking longer to get settled in their rooms. Their flight had left Portland at six in the morning, and it had taken another two hours after they'd landed to drive to Galveston, including a stop at Walmart to pick up spray starch for Mavis and Connie's class.

Lauren sat in a padded wicker chair in one of several conversation groupings in the common space while Harriet went to the bar to get them iced tea.

"Thanks," she said when Harriet returned and handed her a frosty glass. "How long is it until our meet-and-greet?"

Harriet checked the time on her phone.

"It's four o'clock, and our meet and greet is either five or five-thirty. Do you want to go walk around the neighborhood? The historic Strand area is only a block away. That's where the shops are supposed to be."

"In a minute. What I'd like right now is a snack."

Lauren's phone rang, and Harriet recognized from the ringtone it was a work call.

I'll find us something, she mouthed and headed back to the bar.

She ordered a charcuterie plate then sat at the bar to wait while Lauren dealt with her client emergency. A blond young man sat down at the bar next to her. He reeked of alcohol.

"Hi, pretty lady, my name's Michael. Whiskey sour," he said to the bartender and then turned back to Harriet. "You're not here with the groom's party—I'd know because that's me, and we've definitely not met, but I intend to rectify that right now."

He wasn't exactly slurring his words, but it was clear to Harriet the drink the bartender handed him was not the first or probably even the second or third of his day.

"I'm not on anybody's side at the wedding. I'm here with the stitching group."

Michael toppled toward her in an uncontrolled lurch, and she put her hand on his shoulder, pushing him back until he caught his balance.

"Whoops," he said, and had sufficient good grace to blush. "Sorry 'bout that. I started celebrating a little early. The women are off getting their nails waxed or their hair painted or something."

Harriet looked around for help.

"Is your best man around, or any of your groomsmen?"

"No, nope, none. They all have jobs. They'll come for the wedding."

Michael abruptly leaned forward and laid his head on her shoulder. She tried to push him off, but he was a dead weight. She glanced over at Lauren; no help there—her friend was standing by the elevators with her back to the lobby, still on her phone. The bartender looked sympathetic, but he was serving a couple at the other end of the bar and made no move in her direction.

She put her hands on both Michael's shoulders and tried again to force him upright.

"Take your hands off my fiancé!" a big-haired blonde dressed in head-to-toe pink screeched from the top of the entrance stairs. She hurried over to the bar as fast as she could on her stiletto heels, trailed by four similarly coifed and shod women and a thick woman with straight black hair and sensible shoes.

"Take your fiancé off my hands," Harriet retorted and, with a final push, sent him backward, away from her. He would have fallen off his stool if the dark-haired woman hadn't stepped up and caught him.

"Come on, Michael. Nap time for you. Jennifer," she told the blonde, "why don't you take the girls upstairs to clean up and change for dinner?" She turned to Harriet. "I'm sorry. He's normally not so boorish."

Michael laid his head on her shoulder.

"You're so nice to me. I don't deserve you for a sister."

"I'm not your sister," she told him and reached her hand out to Harriet. "I'm Sydney Johnson, and this is my sister's groom-to-be. I'm afraid he's had too much to drink. They're getting married in a few days, and until the rest of his party arrive, he doesn't have much to do."

Harriet dabbed her shoulder with a napkin in case he'd drooled on her.

"No harm done."

"Did he stain your shirt? We can pay for the dry cleaning."

Harriet smiled.

"It's not a problem. I'm fine."

The bartender brought Harriet's plate of snacks.

"Sorry," he said under his breath.

"No problem," she whispered back and took her plate of cheeses and meats.

She smiled and started to turn away, but Sydney stopped her.

"I'm sorry, I didn't catch your name."

"Harriet. Harriet Truman."

"That must be tough."

Harriet sighed.

"You have no idea." She carried the plate of food to the table in front of where she and Lauren had been sitting. Settling into a chair, she leaned back with a sigh and watched Sydney wrestle the groom to the elevators.

"So, what was that all about?" Lauren asked as she slid her phone back into her pocket and sat down.

"Just your everyday garden variety drunk. Apparently, we're sharing the Tremont House with a wedding party. The women were out getting beautiful, and the groomsmen haven't arrived yet, so the groom spent the day drinking."

Lauren selected a slice of prosciutto from their plate and popped it into her mouth.

"I guess he was having his own private stag party."

"Everything okay with your client?"

"Yeah. Some people require a lot more hand-holding than others."

They ate their snack plate and drank tea in silence for a few minutes. Then, Harriet leaned back in her chair.

"Boy, I needed a little protein."

Lauren sighed.

"Yeah, I remember when they used to serve food on airplanes. I loved the cereal and banana. I never ate cereal except on planes."

"What is it Thoreau said?"

"I don't know, enlighten me."

Harriet stared up into the atrium.

" 'Things do not change; we change'."

"I'm pretty sure it was them that took the cereal away, not me."

"Yeah, well, that was the only change quote I could come up with on short notice."

Lauren stood up.

"Come on, let's go across the street to check in for the conference then take that walk."

✂ --- ✂ --- ✂

Harriet took a deep breath as they started down the block. The architecture was nineteenth-century stone and brick. According to her guidebook, it was one of the largest and most historically significant collections in the United States.

"I love the way this place smells. I don't know if it's the water or the sea life or something, but it doesn't smell like our waterfront."

"I think that might be mold you're smelling, from everything being so humid."

"Don't be so cynical. You can almost feel the history of this place in the air."

Lauren looked at her like she was crazy.

"If you say so."

Harriet surveyed the wharf, which was four blocks behind their hotel. Two gigantic white cruise ships sat at anchor. Vacationers bustled up and down the gangplanks, while white-jacketed crew hurried back and forth on all visible decks.

"I guess I didn't realize Galveston was such a cruise port," she commented.

"I'm not sure that's always been the case. I think I read somewhere they've only been here since two thousand."

"I bet having all the cruise visitors has changed the character of this area."

Lauren stopped in front of a gray-and-pink three-story building two blocks from the hotel.

"This is the Hutchings Sealy building," she said and read from the screen of her smartphone. "It says here it was one of the earliest examples of steel-frame construction in Texas."

Harriet sniffed. "My nose says it's the home to a shop with some great-smelling candles. I'm going in to investigate." She turned and climbed the three steps into the shop.

"I'm not really into can…" Lauren looked up a second, interior set of steps to the main floor of the shop. "Hello, linen clothes." She pushed past Harriet, went up the steps and started browsing a rack of shirts.

Harriet pulled a printed flyer from her purse and scanned it.

"I think this is one of the shops on our private spree night. If you wait until then you can get a discount."

A smiling woman came out from behind the sales counter and stood beside Lauren.

"The blue in that shirt really brings out your eye color. I heard you talking. If you'd like, I can put it behind the counter until your shopping night."

"You don't need do that. I know I'm here early."

"It would be our pleasure. Besides, if you pay for it when everyone gets to our shop, it'll prime the pump and get the others to open their wallets."

"Anything for the cause," Lauren said and laughed.

Harriet set a half-dozen square candles on the counter.

"I'm going to go ahead and get these candles today. They smell so good even without lighting them." She held a yellow one up to her nose and inhaled. "They'll make our room smell wonderful."

Lauren sneezed. "Whatever." She slid her phone from her pocket and looked at the time. "We better get going. I'd like to make it around the block before we need to go back for our reception."

The clerk wrapped Harriet's candles in red tissue paper and put them in a small shopping bag.

"I hope you both enjoy your stay in Galveston, and we'll see you in a couple of days."

✂ --- ✂ --- ✂

The hotel property included the Davidson Building across Ship Mechanic Row from the main hotel, and the first gathering of the appliqué conference was in its first-floor ballroom. Harriet and Lauren left the hotel lobby and crossed the street, entering through one of multiple sets of double doors.

Harriet turned slowly around as she took in the curved staircase with its wood-and-brass handrails and bold floral carpeting.

"Wow, you can almost see Scarlett O'Hara sweeping down this staircase."

Lauren scrolled down the face of her phone.

"Yeah, except for the fact that this was a warehouse until a few decades ago. They consulted the historical society when they built the ballrooms and staircase to be sure they were historically accurate."

Harriet rubbed her hand along the brass banister.

"So, this could have come from Home Depot? It looks amazingly old."

"The rich-architect version of Home Depot, but yeah, it was fabricated to look old, but it's probably a lot younger than your house."

"My house may be an old Victorian, but whoever built mine didn't spend the kind of money these people did."

Connie and Mavis came into the lobby and walked over to where Harriet and Lauren were examining the wood-and-brasswork. Connie gazed up the grand expanse of stairs.

"I wonder how old this building is?"

Harriet and Lauren looked at each other and laughed.

"You don't want to know," Harriet told her. "Go with your imagination."

Mavis looked across the lobby and into the ballroom.

"Looks like they're ready for us to check in for our reception. Shall we go get this party started?"

✂ --- ✂ --- ✂

"Why do you need to know how many pets I have?" Lauren asked the woman who had handed her the questionnaire.

A smiling woman with waist-length silver hair stepped up to the sign-in desk.

"It's for our 'getting to know you' event a little later. It's all in good fun, and you're welcome to ignore any questions you're uncomfortable answering, although it may cost your team points if you do."

Lauren scanned her paper.

"That didn't help much."

"I promise, this is not intended to embarrass anyone," the woman assured her.

"If you say so," Lauren muttered.

The room had been set up with round tables, each seating eight or ten people, and a long buffet table arranged down the middle. White-coated waiters bustled in and out, bearing bowls and trays of guacamole, chips, cheese, crackers, hummus and pita bread. A bar was set up at the back of the room where a black-shirted bartender arranged bowls of cut lemons and limes and a similarly dressed woman stacked clean wine glasses on a table behind him.

Harriet finished filling out her survey and glanced at Mavis's.

"Wow, you've been to all fifty states? I didn't know you traveled that much."

Mavis sighed. "I don't anymore, but my husband had a thing about geography. Every summer for years we drove around the country, collecting a state-shaped refrigerator magnet at each stop until we had them all.

Our final trip was to Hawaii." She paused for a moment. "It was our last family vacation."

Connie reached over and patted her hand. Mavis put on a brave face most of the time, but she was still trying to come to terms with the fact the husband she'd believed had died many years before had been living in Europe with another family until his recent actual death.

Harriet was saved from having to comment by a call to order by one of the conference hosts. Four women had organized the appliqué conference, and they each spoke in turn, describing the schedule of events and the locations for various activities.

"As some of you may have noticed, there is a large wedding party sharing the hotel with us," said a small woman with dark curly hair. "They will be having a dinner upstairs in this building tonight, and then the rest of the time, they'll be in the main hotel. The wedding itself will take place in one of the historic churches, so we shouldn't be in each other's way. In fact, with the exception of tonight, you may not even notice them."

Harriet leaned toward Lauren and whispered, "We've noticed them, if that jerk in the bar is part of the group she's talking about."

Lauren smiled. "We're lucky like that."

"I'll give you all a chance to nosh on the tasty snacks the wonderful Tremont people have prepared for you, and then we'll begin our 'getting to know you' activity."

"I'm glad we didn't plan on going out to dinner tonight," Mavis said a half-hour later as she dug in to her second plate of hummus and carrot sticks.

Connie groaned as she watched the hotel staff deliver plates of large cookies to a new table they'd set up at the end of the buffet.

"*Diós mio*. They should have warned us there was dessert."

The dark-haired hostess tapped a water glass with her fork.

"Now, if you all could look on the back side of your questionnaire..." She paused as papers rustled, and the group complied. "...you will find a number. Susan has set a table tent with a number on each of your tables."

Susan, a small athletic woman with a cap of short brown hair, held up a folded card with the number seven on it from Harriet's table to illustrate the point.

"Go to the table that matches the number on the back of your paper, and I will give you your next instruction."

Harriet and Lauren both had the number three, but Mavis had a five, and Connie an eight. They made their way to their new seats.

Their hostess tapped the glass again.

"I'm going to read a number of questions or statements. If you answer in the affirmative, give yourself a point. Some of the questions are worth more points—for instance, if you've ever competed in an Olympics, you get five points. And some—for example, how many grandchildren you have—are worth one point per."

The questions began, and within a few moments, the attendees were laughing like old friends. Everyone was surprised when it turned out there were four beauty pageant winners, including Connie; and Harriet and Lauren exchanged raised eyebrows when they each notched a point for having a PhD.

Three members of the group were medical doctors, and one woman had acted on television, on a soap opera most of them had never watched. A woman with flame-red hair wearing a turquoise shirt with a rhinestone heart outlined across her ample bosom laughed when it turned out she was the only one there who had won a national quilt-show award.

"It was a fluke," she told Harriet and the other women at her table.

Harriet sipped from the glass of ice water the waiter had delivered as the activity continued.

"I'm pretty sure they don't give those awards out lightly. Do you have a picture of the quilt?"

"I'm Stephanie," the redhead introduced herself as she flipped through pictures on her phone. When she found the winner, she turned the screen toward Harriet.

"Wow! I remember seeing this on the front of a magazine." Harriet passed the phone to the others at the table.

Stephanie took her phone back and slid it into her purse.

"I've not entered a quilt in a show since then. It was only the fourth quilt I'd ever made, and I'm just not sure I'll ever make another one that good again. I decided to go out on top."

"It's a fabulous quilt," Harriet said, and the others at the table agreed.

"Now I can relax and just have fun with my quilting," Stephanie said and laughed again. "And this trip is dual purpose. I'm actually attending the wedding at the hotel. It's not till the weekend, so it's perfect."

Harriet picked up her pencil and twirled it in her fingers.

"I've met the groom."

Stephanie looked at her for a moment before speaking.

"Really? I babysat the bride when she was little." She paused. "I've never set eyes on him. But then, I was surprised when I got the invitation. I haven't talked to any of the Johnsons for quite a few years. Not since Jen-

14

nifer was in middle school. I was planning on coming to this conference anyway, though, so I figured why not?"

Harriet wasn't sure what to say about that, and was glad when she was saved by their hostess.

"Okay, campers, time to add up the score for your table. The winning table will be awarded our first door prizes."

Harriet had her head bent adding up her points on the calculator function of her phone, or she might have seen what was coming. As it was, she was defenseless when the bride strode into the room from the lobby and slapped her cheek so hard she almost fell off her chair.

"Stay away from my fiancé," the woman screamed.

Lauren leaped to a protective stance over Harriet, but the woman stormed out, across the lobby and out the front doors.

Mavis stood up. "Someone call nine-one-one."

"And hotel security," Connie added.

Tears streaked down Harriet's cheek, and an angry red handprint was forming on her face. She gasped for breath, and Connie picked up her water glass and held it out.

"Here, take a sip of water," she ordered.

The bartender came over with a maroon cloth napkin wrapped around a handful of ice. He handed it to Harriet, and she pressed it gently against her cheek.

Three men dressed in navy-blue blazers with the Tremont House insignia on the breast pocket hurried through the front doors and gathered around Harriet. One man held some sort of radio in his right hand. The gold name badge on his chest said *Bruce*.

Bruce looked from Harriet to Mavis to Lauren and then addressed Connie.

"Is it really necessary to involve the police in this?"

Connie drew herself up to her full four-foot, eleven-inch height before speaking.

"Harriet has been attacked by a total stranger for no reason, and you are asking if we need the police? She's been assaulted."

"We will do our door prize drawing tomorrow night after show-and-tell," the curly-haired woman announced in a loud voice. The room was buzzing with talk about who had seen what. "Let's go back to the hotel, and if anyone feels like it, in an hour we will have our first pajama party in the room opposite the elevators."

The quilters gathered their purses and filed out of the room.

"Would you like us to call the police?" another of the navy-blazer guys asked Harriet in a strained voice.

15

"We'd be happy to drive you to the local emergency room," the third man offered.

"And of course, the rest of your stay will be on the house," Bruce told her. "If you'd like a room upgrade, I think that could be arranged, also," he added.

The first man leaned in and looked at Harriet's cheek around the napkin-full of ice.

"We have a private physician on call if you'd prefer to be seen at the hotel."

Harriet took the ice away from her face and set it on the table. Her cheek was swelling. Mavis leaned in and studied her then shook her head.

"You need an x-ray at least."

Harriet reached up and gently touched her cheek.

"Mavis is right. I need to have my cheekbone x-rayed, but I'm not interested in having Bridezilla arrested for assault. I'm sure she's stressed about her big day. I did encounter her very drunk fiancé earlier this afternoon, and she clearly misinterpreted what she saw."

The blue-blazer guys all visibly relaxed. Harriet was sure the hotel had seen the wedding of the century slipping through their fingers, not to mention a six-figure or more lawsuit.

Mavis sat down beside her.

"Honey, if you want to go home tonight, you just say the word, and I'll get us tickets on the next flight."

Harriet attempted a smile, then winced.

"I am not ruining our fun week of stitching just because a stressed-out bride took out her frustrations on my cheek unless I have to. Besides, I wouldn't want to leave James here by himself. Let's see what an x-ray shows. If the doctor says it's just a bruise, I'm staying."

"Honey, James is a big boy. He'll understand if you want to leave."

Harriet looked at her.

"If I told James I was hurt badly enough that I have to leave, he would insist on coming with me."

Connie raised her eyebrows and turned to Lauren.

"I didn't realize things had progressed that far."

Lauren smirked.

"You don't know the half of it."

"You guys can stop talking about me like I'm not here," Harriet said. "James and I are just friends, but since it was his idea for us to come here, I know he'll feel responsible."

Bruce turned away and spoke into his radio. He let out a long breath as he turned back to Harriet and her friends.

"I've called the ER and arranged for you to be seen immediately. Our limo will take you there, and our rep will stay with you and take care of all the expenses."

"I'd like my friend to come with me," Harriet tipped her head at Lauren, "And, Mavis, please let *me* tell Aunt Beth after I've seen the doctor and can assure her I'm fine. You and Connie should go ahead and go to the night stitching activity. We'll let you know when we're back."

Mavis's brows pulled together.

"Connie and I will take a cab and meet you there." Her tone told Harriet there would be no argument.

Bruce looked over Harriet's head and out the front windows.

"There's the car. Shall we go?"

Chapter 3

Harriet checked her watch as she got out of the limo in front of the hotel. Lauren collected both their purses and followed her out of the car.

"Do you want to stop in the cafe and get something to eat before we go up to the room?" Lauren asked as they crossed the hotel lobby.

"Didn't I hear someone say there would be homemade cookies at the pajama party tonight?"

"Yeah, you did."

"I can hold an ice pack on my face down there while I'm eating a cookie just as well as I can sitting upstairs alone in our room."

"They said the pajama party is in the room opposite the elevators," Lauren said and turned around. "We can just go on in, if you want."

Harriet turned toward the conference room doors.

"I can't stitch one-handed, so I'm good. Did you want to get your project?"

"I say we go straight for the cookies. After tonight's excitement, I'm not really in the mood to stitch."

Barb DePan and Ann Purgason, the conference organizers, came over as soon as Harriet stepped through the door.

"Are you okay? Is there anything we can do for you?" Barb asked.

Ann pulled out a chair at the closest table.

"Here, sit down."

Harriet settled in the chair and put her ice pack down on the table.

"I'd really like a cookie. Chocolate, if that's an option."

Before she'd finished speaking, a woman whose hips said she knew her way around a cookie table brought a paper plate filled with a selection of cookies and put it in front of her.

Harriet looked up at her.

"Thank you so much. I'm Harriet, by the way."

"Alice," the woman said and held out her hand. "How did it go at the hospital?"

Harriet picked up a chocolate-frosted chocolate cookie and took a bite before she answered.

"I have a small fracture on the edge of my eye socket where her ring hit, but nothing is displaced, so for now there isn't anything for them to do."

"I imagine they gave you some pain meds and decongestant and maybe an antibiotic."

She smiled with the half of her mouth that wasn't swollen.

"Are you a doctor?"

Alice joined her at the table, setting a cookie down on a napkin.

"No, I'm an ER nurse in a college town. And believe me, I've seen more broken faces than I care to remember. Usually from Friday-night bar fights." She bent and scanned Harriet's eye and the surrounding area. "If nothing's out of place, it should heal just fine. Be sure to take the decongestants they gave you, and if you *have* to sneeze or blow your nose, keep your mouth open. You don't want any pressure to build up anywhere in your face. Did they give you steroids for the swelling?"

Harriet nodded. "They said I only have to take them if the swelling doesn't go down in the next couple of days. And I'm going back so they can take a look for themselves the day after tomorrow."

"Don't expect it to be better in two or three days. You're going to be puffy for a while."

The door opened slightly, and a woman peeked in and scanned the room before opening it all the way and entering. It was the woman with the sensible shoes from the bar—Sydney Johnson, the bride's sister.

She came to Harriet's table and sat down.

"Are you okay?" she asked. "I'm so sorry for my sister's terrible behavior. Is there anything the family can do? We'd like to pay your hospital bill and for anything else you might need."

Connie and Mavis arrived and joined Harriet.

"I think you and your family have done enough, thank you." Mavis said, glaring at the woman as she spoke.

"Why don't you and Connie go get your cookies and then come sit down," Harriet suggested.

19

Mavis hesitated, and she and Connie looked at Harriet, then Sydney. They finally turned without speaking and walked to the back of the room and the cookie table.

Harriet watched them until they were out of earshot then looked back at Sydney.

"The hotel is handling my medical bills. Maybe you should talk to them."

Sydney's shoulders sagged, and she sighed deeply.

"I'll do that. If there's anything else…"

Sydney pulled a man-style wallet from her pocket and extracted a card, writing a phone number on the back. "You can reach me at this number." She put her hands on the table and started to push herself to her feet.

Harriet gave her a half-smile.

"Why don't you sit down and have a cookie while you're here?"

"Oh, I couldn't impose," she said. She fingered the edge of her shapeless tunic with her left hand.

Lauren gave Harriet a look that said "Are you kidding?"

"Yeah, she couldn't impose."

"Oh, come on." Harriet insisted. "You weren't the one who whacked me. And it couldn't have been a picnic dealing with the drunk groom."

Connie and Mavis had returned with their cookie plates; Lauren looked to them for help.

"I think her drugs are talking."

Sydney smiled at Harriet.

"You are way too kind, and you're right—dealing with Michael is no picnic. I wish I could say his behavior is an isolated incident, but unfortunately, that would be a lie."

"Why is your sister marrying him?" Lauren asked.

Sydney's lip curled up on one side.

"She says she loves him."

Lauren rolled her eyes. Mavis took a bite of a butterscotch cookie and chewed.

"If he drinks like that on a regular basis, the marriage isn't likely to last long," she said then.

"Have you tried to talk to your sister?" Connie asked.

"No one wants to hear what the resident old maid has to say, least of all my sister. My mother considers me the one great failure in her life. Besides, Jennifer knows what side her bread is buttered on. She gains a sizable inheritance when she marries Michael and produces an heir."

Harriet picked up another of the double chocolate cookies from her plate and handed it to Sydney.

"This'll help."

Sydney smiled.

"Thanks. I wish it was that simple."

Stephanie came over to the table.

"How's your eye?" she asked.

"Slightly broken, but they tell me it will heal just fine."

"Well, that's a relief. It would be terrible if you came down here for a fun week of stitching and went home permanently maimed."

Connie sent her a warning look, but Stephanie didn't seem to notice. She turned to Sydney.

"Hi, Sydney. I don't know if you remember me, but I used to babysit you and Jennifer when you were little."

Sydney gave her a forced smile.

"Of course I remember. Your red hair is hard to forget. Jen wanted to dye her hair that color in junior high, but Mama wouldn't let her. I didn't know you and Mama were still in touch."

Stephanie's cheeks turned pink.

"I haven't heard from your mother in years. Frankly, I was surprised when I received an invitation to your sister's wedding."

"Mama doesn't have a lot of friends."

Stephanie shook her head.

"I guess that explains it." She turned back to Harriet. "I better get back to my stitching. I just wanted to see how you were doing. I hope you feel better tomorrow."

✂ --- ✂ --- ✂

"Are you going to take the hotel up on the room upgrade?" Lauren asked as they got off the elevator and started down the hallway toward their room.

Harriet sighed.

"Maybe that'll sound like a good idea tomorrow, but tonight I just want to ice my face down and go to bed."

Lauren slid the room key into the door lock. When the hotel had been repaired in 2008, after Hurricane Ike, many of its features had been up-graded to contemporary standards, including door locks that now opened with keys embedded with a computer chip so they functioned like a swipe card but looked like a key.

"I'd like to see what the upgrade room would look like," she said as she dropped the key into the pocket of her hoodie.

Harriet looked around their room. The ceiling had to be at least eigh-teen feet overhead. Two queen beds with iron frames sat opposite a small sofa and coffee table. An antique armoire had been modified to conceal a flat-screen television. Beside the entry door was a large walk-in closet. The bathroom had a steam-heated towel rack beside the deep bathtub-shower combo.

"This looks fine to me. I'm not sure what else we'd need." She crossed to a round glass table in the corner of the room and picked up the ice bucket. "I'm going to go get some ice for my face. Don't lock me out." Just to be sure, she flipped the door's bar guard out before she closed the door behind her, so it couldn't shut completely.

The hotel rooms were arranged around the lobby atrium, and Harriet had to cross a short open walkway to the opposite side of the building to find the room that held the ice machine. She mentally shook her head as she looked down into the lobby and saw the groom once again draped against the bar, downing a drink.

A hotel maid was pushing her cart along the hallway a few doors down from the ice room, and Harriet nodded as she passed her. An older hotel maintenance man emerged from one of the rooms, and as she filled her bucket with ice, she heard him scolding the maid.

"That was weird," she told Lauren when she'd returned to their room and was refilling her eye bag with fresh ice. "I overheard a maintenance guy arguing with the hotel maid in the hallway. They were speaking Cajun, but I'm pretty sure I got it right. A large part of the language is French."

"How could I forget? You're the Rosetta Stone of our group. What were they arguing about?"

"He was reprimanding her for 'bothering with the quilters.' He told her to focus on the wedding party."

Lauren rinsed her toothbrush and tapped it on the edge of the sink before setting it down on a folded washcloth and stepping out of the bathroom to go to her bed.

"That makes a certain amount of sense. I mean, the wedding party is likely to have bigger tippers."

Harriet held the fresh ice pack to her face.

"But he said 'don't bother with the quilters.' I'm pretty sure the hotel expects her to clean every room on her schedule no matter who occupies the room."

"Maybe they do something extra, like put chocolates on the pillows at night, or fold their towels into animals the way they do on a cruise ship."

"The chocolate I can believe, but towel animals in an elegant old hotel like this one? Somehow, I doubt it."

"I guess time will tell. And speaking of time—do you want to shower first or second in the morning?"

"I'll take second so I can ice my face beforehand."

"Let's hope the rest of our trip is less eventful."

"Amen to that."

Chapter 4

Connie and Mavis were seated at a large round table in the banquet room across the street from the hotel when Harriet and Lauren entered and went directly to the continental breakfast buffet. Lauren placed a flaky chocolate-filled croissant on her plate and watched as Harriet picked up a carton of yogurt.

"We could probably get one of the kitchen people to stick one of these in a blender for you," she said with a chuckle.

"Oh, yeah, yuck it up. You just wait till you need help," Harriet said, speaking carefully so as to not jostle her cheek.

She picked up a spoon and joined Mavis and Connie.

"Oh, honey," Mavis said. "Does that feel as bad as it looks?"

"Let's see," Connie said. Harriet turned her cheek toward her friend and leaned in slightly. Connie carefully examined the injury.

"Well, it doesn't look like the swelling is any worse than last night. Were you able to sleep at all?"

Harriet sat back.

"I definitely could tell when the pain medication wore off, but I got up and took another dose and went back to sleep."

"Does anyone have any idea why the woman attacked you so viciously?" Connie asked her.

"No idea, other than what I told you all about encountering the drunk groom in the bar. It's crazy."

Mavis leaned toward Harriet.

"I'm trying not to overreact, but I'd feel better if you two would give me a copy of your room key. Connie and I will do the same for you. I

24

want to be able to check on you if I can't raise you on your phone. If one of us has been attacked when we've only been here for a day, who knows what else is going to happen."

Lauren came back to the table, carrying her pastry plate on top of a cup of tea in one hand and another cup of tea for Harriet in the other.

"I'm assuming the drugs have your mind muddled, and that's why you forgot to get a drink. Anyway, I brought you a cup of tea."

Harriet took the cup.

"Thanks, I did forget about it. By the way, we're getting a spare room key for Mavis, and they're doing the same for us."

"Why?" Lauren asked.

Mavis took a deep breath and started to explain.

"Never mind," Lauren told her. "It's fine. If Harriet wants you to have our key, fine."

Harriet gave her an *I'll tell you later* look, and Lauren gave a slight nod of acknowledgment.

Mavis watched Harriet carefully eat her yogurt.

"Are you sure you don't want to press charges against that young woman? It's not too late."

Lauren looked at Harriet.

"You keep eating—at the rate you're going, we're barely going to have enough time for you to finish. I can tell Connie and Mavis your objections, since we had this same argument last night before we went to sleep and again this morning before we walked over here."

She turned to the two older women.

"Harriet thinks the Galveston police will call the Foggy Point police and ask about her. This might be problematic unless Detective Morse is the one to answer the phone, which we all know is unlikely, since she's a detective, not a desk sergeant.

"They will tell them that our friend here has been involved in a few too many crimes locally for it to be coincidence. They may even throw in the fact she has been warned each and every time to keep her nose out of police business."

Harriet set her spoon down.

"At the very least, they might look me up on the internet, and once again, they'll see that I've been involved in more crimes than is seemly in such a small town."

Connie brushed muffin crumbs from her fingers.

"None of those situations are your fault, and if the police were honest, they'd admit your involvement often resulted in the right person being convicted. Someone they hadn't identified or didn't have enough evidence to even look at."

"I get it that they don't want average citizens involved in their work," Harriet said. "And if any of our situations hadn't involved friends or family, I'd have been the first one to step aside and let them do their job." She picked up her spoon again. "I'm not willing to stand aside and watch while they jail one of our friends."

Mavis patted her hand.

"No need to get riled up. And I do understand your concern. I just worry that gal who slapped you may be getting away with this sort of behavior because she's young and pretty or has rich parents. What if she does something worse?"

Harriet sighed, but her friend James Garvin, proprietor and chef of The Cafe on Smugglers Cove in Foggy Point, came into the room before she could respond. He looked around, and when he found Harriet he hurried to her table, crouching beside her chair.

"Harriet, what happened?"

"A stressed-out bride whacked her in the face," Lauren answered for her. "Harriet was hit on by a very drunk groom, and the bride misinterpreted what she was seeing when she came on them in the lobby bar."

"That's terrible!" He looked at Harriet's injury. "Do you need anything? I'm guessing you've already been to the doctor." He turned to Lauren. "Does she need anything?"

Harriet scraped the last bit of yogurt from her container and popped it in her mouth.

"Sorry, eating is a little slow," she answered for herself. "Yes, I've seen a doctor and had an X-ray, and they said as long as the swelling and discomfort decrease gradually and nothing else develops, I should be good as new in a few weeks."

"And since she needs to sit still while her cheekbone heals," Mavis added, "she might as well be stitching."

Harriet gave James a half-smile and touched his pant leg.

"Don't you look cute in your hound's-tooth chef pants. Do they make you wear a hat?"

James's face turned red.

"Yes, they do. And when we get to the kitchen, we have to put on these double-breasted coats, even though it's a million degrees here."

Lauren stood up.

"This is all fun, kids, but we have to go upstairs to our classrooms."

James stood and gave Harriet a tender look.

26

"I've got to get to class, too. I know you guys are on your own for dinner tonight, so I came by to see if I could steal Harriet. There's a restaurant I want to try out."

Mavis smiled.

"If you promise to do a better job of keeping her out of trouble than we've done, then I guess she can go."

Harriet looked at her.

"I'm here, in case none of you have noticed. And I don't need anyone's permission."

Connie smiled.

"Of course you don't," she said. "I think it's a good idea for you to go have some fun."

Everyone got up and headed for the door, Lauren beside Connie.

"Are you saying we aren't fun?"

Connie eyes twinkled as she smiled.

"Not as much fun as he is."

✂ --- ✂ --- ✂

Harriet was surprised to see Stephanie sitting in their classroom. She'd assumed the woman would be in the more advanced classes. She said as much to her when she'd sat at the table behind hers.

"Oh, I don't sign up for the most challenging classes. I go by whether I like the project or not. I like the pillow you can make with the piece we're doing in this class, so here I am."

Lauren sat down beside Harriet.

"I definitely went by difficulty level. I'm not a great appliqué-er."

"Yet," Harriet added for her. "We expect to be much better after we learn all the tricks this week."

"Says you," Lauren shot back.

Harriet turned back to Stephanie.

"You know the bride and her family, right?"

"I did know them. We haven't really been close since they moved out of our neighborhood. I barely recognized Sydney. Once they started making money, we were left in the dust. They moved to a mansion in the Isle of Hope neighborhood and joined more elevated circles."

"And yet you scored an invite to the wedding of the century," Lauren pointed out.

Stephanie smiled.

"Judith didn't have many friends in our neighborhood, and I'm pretty sure her style didn't play well with the old-money types in the Isle."

"What do you mean—her 'style'?" Harriet asked.

27

Stephanie laughed.

"I'm guessing you haven't met her."

Harriet shook her head.

"She has one goal in her life, which she's never really going to achieve. She wants to be old Southern money, and no amount of new money is going to buy her way into that club. Her paying Jennifer's way into every social club hasn't helped, either."

"Wait," Lauren said. "I thought you hadn't seen Jennifer since she was little."

"I haven't. One of my friends runs a neighborhood coffee shop in Isle of Hope—it's a ritzy neighborhood in Savannah. She hears everything, including the other young people in the neighborhood talking about Jennifer and her obnoxious mother."

A thin woman with long curly gray hair came to the front of their class room and cleared her throat.

"Everyone plug your lamps in and open the pattern that is laying on your desk."

They did as instructed, and she began explaining the design they would be doing—a floral pattern with leaves in several shades of green. Their first step was to transfer the image to their background fabric and the task required enough focus that further discussion of Jennifer and her family was precluded.

Harriet smiled as James drove up in his rental car.

"Thanks for waiting with me," she said to Lauren. "I would have been fine with the troop of bellmen here."

Lauren rolled her eyes.

"Not according to Mavis and Connie. And by the way, you better call your aunt because those two are not going to hold out much longer."

Harriet gave the half-smile.

"I'll call her as soon as I get back from dinner."

"Try to stay out of trouble."

Harriet stepped off the curb when the car stopped.

"Don't worry. Nothing else is going to happen."

"Famous last words."

James had gotten out and was holding the passenger door open.

"What are famous last words?" he asked when they were both in the car.

"Oh, Lauren is just urging me to be careful. This…" She pointed at her swollen cheek. "…is definitely a freak accident."

"I wouldn't call it an accident. Sounds like it was an assault," James said as he turned onto Broadway, and headed for the Seawall area of the island. "Didn't the woman hit you?"

Harriet sighed.

"I'm tired of talking about it."

"Can I say one last thing?"

"Fine. Out with it."

"If anything like this happens again—ever—would you please call me? Or have Lauren or someone call me?" He looked at her. "I mean, even though we haven't known each other all that long, you're kind of growing on me."

She carefully smiled.

"You're kinda growing on me, too."

He grinned at her.

"Good, I'm trying."

"Where are we going to dinner?" she said, changing the subject.

"We're going to a Galveston icon. It's called Gaido's, and it's been in business since nineteen-eleven. They use locally sourced seafood and hand-prepare everything. And I'm told they have a fantastic dessert menu."

"Now you're speaking my language."

Harriet watched out the window as James turned onto Seawall Boulevard, which ran parallel to the beach and along the top of the seawall that had been built after a hurricane had swamped the island back in 1900, killing six thousand people.

"This is amazing. It's so different from the area where we're staying." She pointed out her window. "Look, is that a dolphin?"

James laughed.

"I can't look—at least, I can't look without driving over the edge. But our hosts told me dolphins are pretty common around here. Some people think seeing a dolphin in the surf brings you good luck."

"Really?" She looked at him.

"That's what they say." James guided the car into a busy parking lot. "Here we are."

Harriet got out of the car and stood looking in amazement at the giant fiberglass crab perched on the roof of Gaido's.

"That's impressive. I like the blue claws."

"Don't judge until we get inside. You might be surprised."

He was right. After seeing the outside, she was expecting a casual beach interior, but it was the exact opposite. Round linen-covered tables were ringed with leather-upholstered chairs, and a large display case showed off an impressive collection of leaded cut-glass bowls and vases.

29

They were shown to a table, and the maître d' held out Harriet's chair and set the navy-blue napkin in her lap.

"Okay, I am surprised," she said when the man was out of hearing range.

"I told you. Never judge a book by its cover."

"I stand corrected," she said and smiled. Looking at him, she could almost forget about the pain in her face.

※ --- ※ --- ※

Harriet set her dessert fork down on the table.

"I can't eat another bite."

James dipped his into their shared pecan crunch.

"It'll be tough, but I guess I'll have to finish it myself."

"If I were around food all the time like you are in your restaurant, I think I'd weigh a thousand pounds."

James chewed his last bite of pecan and set his fork down.

"If you worked in a restaurant, you'd be on your feet all day, running from one end of the kitchen to the other. Besides, I run most mornings, too."

"I didn't realize you were a runner."

"I am. I was going to ask you if you wanted to go together sometime, but I'm afraid you might be faster than I am."

"I doubt that," she told him. "I do just enough to work off my quilt group's baking habit."

He reached across the table and took her hand.

"Are you okay, really? I know you're telling your friends everything is fine, but I'm guessing you don't want to spoil their week."

"My eye socket hurts, but it's going to feel bad no matter where I am, so I might as well have the distraction of learning how to appliqué."

James rubbed his thumb across the back of her hand.

"I don't like to see you hurting."

"I feel sorry for the bride. She's marrying a lush just so she can claim an inheritance."

"Sounds like she's being greedy, in which case, maybe she's getting what she deserves."

"If it's her choice. The way her sister was talking last night, it might be the mother pushing her into it. Oh, and she has to produce an heir."

"Geez, I can see why you feel sorry for her."

Harriet pulled her hand back and sat up straight.

James looked at her.

"What's wrong?"

30

She leaned back in, took his hand again and lowered her voice to a whisper.

"Don't turn or anything right now, but over your left shoulder is a couple. The woman was in my class today, and the guy she's with is none other than The Drunken Groom." She casually knocked her fork onto the floor to James's left. "Dear, could you please pick up my fork?" she said in a louder than normal voice.

He turned his head slightly to see the couple as he fumbled with her fork on the floor.

"My, my, my, they're looking cozy, considering he's about to be married to someone with a temper in a few days."

"He's holding her hand," she whispered as James handed her the fork.

"I'm confused," he whispered back. "If they're holding hands, can't we?"

She laughed.

"Of course. That was just my 'I'm shocked' reaction." She put her hand back on the table, and he took it again. "I can't believe he'd be cheating on her before the wedding, and on the day after she reacted so badly when she just *thought* I was putting the moves on him. Who knows what she'd do if she actually found him out with someone else."

James wiggled his eyebrows up and down.

"You can put your moves on me."

"I already have. Can't you tell?"

He laughed. "Try again, and I'll let you know. Let's go walk on the beach before I take you back for your stitching party."

✂ --- ✂ --- ✂

Harriet wiggled her bare feet in the wet sand at the water's edge.

"Wow, this is so different from our beach at home."

James smiled at her.

"You mean the fact the water is as warm as bathtub water? Or are you thinking of the rocks that cover the water's edge in place of sand and pass for a beach in Foggy Point?"

"Both, I guess."

He put his arm around her shoulders, and she leaned into him as they began walking along the beach.

"Another one of my classmates is invited to the wedding," she told him. "She used to babysit the bride when she was little, but she's never met the groom."

"If the bride is so stressed she'd whack a stranger in the face, I'm guessing the marriage will be doomed."

Harriet laughed.

"You think? If he's stepping out on her already and they're not even married, it can't be good."

"Well, when I get married, it will be for one reason and one reason only. I'm going to be so in love with my bride I can't conceive of spending another minute without her."

"That's a pretty lofty ideal."

"So I'm told. My friends tell me things mellow a little after you put a ring on it."

"It could be why you're not married yet."

"Maybe. With the restaurant, I don't have much time to think about it. What about you? Do you see yourself getting married again?"

"I don't know. I always thought I'd grow old with Steve. I never imagined he would die from a congenital heart defect before he was thirty-five. Since then, I guess I've assumed I'd be alone. To tell you the truth, I've been so angry at Steve for leaving me, I haven't allowed myself to consider what comes next."

"I notice you said you're angry at him for *leaving* you. Didn't he die?"

"You caught that, huh? He did."

"And you're angry at him for that?"

Harriet stopped and turned to face him.

"You know, just lately I've started letting go of the anger. I thought I was mad because he didn't tell me about his health problems, but I've come to realize my anger has really been about feelings of abandonment. I've told you about growing up in boarding schools, except for the few times I got to stay with my aunt Beth. When Steve and I got married, I felt like I finally had a real family, even if it was just the two of us. I guess it made me angry to have that taken away, and it was easy to blame him."

James gently kissed the uninjured side of her face.

"I'm sorry you've had such a rough time."

Harriet sighed.

"I'm finally accepting that stuff just happens. It wasn't anyone's fault."

He put his arm over her shoulders again and turned her to walk back down the beach.

"That's true, but it doesn't make it hurt less."

"How'd you get so wise?"

He laughed.

"I'm not very wise. I'm the guy who's never been married, remember."

"Some girl is going to be lucky to have you, when the time is right."

It was James's turn to sigh.

32

"That's what I'm hoping."

They returned to the car, and James held the passenger-side door open for her.

"Will I see you tomorrow? We don't have to do anything if you're not up to it. I just want to see you're okay with my own eyes."

"Sure. I have to go get my face checked at the hospital in the afternoon. I'll be back to go to dinner with Mavis and company, and then we go shopping on the Strand. Several shops are staying open late just for us."

"I'll try to make it before you go to dinner. Do you know where you're going?"

"No, I think it will be a game-time decision. Gumbo Bar is one option, and The Black Pearl is the other. Ultimately, we'll go to each of them, but I think we need to see where our classmates are going and then go to the other one so we don't overwhelm the smaller restaurants."

"Okay, I'll check when my class gets out. If I miss you, I can come after you finish shopping. I won't be able to stay long—the other cooks and I are practicing making roux tomorrow night."

"That sounds fun."

He looked at her.

"Are you mocking me?"

Harriet gave him her half-smile as he shut her car door.

Chapter 5

Mavis and Connie were in their usual spot at the round breakfast table the next morning when Harriet and Lauren came into the banquet room, gathered their food and sat down next to their friends.

"I'm glad you finally called your aunt," Connie told Harriet.

Mavis pinched a piece off her roll, popped it into her mouth and chewed thoughtfully.

"It was everything we could do to keep her from jumping on a plane and coming down here," she said.

"At one point she was going to send Jorge down here to get you and drive you back," Connie added.

Harriet looked up at the ceiling, then shook her head.

"That would have been just great."

Mavis reached over and patted her hand."

"Don't worry, honey, we talked them out of it."

"Jorge wasn't keen on the idea, anyway," Connie said.

"I think we've got her calmed down—for now," Mavis finished. "Just make sure you call her every day."

Harriet sighed.

"I can do that, I guess."

Lauren sipped her coffee and set her mug down.

"We were so occupied with your call to your aunt, I forgot to ask where your chef took you to dinner last night."

Harriet told them about Gaido's and the illicit lovers they'd observed there. Lauren set her napkin on the table beside her empty plate.

"Wow, this wedding stuff keeps getting better and better. It sort of makes you wish we were invited."

Mavis pressed her lips together.

"Not me. We've had enough drama in our lives without going out and looking for more."

Harriet swallowed a bite of yogurt.

"I'm with you. A jealous bride and a philandering groom are a recipe for disaster, if you ask me. On another topic, have any of you heard about the possibility of a ghost tour one evening? I heard some of our classmates talking about it in the lobby while Lauren was checking her voicemail."

Mavis and Connie shook their heads.

"I'm going to stop answering my phone in the lobby," Lauren said. "I'm missing all the good stuff."

"Want to go look for the elusive *loups garous* with them?" Harriet asked her.

"I have no idea what you just said, but sure."

"*Loups garous*. It's *werewolf* in Cajun French."

"Whatever."

Connie stood up.

"Shall we meet down here to go to lunch?"

Harriet stood up, too.

"I'm going to swing by the restroom and wash my hands, so I'll see you two…" She nodded to Mavis and Connie. "…at lunch and…" To Lauren: "I'll meet you upstairs."

"I don't suppose you know where Michael is," Jennifer Johnson shouted as she stormed through the entrance doors to the classroom building. Harriet was waiting for her friends at the bottom of the staircase and looked around for somewhere, anywhere she could go to avoid the inevitable confrontation. Unfortunately, she was too far from the banquet room door, and the restrooms were even farther away across the lobby.

She held her hands in front of her and backed up.

"I've been in class all morning. I just came down here to meet my friends for lunch."

"I can't find him, and he's supposed to get fitted for his tux," Jennifer wailed, and then she burst into tears.

Harriet surveyed the entrance lobby again, hoping Sydney or the bride's mother or *someone* would appear out of anywhere to help her out. She had no idea why Jennifer thought Michael would be in the annex building with the stitchers, but before she could point this out, Sydney burst through the entrance doors.

"Come on, Jennifer," she said and wrapped a plump arm around her sister's shoulders. "Your friends are waiting for you to go to the spa at the Hotel Galvez. What are you doing over here bothering Harriet?"

"Michael's missing. He was supposed to go get measured for his tux, and the rental place called me with a question about the cummerbunds, and they said he hadn't been in yet." Fresh tears ran down her face.

Sydney pulled a tissue from the pocket of her cotton skirt and handed it to her sister, keeping her arm around the younger woman while she wiped her eyes. She looked over her sister's shoulder and mouthed *I'm sorry* then turned back to Jennifer. "You go on with your friends, and I'll find Michael."

Jennifer snuffled and wiped her nose. She attempted a smile.

"You're the best."

Lauren descended the wide staircase as the sisters were going out the door.

"What was that all about?"

"You don't want to know. More bride drama."

"Why were they over here? Apologizing?"

"Not that. But, who knows? I don't care, as long as she keeps her hands to herself."

Harriet turned toward the class supply store that had been set up at the back of the lobby.

"Let's check out the thread donuts while we wait for Connie and Mavis," she said, referring to the circular rubber holders that held a range of thread colors wound on sewing machine bobbins.

✄ --- ✄ --- ✄

Stephanie came down the stairs before Mavis and Connie appeared.

"Do you have anyone to go to lunch with?" Harriet asked her.

"No, I was just going to go over to the hotel."

Lauren turned from inspecting the bobbin holders.

"We're either going to the Gumbo Bar, which is obviously gumbo, or the Black Pearl, which is I-don't-know-what, but everyone says it's wonderful."

Connie joined them as Lauren was talking.

"There's a big group from our class going to the Black Pearl, so I think we should try Gumbo Bar today."

"Sounds good to me," Harriet said. "I think that might be easier for me to eat anyway."

36

Mavis arrived, and when everyone had done a turn in the bathroom, they headed out for the six-block walk.

Harriet fell in beside Stephanie.

"Tell me—do you think Jennifer is dangerous? I ask because I just had another encounter with her, and I wasn't sure if I should run or just ignore her."

Stephanie kept her eyes on the sidewalk as she walked and was silent for a long moment.

"If *Judith*, her mother, had attacked you, it would make sense. and I'd say you were right to fear her. I'm having trouble seeing Jennifer in that role. She's a spoiled girl, to be sure, but she's more of a 'stand there and wring her hands' type if things aren't going her way. In spite of the fact we all witnessed her attack you, I still have trouble believing she did that."

Harriet turned her bad eye so Stephanie could see it.

"There's no doubt in *my* mind. She whacked me a good one."

"And if she could do that, then I guess I don't know her at all, so maybe you *should* fear her."

Lauren had been behind them, but she pulled up even with them.

"In other words, you don't know anything that can help us."

Stephanie couldn't meet her eye.

"Stop it," Harriet told Lauren then turned to Stephanie. "Ignore her. She's being over-protective. It's not your fault you can't predict the actions of a girl you haven't seen for decades."

Stephanie shook her head.

"I wish I could be more help. Like I was saying, it seems out of character for the girl I knew."

"Well, people change," Harriet said. "Look." She pointed to a sign halfway up the block. "There's the Gumbo Bar."

✂ --- ✂ --- ✂

"Wow, that was different than I expected," Connie said. "In the lunchroom at school they used to serve something they called gumbo. It came out of a can, and it wasn't dark like this."

Harriet smiled.

"That's because most people think anything with okra in it is gumbo. I've learned from James that it's actually the browned roux that's the hallmark of good gumbo. He says the roux should be the color of mahogany. He also told me it has to include the 'holy trinity'."

"What on earth is that?" Lauren asked.

"It's the basis of all Cajun/Creole cooking—chopped onion, celery and bell pepper."

37

Mavis shuffled her purse onto her arm when she'd finished paying her bill.

"I've never had Cajun cooking before. This was delicious."

Harriet laughed.

"Well, you'll have plenty of opportunities in the future. James plans to introduce it to his restaurant menu."

"All the time?" Lauren asked.

"No, I think he'll do it at special times. Like during Mardi Gras, maybe." Connie led the way to the door.

"Sounds good to me."

✂ --- ✂ --- ✂

There was no medical reason for Lauren to accompany Harriet to her follow-up doctor appointment, but when Harriet exited her class in the afternoon, her friend got up and left with her.

"I can take myself to the doctor."

"With that crazy bride and now a possibly missing groom, I think we need to travel in pairs."

"Hey, who are you trying to kid here, me or you?"

"Okay, so I'm getting cramps in my fingers and my curves have elbows."

"What?"

"That's what the teacher called the points I'm getting in what should be smooth curves."

They crossed the street into the main hotel lobby.

"Shall I call the limo for you?" the desk clerk asked before Harriet reached the counter.

"Your reputation precedes you," Lauren whispered.

"I suspect the nervous hotel manager told the desk staff to keep an eye out for a woman with a massive black eye needing a ride to the hospital and to give her anything she wants. Yes," she told the desk clerk, "but we'd like to take our sewing things up to our room before we go."

The clerk motioned to a bellman.

"Robert can take those to your room for you, if you'd like."

Harriet smiled at Lauren and handed over her bag.

"Thanks," she said and turned to Lauren. "On the way back, let's go to the store where you found your top."

Lauren checked the time on her phone.

"It will probably be too early, especially if you get the VIP treatment again."

38

"I know, but I've been thinking about a shirt I saw, and I'd like to either buy it or put it on hold before it disappears. I'll need to ice my eye after the doctor, and I'm afraid it'll be gone if I can't shop until after that."

"It doesn't matter to me, as long as we work a dinner snack into our adventure somewhere."

✄ --- ✄ --- ✄

Harriet held her phone out in front of her and pressed Aunt Beth's number on speed dial, followed by the speaker button.

"Can you hear me?" she asked when her aunt answered.

"I can hear you, but I'd like to see you. Can't you put me on video chat?"

Harriet told her it wasn't possible when they were in the hotel limo. She recited what the doctors had told her, which was that nothing had changed and to see her own doctor when she returned to Foggy Point.

"You still want to go by the clothing shop before we go back to ice your eye?" Lauren asked when she'd ended the call.

"Yes, I do. I have a black eye, I'm not crippled."

Lauren threw up her hands.

"Okay, okay. I just don't want the wrath of Mavis and Connie coming down on me if your eye gets worse."

Harriet sighed.

"I'm fine."

Lauren leaned forward to speak to the driver.

"Can you take us to Tina's on the Strand?"

"Yes, ma'am,"

"Thanks."

✄ --- ✄ --- ✄

Harriet led the way up the steps into the shop. A well-dressed woman with dark hair and a name tag that read *Boyce* stood at the top of the interior stair landing.

"My goodness, what happened to you?" she asked.

"Would you believe I ran into a door?"

"Whatever you say, honey. How can I help you?"

Lauren explained Harriet's desire to put a shirt she had spotted the last time they were there on hold until she could come back with the quilting group, and after Harriet had taken the time to ice her eye.

Harriet went over to the shirt rack and found the one she was looking for—a red-orange linen number with a flared bottom edge and bell sleeves.

Suddenly, a woman knocked into her, her arms full of clothing.

39

"Get away from me!" Harriet shouted—it was Jennifer.

The two women glared at each other.

"What is your problem?" the bride hissed. She shoved her garments into Boyce's arms. "I'll take all of these. My sister will take care of it." She said this over her shoulder as she strode out.

Sydney appeared from the dressing room area, looking apologetic.

"I'm so sorry for my sister's rude behavior. I seem to be saying that a lot, but I really am sorry. She's under a lot of stress, and I'm afraid she's not handling it very well."

Harriet glared at her. Sydney sighed.

"Okay, you're right. She's spoiled and pretty much rude to anyone who doesn't fawn over her."

Boyce set the clothes on the checkout counter and turned back, rubbing her hands together.

"We've got wine for tonight, and if you'd like, I could open a bottle early."

Harriet smiled at her.

"Thanks, but that's not necessary. Besides, it's not allowed with the meds I have to take for this." She pointed at her eye, then turned to Sydney. "I'm sorry. I know you can't control your sister's behavior."

"How about I let you take your shirt now at the discount," Boyce suggested, "and I'll even give you the shop quilter gift."

"That would be great. I plan to join the shopping tour, but I'm on my way back from the doctor, and they were on me about not icing and resting enough."

"Don't you worry," Boyce told her. "We'll fix you right up."

χ --- χ --- χ

"You do realize we could have walked back to the hotel quicker than it's taking us to use the limo," Lauren said a few minutes later as they waited for the vehicle to circle the block so it could pull up to the curb in front of the shop.

"I know, but the hotel manager feels bad, and he's doing everything he can to make it up to us."

"I don't know about you, but this 'kill-her-with-kindness' business is starting to annoy me."

Harriet grinned her half-grin.

"That's because you're not getting the good stuff." She pulled a tube of French lotion and a bar of scented soap from the bag that held her shirt.

"Is that the shopping prize?" Lauren asked her.

"No, that one's a scarf. This is a bunch of feel-better goodies. There's a note from the shop manager. 'I hope your visit to Galveston gets better, and you'll come back again,'" she read. "'Enjoy this little get-well token.' This definitely is going to help me think better of these folks—and I was liking them pretty well already."

The limo finally arrived and, after another trip around the block, deposited them in front of the hotel.

"Will you be okay getting your ice by yourself?" Lauren asked as she climbed out of the back of the car.

"Of course. Where are you going?"

"I saw a candy store on the Strand. Our brochure says it's a nineteen-twenties' style confectionary. And they have chocolate. I'm pretty sure your eye will heal faster with a liberal dose of chocolate."

Harriet smiled so widely her face hurt.

"That sounds like a worthy mission. I'll be fine."

With the ice machine across the walkway from her room, it would have been convenient to stop on her way in, but she didn't have anything to carry the ice. As she started down the hall with the bucket, she saw the same housekeeper she'd observed earlier, this time with a younger man. Their backs were to her, and they were arguing in Cajun French.

"I'm putting it back," the girl said, and held up a necklace that looked a lot like the one Connie had worn the day they'd arrived.

"Then *you* can tell Paw-Paw why we don't have anything tonight."

Harriet wasn't sure she was translating perfectly, but they were standing in front of Mavis and Connie's room holding what appeared to be Connie's necklace.

The young man—Paul, the young woman had called him—turned and went the opposite way down the hall. The girl went into Mavis and Connie's room. Harriet patted her pockets. She'd put her own room key in one pants pocket, and the one Mavis had given her in the other. She pulled it out and followed the girl into their room.

The girl screamed when Harriet entered and shut the door. She held her hand against her chest.

"You scared me," she said in accented English, her eyes cast downward. "Are you a friend of the women who stay in this room?" She looked up and saw Harriet's face and the color drained from her own. "You are her? The one the bride attacked?" Tears filled her eyes. "The manager will fire me. He told us we were to do everything to make your stay perfect. He said if one thing wasn't just right, we would be fired."

"Listen..." Harriet looked at the name badge on the girl's shirt. "... Odette. What I want to know is what were you doing standing in front of

41

my friend's room with my friend's necklace in your hands and arguing with some guy about putting it back."

The girl's eyes got wide as she realized Harriet had understood the conversation.

"And why will you be in trouble with Paw-paw, whoever he is?"

The girl took a deep breath.

"That is family business. I'm in your friend's room with her necklace because I found it in the dirty towels. I was unloading my cleaning cart, and it fell out. This is the last room I did, and the towels were on the top of my pile."

"How about I call my friends in the security department and see what they think?"

Odette started crying again.

"Please. I need this job. And see?" She pointed to the table where she'd set the necklace. "Your friend's necklace is here."

"How do I know this isn't a trick to distract me from the real things you stole?"

"I didn't steal anything, I swear. Please."

Harriet glanced around the room. She couldn't tell if anything was missing. Connie and Mavis didn't tend to leave things lying about when they weren't in their room, which is why she was sure Odette hadn't found the necklace in their towels. But she realized reporting the return of something didn't make a lot of sense. And Odette did appear to be in fear for her job.

She sighed.

"Okay, I won't tell your boss for now, but I'm telling my friends about this, and they may decide to talk to security, your boss or both."

The relief was visible on Odette's face.

"Thank you so much." She pointed at the ice bucket in Harriet's hand. "Can I get some ice for you?"

"No, I think you've done enough, thank you. Just leave."

Odette wrung her hands and didn't move.

"Go. Return jewelry to someone else's room."

Odette did something that was halfway between a curtsy and a bow, then turned and all but ran out of the room; Harriet waited a few minutes to give her time to leave the floor. When she finally went out, the corridor was empty, so she retrieved her ice and returned to the room without seeing anyone else.

Lauren came in as Harriet was filling her ice bag.

"Did you make the ice yourself? I figured you'd be halfway through your icing session by the time I got back."

"You haven't been gone that long. And no, I didn't make the ice by hand. I did have an interesting encounter."

"Wait, sounds like this story requires chocolate." She pulled two small brown bags from a large white one and tossed one to Harriet, then sat down opposite her.

"Okay, spill."

Chapter 6

Harriet went into the bath room and tossed her bag of half-melted ice in the sink. She glanced at the time on her phone.

"I suppose we should go catch up with the shopping group."

Lauren closed the lid on her laptop.

"Let's swing by and put in an appearance at the shops, and then move on to that Starbucks that's near there. They close at seven, but we've got time if we don't linger at the stores."

"Sounds like a plan," Harriet said and put on her light-weight cardigan.

Lauren reached into her pocket and pulled out a folded piece of paper.

"I forgot—I found this sticky note on the floor outside our door—James must have left it when you were gone getting ice, and it fell off."

"I didn't notice it when I came in. Do I even need to read it?" Harriet said and laughed.

"Hey, he stuck it on the door for anyone to see—I'm the one who folded it. And, yes, you need to read it. It's his schedule, and when he'll be back by."

Harriet shook her head and retreated to the bathroom to brush her teeth and gently wash her bruised face before they left.

They found Mavis and Connie in a gift shop a block down from Tina's. Connie had a new grandchild on the way, so she was immersed in the baby gift area, while Mavis perused kitchen accessories.

"What did the doctor say?" Mavis asked the minute she saw Harriet enter the store.

44

Lauren came up and answered for her.

"More rest, more ice, but otherwise she's fine."

Harriet turned to glare at her.

"I can speak for myself."

"Yeah, but it would take you longer, and we're on a tight schedule."

"Why is that?" Connie asked.

"We haven't eaten yet, since we've been following orders and icing. Our plan is to go to Starbucks if we can get there before they close at seven," Lauren told her.

Connie joined them, a set of embroidered onesies in hand.

"We got a snack in the hotel cafe before we came shopping. Are you two coming to the pajama party stitching tonight?"

Harriet waited to see if Lauren was going to answer before speaking.

"James wants to stop by, but otherwise, I think we're planning on coming."

"You girls run along, then, and we'll see you there," Mavis said. "You can give us a more complete report on what the doctor said."

"Sure," Harriet said. "Also remind me to tell you something weird that happened while we were at the hotel."

✂ --- ✂ --- ✂

Harriet set her stitching project on the big round table and went to load a paper plate with the homemade treats on the buffet. She was dressed in the flannel pajama pants her aunt had made.

"These look delicious," she said when she'd returned to her spot between Mavis and Connie.

"Someone did a lot of baking before we got here," Connie commented. She'd chosen to wear a purple warm-up suit in lieu of pajamas.

Mavis took a bite of a ginger cookie.

"Now, what was it you were going to tell us about something that happened at the hotel? That bride hasn't been bothering you again, has she?"

"No, nothing like that." Harriet described her encounter with the young housekeeper.

Connie stood up.

"I'm going to go look."

Mavis pressed her lips together.

"We were just up there after shopping. I'm sure we'd have noticed if something had been disturbed. The most valuable thing I brought with me is my phone and my stitching tool bag." She held both items up. "The rest is just clothes. I'm betting a young woman isn't interested in a bunch of old-lady things."

45

Connie sat back down.

"You're right. Both of the necklaces I brought are obvious costume pieces. One is made from sewing machine bobbins and the other is plastic beads covered in quilt fabric. Anyone can see they aren't worth anything. It *is* very curious, though. I definitely did not leave either one outside my suitcase."

Harriet popped a lemon-drop cookie into her mouth and let it melt into nothingness.

"Something weird is going on. I'm not sure what, but I don't believe for a minute that girl was returning the necklace."

Lauren took a sip from the bottle of water she'd brought from their room.

"This whole place is weird, if you ask me. And I thought that before we found out the hotel and pretty much every other building on this island is haunted."

Alice the nurse came in and stopped at their table.

"How did your doctor appointment go?"

"It was fine. They said I need to rest and ice a little more. I guess they thought the swelling should have gone down more than it had."

Alice examined her eye.

"Maybe. Everyone's a little different when it comes to how they heal. Some people are quick, and others take a little longer. I'm not a doctor, of course, but it seems like it's on track to me."

"Did we miss anything from class while we were gone?"

Alice laughed.

"No. We struggled along trying to stitch our stems down smoothly."

Harriet held up the green leaf fabric and off-white background she'd been stitching together.

"Did the teacher reveal any more secrets that could help me here?"

"No, she repeated the demo a second time, but there wasn't anything new."

The door opened again, and Sydney entered, a canvas bag over her arm.

"Is it okay if I join you guys? I brought my stitching." She held up a floral-pattern cloth tote.

Barb the conference organizer came over as well.

"Feel free. We have plenty of cookies. Be forewarned, though, the light in here isn't very good. We let our conference attendees know before they came, and as you can see, lots of people brought personal lamps."

"I bought one of those lights that hangs around your neck from your vendor in the lobby of the building across the street this afternoon."

Barb smiled at her.

"You're set, then. Enjoy."

Mavis looked at the quilt block Sydney pulled out of a small project bag.

"What are you making?"

The background fabric was a white tone-on-tone floral. Sydney was appliquéing a curved strip cut from a medium gray all-over print on to it. She held the block up so they could see the completed portion. A clear green diamond connected the arcs.

"It's a modern double wedding ring."

Connie leaned closer.

"I haven't seen that done before."

Sydney smiled.

"I'm not sure it has been done. My quilt group at home wanted everyone to do a modern quilting project, but I wasn't inspired by the patterns we found. I just don't get the whole modern thing. There were patterns with three circles of print fabric on a white background, or patterns of colored rectangles on a solid background. If I was a long-arm quilter, I could get excited about all that blank fabric to stitch patterns on, but I hand-piece. I decided to do a traditional pattern in a modern color palette."

"You're not the only one," Mavis said. "Harriet's aunt and I went to a quilt show a couple of months ago, and we noticed several modern quilt entries that were just what you're doing. Not the same pattern, but using more traditional pieced blocked patterns with modern quilt colors."

Harriet stopped stitching and looked at Sydney.

"I *am* a long arm quilter, and I'm not sure I get it. If I wanted to show off my stitching ability, I'd make a whole cloth quilt and forget sewing a few colored circles on it."

"I'm killing two birds with one stone. I'm making the quilt for my sister. Obviously, I'm behind schedule, since the quilt is still in pieces, and she's getting married in a few days; but it keeps my mother quiet to see me working on it."

"Does your mother quilt?" Connie asked her.

"No. She likes the look, though. When she wants to give a hand-done quilt to someone as a gift, I get to make it."

Lauren looked at her.

"That must be annoying."

Sydney shrugged.

"I never have to spend any money on fabric." She sighed. "And I don't have anyone to make quilts for, anyway."

Lauren was about to ask another question, but Mavis squeezed her arm; and when Lauren looked up, she shook her head, quieting her.

The group stitched in silence until Barb, their hostess, stood up to make an announcement. The other hostess, Ann, pulled a brightly patterned shopping bag from under the cookie table and sat it on the floor next to Barb. Susan, the third conference organizer, started handing out tickets to everyone.

"We've decided as a special treat this year we're going to have door prizes that are only for the hearty stitchers who stay up late at our pajama party."

Barb was midway around the first table, collecting tickets that now had names written on their backs, when two uniformed policemen stepped into the room.

"Sorry to interrupt," the taller of the two said. "There's been an incident in the hotel, and we're going to need you all to stay in this room until further notice."

"What sort of incident?" Barb asked; as the rest of the group began talking.

"An officer will be back to question all of you shortly."

He stepped back out into the corridor as the second officer looked at his notepad.

"Is one of you Sydney Johnson?"

The color drained from Sydney's face as she raised her hand.

"I'm Sydney."

"I'm going to need you to come with me."

She gathered her stitching and stuffed it into her bag. Harriet quickly wrapped the remaining cookies on her plate in a napkin and dropped them into the front pocket of her bag.

"You might need sustenance," she said.

Sydney glanced at her, eyes wide and her face white, and then followed the policeman out of the room.

✂ --- ✂ --- ✂

A half-hour passed with no return of the police, or anyone else. Barb stood up.

"I don't know what's going on, but as my mother always told me, don't borrow trouble. In that vein, I'd like to go ahead with our prize drawings. Where did we leave off with collecting tickets?"

Half the women at the first table raised their hands, and Susan went there to resume her ticket-taking. Ten prizes that varied from patterns designed by the teachers to specialty scissors that enabled a quilter to snip slits in tiny seams were distributed with much fanfare and discussion.

Harriet examined the stack of folded fat quarters she'd been presented when her name had been called.

"Well, now I have some modern quilt fabric to try out."

Mavis reached over and stroked the smooth cotton.

"It's nice fabric."

Connie took a bite of her last cookie and sat back in her chair, glancing at her watch as she did.

"I wonder when they're going to let us out of here. It's past my bedtime."

Harriet pulled her phone from her pocket and looked for a message.

"I can only imagine what they told James. He was planning on coming by after he got done with his cooking."

Mavis stood up.

"I'm going to go ask Barb if she can find out anything for us. I need to go to the restroom, and I'm probably not the only one, given how much water and tea we've all been drinking."

She went to the small table in the corner where the organizers were sitting. Connie gathered up their empty paper plates and used napkins and took them to the wastebasket by the door.

As soon as Connie was out of earshot, Lauren pulled her phone from her pocket, tapped it awake, and held it out to Harriet. Harriet took it and read the text message on the screen. It was from James.

> Not letting anyone out of hotel. In elevator when it happened. Held in conference room for questioning. Food brought in, slipped out with service people. Get Harriet out. Meet at my car on Kempner Street at Market. Turn Harriet's phone off.

She slumped in her chair.

"So, what does this mean?"

Lauren shrugged.

"It's pretty self-explanatory. Do you trust him?"

"Why do I need to get out of here? He didn't say you or Mavis or Connie. He said *I* need to get out."

"This is just a guess, but he likes you a lot more than he likes the rest of us."

"It's got to be more than that. And to answer your question, yes, I trust him."

Lauren squashed a cookie crumb on the table in front of her.

"I do, too. And he's a nice guy. If there was a general threat, he'd have a plan for all of us. There's something up with him texting me and not you, which again points to you specifically being in trouble."

"We need to tell Connie and Mavis. If we're allowed to go to the restroom, maybe they can create a diversion so we can get out of here."

Connie and Mavis returned to the table. Harriet quickly told them what had transpired. Connie looked toward the door.

"Barb called the front desk and asked them to find someone in control and get them to authorize a potty break."

Mavis frowned and shook her head.

"I don't like breaking the law, but I trust James. If he thinks you need to get out of here, he must have a good reason. And given the whole attack-by-the-bride nonsense, I'm starting to think there's something going on we're not privy to, and I mean more than whatever just happened. Hitting a total stranger to the point she has to go to the ER doesn't make sense—I don't care how stressed she is. People get married all the time without assaulting people they don't know. I don't want you getting caught up in that woman's crazy affairs any more than you already are."

"*Diós mio*," Connie said. "Are you suggesting we help Harriet escape?"

Mavis smiled grimly.

"If all the crime shows I've watched are correct, the police can't hold you unless they read you your rights and tell you you're in custody. I believe we are all free to go if we really want to. I'm not suggesting we do that, but I think if Harriet wanted to slip out while we were on our bathroom visit, she'd be within her rights. And since none of us knows anything about what's going on in this town, it shouldn't matter." She looked at Harriet. "You *don't* know anything about the bride or her family we don't, do you?"

"I already told you about James and I seeing the groom out with a woman not the bride. Other than that, I don't know anything."

"Yeah, except for the fact that the groom is a jerk and the bride a fool," Lauren added.

Connie scanned them each in turn.

"Do we all trust that James has Harriet's best interest in mind? I know Harriet believes it, but what about you two."

Lauren nodded.

"Yeah, I do. I can't imagine he'd make this sort of suggestion without a good reason."

Mavis chewed on her lip.

"Okay," she finally said. "I can't believe he'd suggest this if it weren't important. And, if we're going to do this, I have an idea."

Barb came back followed by a uniformed officer.

"Officer Wilson is going to escort us to the larger conference bathrooms upstairs. You can take your purse, if you want, but leave your stitching stuff here. We'll be coming back."

The quilters complained to each other about the unfairness of it all and asked Barb if anyone could tell them what had happened. Barb held her hand up, and after a moment, people noticed and fell silent.

"Susan and Ann and I don't know what has happened, and the police aren't telling us. They don't want us to talk about whatever it is until they question us. After we take our break, they're going to take us out one at a time. We won't be allowed to return to this room when we're finished, so when it's your turn, take all your stuff with you. I think I speak for the whole organizing team when I say how sorry we are that we're in the middle of…" She gestured with both hands. "…whatever this is."

Harriet and Lauren positioned themselves behind Mavis and Connie at the back of the group. As they reached the bellmen's station, Mavis gave a little cry and crumpled to the floor. Connie knelt beside her and pulled a prescription bottle from her purse. She cracked it open and slid a pill under Mavis's tongue. No one else could see it was a cough drop.

"Give her some space," Connie said in a loud voice. "She'll be okay as soon as her medication kicks in."

The quilters stepped back. The clerk at the desk came over to help.

While everyone was focused on Mavis, Harriet and Lauren slipped through the door behind the bellmen's station. Mavis had explained she'd watched one of the bellmen take a woman with a walker through there the day before, emerging onto the sidewalk in front of the hotel a few moments later, avoiding the main entry stairs.

"Wow, this was a good catch by Mavis. I hadn't noticed anyone using this entry. I guess it's how they deal with ADA accessibility." Lauren glanced at a map she'd opened on her smart phone. "The most direct way to James takes us in front of the main entrance. Let's go to the right and circle around the back of the hotel. It'll be an extra two blocks, but we'll be on darker, quieter streets."

Harriet headed out in the direction indicated.

"This makes no sense. Why are we avoiding the police?"

"Hopefully, James is going to explain all this. If I were to guess, I'd say he thinks you're in danger. Maybe the bride is rampaging. Maybe he heard her threaten you further. I don't know. If you stop talking and start walking faster, we can find out."

As soon as they turned the corner, Harriet broke into a jog.

"Turn right at the next corner," Lauren called out. She pulled her phone from her pocket and dialed James as she, too, started jogging. "We're headed your way, four blocks out," Harriet heard her say.

It felt like an eternity had passed before Harriet spotted the rental car sitting at the corner of Kepner Street at Market with its running lights on. The driver's side door opened, and James got out. He pulled her into a quick embrace.

"Thank heaven you're safe," he said and led her to the front passenger side door, quickly helping her in before returning to the driver's side.

"You better get in, too," he told Lauren and she did.

He pulled away from the curb and continued on Market Street, heading toward the ferry landing. Harriet twisted to face him.

"James, what are we doing here?"

When he didn't answer immediately, Lauren leaned forward from the back seat.

"Yeah, James, what *are* we doing here?"

He looked into the rearview mirror, clearly checking to see if anyone was following them.

"It's a long story, and I'll tell you everything when we get onto the ferry."

Lauren sagged back in her seat.

"This better be good," she muttered.

"Doesn't the ferry go to the Boliver Peninsula?" Harriet asked.

"It does," Lauren answered when it became apparent James wasn't going to.

A ferry was docked at the landing; James drove onto it and turned the engine off.

Chapter 7

The Boliver ferries weren't anything like their Puget Sound counterparts. For one thing, they were much smaller, with single open car decks that could hold three rows of cars per side.

Harriet looked up. There was a narrow structure that housed a pilot house on each end and a public seating area in the middle. An outdoor viewing deck circled the whole upper level. Most of the passengers locked their cars and headed up the stairs.

"Let's get out," James said. He led the way to the side of the boat. "I'm sorry to be so cryptic, but it was important for us to get out of town before anyone could question us."

Lauren looked out over the dark water.

"What happened?" she asked, her voice rising with her frustration.

Harriet put a hand on her arm.

"Keep your voice down."

"If he doesn't tell us what's going on—and I mean right now—I'm going to call nine-one-one myself and tell them where we are."

James sighed.

"I'm sorry. I guess I'm avoiding telling you anything because now that we're on the ferry my plan seems crazier than it did when we were being held in separate rooms under police guard. I couldn't think of anything else at the time."

Lauren started to speak, but he held his hand up to silence her.

"Let me start at the beginning, before I lose my nerve," he continued. "Earlier this evening, I was going up to your hotel room to see if you'd gotten back, like I said in the note, but before I got there, I saw Harriet

53

go into another room." He looked at her. "I wasn't sure it was you, but I heard someone say 'Harriet, what are you doing here?' and then you went into the room, and the door closed. I went to the door and knocked, but no one answered. I thought it was weird, so I went back down the hall and knocked on your door. No one answered there, either, so I left."

"I went into Connie and Mavis's room, but that was a lot earlier," Harriet told him.

"I told you it seemed weird. Let me finish before we figure that part out. I went and did my roux practice session, and we got done early enough I decided to come back and see how your doctor visit went. I was getting off the elevator on your floor, and I heard screams, and a woman came out of that same room you'd gone into screaming for someone to call nine-one-one."

"*What?*" Lauren and Harriet said in unison.

"Yeah. I was pushed back into the elevator by a hysterical older woman who hit the down button and was screaming about her 'baby.' We got off the elevator in the lobby, the woman yelled her daughter Jennifer had been murdered, and the bellmen locked the front door. A security officer appeared, and those of us from the elevator were hustled into a conference room. I don't know what they did with the people from the lobby."

Harriet grabbed the side rail of the ferry with both hands. The water was becoming choppy, and she stumbled briefly before regaining her balance.

"And you think I killed her?"

He put his hands on her shoulders.

"Harriet, no. I know you didn't kill anyone. I don't want to scare you, but they're going to talk to everyone in the hotel and with the bride doing that…" He pointed to her eye. "… the police are going to want to talk to take a closer look at you."

Lauren ran her fingers through her long hair and twisted a strand around her index finger.

"Oh, geez, she's going to be suspect number one."

James glared at her. Harriet sighed and her whole body sagged. She clutched the railing tighter and he put his hands on her shoulders gently kneading the muscles.

"She's right. Especially if they interview you and find out you think I went into her room."

"I'd lie about it in a heartbeat if I could, but I'm not a good liar. They'd know, and then they'd wonder what I was trying to cover up, and you'd be in more trouble. The housekeeper saw me on the stairs, but I don't know if she was close enough behind me to have seen what I saw or if she'll tell them I was up there banging on the bride's door."

Harriet shrugged his hands off.

"So, what are we doing here?"

Lauren looked up from her phone, which she'd pulled from her pocket, presumably to look for news of the event.

"Yeah, what are we doing?"

"Don't get mad, but this was all I could think of." He took a deep breath. "In Louisiana, you can get a special marriage license for five dollars, allowing you to marry immediately. If we're married, I can refuse to answer questions about you."

Harriet gasped and spluttered as she tried to regain her breath.

"What?" she croaked.

"We only have to do it on paper. If we both swear we consummated it, no one can prove we didn't. This way, as I said, I won't have to say anything."

"What about the cleaning woman?"

"She was in that room where they keep their carts when I came the second time and seemed pretty scared when the woman ran out of the room screaming. She started crying and saying something in French, and I don't know how we'd figure out if she saw anything. All I know is, I don't want to be the one who testifies against you."

Lauren finished making a call and slid her phone back into her pocket.

"You did the right thing," she said. "I just called Robin, and she said neither one of you should talk to the police until you have legal representation."

Harriet looked at her.

"Can we do that?"

"Doesn't that make us look guiltier?" James asked before Lauren could answer.

"First of all, since she's a lawyer, I don't think Robin can recommend something like that if it isn't legal," Lauren pointed out. "Something about being an officer of the court. But I did ask that question—actually, both of your questions—and Robin says it's the lesser of two evils."

Harriet leaned against James. She hadn't ruled out the possibility of marrying again; she just hadn't thought it was going to happen anytime soon. Having been in a relationship with Aiden Jalbert, the veterinarian her friend Carla worked for, that was in the process of ending badly, marriage was the last thing on her mind. And to James?

She needed time to think.

"Wow."

Lauren turned to watch the approaching lights of the Boliver ferry landing.

"Oh, and Robin is getting on the first flight out in the morning. She can't represent you in Texas, of course, but she's contacting a law school friend who lives in Houston and owes her a favor. Something about a really ugly bridesmaid dress."

"Did you tell her about James's plan?"

Lauren gave her a wicked smile.

"She said congratulations and not to worry, you can have it annulled when you get back to Foggy Point."

Harriet stared at Lauren.

"She didn't really say that, did she?"

"Well, not in those words, but she did say it wasn't a bad idea. She pointed out it doesn't solve all the problems, but it does stop James from putting you directly in the cross-hairs. And it buys her time to get a legal team assembled, if that's what it comes to. I did ask her the annulment question. She said probably, depending on what happens between now and then." She raised her eyebrows. "If you know what I mean."

"She did not."

Lauren laughed.

"Okay, she said she'd have to check, but at the very least, you could get a divorce. She did reiterate it was important that Harriet not become the simple solution to their crime. Since the bride isn't from Texas and neither are you, Robin is afraid they'll take the easy way out and not bother with the real killer. Besides, I've always wanted to be a bridesmaid."

James narrowed his eyes.

"I'm glad you're getting a laugh out of our problems."

Lauren stopped laughing.

"Sorry, it's how I cope."

Harriet looked out over the water.

"I've got to call my aunt," she said finally.

Lauren offered her phone, but Harriet pulled her own from her pocket. She walked along the railing to create some space between herself and her friends and then dialed. She described the situation then listened to her aunt's advice before signing off and rejoining the others.

"Well?" Lauren demanded.

"She surprised me. She said there was no question—I have to marry James if there is even a chance it can keep me from being arrested for killing the bride."

James held his phone up.

"For what it's worth, I called my mom, too."

"Oh, James, I'm sorry. I've been acting like this is all about me, but you're getting married under duress, too."

He smiled.

"I guess I don't see it as quite the huge sacrifice that you do, but yes, I'm getting married, too. I explained the situation to my mom, and she said she was proud of me for wanting to protect you from injustice."

Lauren started toward the car.

"We're getting close to the dock. I called Mavis and Connie while you two were calling home. I'll tell you what they said when we're settled again."

James steered the rental car off the ferry and headed east on Highway eighty-seven, the only real option when you got off a ferry at the Boliver landing. The peninsula was sufficiently narrow they could see the Gulf of Mexico out the passenger side of the car and the channel leading out of Galveston Bay from the driver's-side windows at the same time.

Harriet turned to the back seat.

"So, what's going on back at the hotel?"

"Well, they haven't asked Connie or Mavis where you are. Their sense is the detectives are busy with the wedding party while lower-level police are interviewing the people in the lobby and the hotel employees. Mavis thinks they're waiting to talk to them until later because they don't see them as likely suspects. They figure if and when someone mentions the potential bride-whacking Harriet that will change."

Harriet faced forward and leaned her head against her seat.

"I wonder if we can get this done and get back there before they get to us."

James looked into the rearview mirror at Lauren.

"Look on your phone and find us an all-night pharmacy in Beaumont. I'm pretty sure that's the first town we'll come to that's large enough to have one. We need to get ice packs for Harriet's eye."

Harriet closed her eyes.

"See if they have a twenty-four-hour Walmart instead. I know this isn't a real wedding, but I'd like to wear something besides pajamas."

Lauren tapped on her phone.

"No problem. Walmart is everywhere."

"How are we getting around the waiting period?" Harriet asked after a few silent minutes had passed.

"We're getting a special license," James reminded her. "My classmate who told me how to do this has an uncle who's a judge, and he can waive the waiting period for us."

Lauren's phone chimed, and she opened her text messages.

"Robin says to tell her which courthouse our judge works out of, and she'll fax a copy of Steve's death certificate to them—your aunt is going to your house to get it from your lockbox. Robin says they can't let you marry unless they have a copy attached to the license. She called James's mom to make sure he's free to marry, too."

"She could have just asked me," he said without taking his eyes off the road.

Lauren laughed.

"I can see the Threads now. They've probably all swung into action, looking up Louisiana law, making tea, warming cookies. Kinda makes you wish we were there."

"If we were there, there'd be no reason to meet, so best that we're here," Harriet said.

They drove on for another hour, each lost in their own thoughts. Then, James pulled the car into the parking lot of an all-night gas station and convenience store.

"I don't know about you ladies, but I need a break and something to drink."

Harriet and Lauren headed for the restroom while James pumped gas.

"Probably best if you stay in the background," Lauren told Harriet. "You look a little scary for people who aren't used to your eye."

"Good point. Can you grab me some sort of bottled tea and whatever frozen food they have that I can ice my eye with?"

She returned to the car and waited while Lauren and James bought drinks and snacks. Lauren opened the back door and climbed in, tossing her a bag of frozen okra.

"This is all they had, so I hope it works for you."

"It's great," Harriet said and held the bag up to her eye. "What do you think is really going on here?" she asked when they were on the road again.

"You mean in the car tonight?" Lauren asked.

James glanced at Harriet.

"I think we're really getting married so I can't be compelled to say anything incriminating about you."

Harriet set her okra down on the seat.

"Geez, guys, I know why we're *here* tonight. What do you think is going on at the hotel? I mean, the bride whacking me and then ending up dead."

Lauren sighed.

"That's a very good question. Let's review what we know."

"Was Harriet being attacked the first thing that happened?" James asked.

Harriet turned sideways.

"The groom hitting on me and the bride being rude about it was the first thing that happened. *Then* the bride hit me."

Lauren pulled a notebook from her shoulder bag.

"I think I need to write this down. First the drunk groom, then the hit. And then we met the long-suffering sister and learned the marriage is possibly not a love match."

"They were looking for the missing groom one day," Harriet added. "Do we know if they ever found him?"

Lauren wrote "missing groom" and put a question mark.

"Let's not forget the staff," Harriet said. "I don't know if they connect to the bride's death, but the whole business about supposedly returning Connie's necklace seems fishy, and the conversations I heard when they were speaking Cajun struck me as odd."

James drummed his fingers on the steering wheel.

"Can you connect the staff people to the bride and groom in any way other than me seeing one on the stairs when faux-Harriet went into the bride's room?"

Harriet shook her head, and Lauren wrote "connection between Cajuns and bride."

"Who do we think the me lookalike is or was?" Harriet asked.

"That's another good question," Lauren said.

"Do you guys still want to stop at a Walmart?" James asked as they passed a sign telling them Beaumont was coming up.

Harriet crunched her bag of okra in her hand.

"This is working fine as ice. I say we keep going. We can buy clothes in Louisiana."

Lauren looked up from her phone.

"Works for me. I don't see anything on the Houston news station about the murder at the hotel. I was just thinking about calling Mavis again to see what's going on."

"Do it," Harriet said.

"I'm putting you on speaker phone," Lauren said when she'd dialed up Mavis. "What's going on there?"

"Let me ease away from the crowd," Mavis said and presumably did so.

"*Dios mio*," they heard Connie say, then a rustling noise.

"Okay," Mavis said. "You're on speaker here, too. We haven't made it out yet, but two police officers started doing quick interviews just outside our door. They seem to be taking everyone's name and home address one at a time and then letting them go."

"Has anyone said anything about the murder?"

"Not directly to us. We heard from the hotel employees who brought us coffee and tea earlier that they think the bride was killed sometime early in the evening, possibly while we were shopping."

"That's why we're all being questioned," Connie said.

"Everything okay with you three?" Mavis asked.

"We're just driving," Lauren told her.

"Oops, I've got to go, they're questioning the people at the table before ours." Mavis disconnected the call.

James looked over at Harriet.

"No news is good news, huh?"

She stared out the window.

"I was hoping they'd decide she'd been killed while we were in the stitching room."

"I was hoping they'd arrested the groom," Lauren said. "Aren't you most likely to be killed by your loved ones?"

On that happy note, they fell silent again while James drove on through the night.

Chapter 8

Harriet stood in front of a rack of dresses in the Walmart in Alexandria, Louisiana.

"Why can't stores stock the clothes you need now instead of always being a season or two ahead?"

Lauren pointed to a rack at the back of the women's clothing section. It had a large forty percent-off sign attached to its crossbar.

"I think those are the summer options. Come on, let's see what they have."

Harriet pulled a lime-green lace number from the section marked with her size.

"What about this?"

"You're joking, right?"

Harriet smiled.

"Maybe I should have stayed in the fall section. The black or gray would go with my eye."

Lauren dug through the rack, studying each selection before rejecting it and taking the next one. She finally stopped and handed her a lavender floral wrap dress.

"How about this one?"

Harriet took it from her and held it up to her body.

"Not bad. See what else there is."

Lauren handed her two more summery dresses.

"That's it, so take your pick."

Harriet ended up with a simple sheath in a rose-colored cotton blend. She took it to the dressing room and came out a few minutes later.

"Well?" Lauren asked.

"Not something I'd normally pick, but under the circumstances, I think it's wonderful."

"James texted while you were trying the dress on. He got us rooms at a motel two blocks from here."

"Let's grab an ice bag on our way out."

Lauren took the dress from her.

"I'll go get that while you go find a pair of shoes."

"I'd rather go barefoot than wear cheap shoes."

"And I'd rather be in my hotel room in Galveston with nothing but stitching on my mind, but neither of those things is happening. We will not upset the judge who is doing us a great favor by waiving your waiting period and putting you first up on his already booked schedule."

Harriet sighed as she turned and headed to the shoe department.

✂ --- ✂ --- ✂

Lauren threw the Walmart bag on her bed and plopped down beside it.

"I can't believe this hotel only costs forty-nine dollars a night."

Harriet found the mini-fridge and put her bag of okra in the tiny freezer compartment.

"I can't believe I'm spending my wedding eve in a forty-nine-dollar-a-night motel."

Lauren reached into the shopping bag and pulled out two diet Dr. Peppers.

"I know it isn't your traditional bachelorette party, but I can play a wedding movie on my tablet for us. How about *The Wedding Crashers*? Or maybe *My Big Fat Greek Wedding*?"

"For once, I'm glad you carry your tablet everywhere you go. I need something more mellow, though. Can you find *The Wedding Singer*?"

"Easy peasy." Lauren brought her tablet out, tapped it awake, and began searching for the movie.

Harriet went into the bathroom to get glasses for their soda.

"Hey, look what I found." She held up a cellophane-wrapped package. "They gave us a bag of microwave popcorn." She opened it, unfolded the bag and set it on the glass tray in the little microwave. While it was popping, she brought two washcloths over to the nightstand along with the glasses. She grabbed the pillows from her bed and tossed them onto Lauren's to make a backrest for herself.

"This is much more my style than my first bachelorette party. The wives and girlfriends of Steve's friends took me out and pretty much did every cliché party trick."

62

"Do tell. Did they have a male stripper?"

"Oh, yeah—two of them." She shuddered. "It was perhaps the most painful night of my entire adult life. And not because of the guys. Having grown up mostly in Europe, I find nude men and women at the beach normal. It's just how it is over there. My 'friends'..." She made air quotes. "...acted like they were in junior high. They giggled and poked the dancers, and stuffed money in their g-strings." She shuddered again.

Lauren sighed. "I didn't grow up in Europe, but I never got that whole nude male dancer thing. It's so demeaning to all parties involved."

"I agree," Harriet said and went to fetch the popcorn.

Lauren scanned the room.

"With a little warning we could have gotten something better, but I guess it is what it is."

Harriet attempted a smile.

"Let's not over-think it." She set the popcorn on the nightstand, poured two glasses of soda and sat down on the bed, handing one to Lauren. "Let's just watch our movie and then try to get some sleep."

Lauren propped the tablet on a pillow between them and grabbed a handful of popcorn.

"You got it."

✂ --- ✂ --- ✂

Lauren was sitting at Judge Metoyer's computer when James and Harriet entered his chambers.

"I recommend you develop a more complicated password and change it on all your accounts. Whoever was trying to hack you didn't make it all the way in, but they shouldn't have gotten as far as they did."

"Thank you so much. If there's ever anything I can do for you, let me know."

"If you can get these two lovebirds married, we'll be even. And if your problem here persists, call me anytime, day or night."

The judge was wearing a blue seersucker with white shoes and belt. He peered at James and Harriet overtop his wire-rimmed glasses.

"My nephew tells me you own a restaurant in the Northwest," he said to James.

"Yes, sir, I do. We'd love to have you come for dinner if you ever get up our way."

"Thank you, I may just take you up on that. The missus has been after me to take her up north for some time." He turned to Harriet. "And you, young lady. What do you do at home? Are you also in the restaurant business?"

"I'm a quilter. I mean, I have a commercial machine and quilt other people's quilts for them."

"I'm going to show my age here, but I'm guessing women don't sit around a frame in the church basement and quilt by hand anymore?"

Lauren and Harriet shared a look and then laughed.

"Yes, people still do that on occasion. We did one that way last month. But with queen- and king-size beds, most people have someone like me machine quilt their project on a more industrial-style machine."

The judge sat down and indicated Harriet and James should step up in front of his desk.

"You three didn't come here to educate an old man, so I suppose we should get this done." He looked at the papers in front of him on his desk. "Okay, so we've seen copies of your birth certificates, and…" He looked at Harriet. "…the death certificate of your first husband. I'm sorry to hear you were widowed at such an early age."

He studied the papers more.

"It looks like everything is in order. In lieu of counseling, I'm obligated to ask you if you're sure you want to do this, and if both of you are entering into this arrangement of your own free will."

They both nodded the affirmative.

"Will we be having rings?"

Harriet started to shake her head but stopped when she saw James dig a small box from his pocket. His mouth curled into a slight smile.

"Walmart," he said.

The judge took the box.

"I'm not sure what you were expecting, but I have a few words to say and then if you have your own vows, you can speak them to each other. If not, I'll lead you through the vows we've written, and then we'll do a ring ceremony."

A knock on the door interrupted him.

"Come in," he intoned.

His clerk bustled in with a large bouquet in her hands. She handed it to Lauren, who gave her a wad of cash in exchange.

"Thank you."

Lauren in turn handed the flowers to Harriet.

"Her sister is the local florist," she said by way of explanation.

The judge waited while Harriet took one of the flowers and slipped it into the pocket of James's white shirt. He looked at each of them and smiled.

"Are we ready?"

They nodded again, and he began the wedding ceremony.

Harriet tried to stay in the moment, but it was hard not to think about her first wedding. Her parents hadn't been there, of course. They'd been too involved in their careers to take time off for something as trivial as their only child's wedding. Steve's parents had been wonderful, and of course, Aunt Beth had been there. Her dress had been simple—an off-white silk embroidered with small lavender flowers. She'd splurged on a pair of custom pumps made from the same silk. And the biggest difference—she'd loved Steve more than life itself.

James took her hands, squeezing slightly before repeating after the judge.

✂ --- ✂ --- ✂

The drive back didn't seem as long as the drive to, and the scenery was better. Lauren had her tablet in her lap and papers spread out in the back seat. Harriet turned to say something to her, but she was deep in a work problem.

James smiled at her.

"Have you thought about what you're going to do about your name? I mean, you could take mine. It would save you having to explain why you were named after the thirty-third president of the United States. Or we could be progressive and both hyphenate."

Harriet laughed.

"Clearly, you've given this some thought."

"We've had a few miles to think about things. Haven't you thought about it?"

"No offense, but I haven't thought about our marriage since we finished our I-dos. I've been obsessing about how and why we've been dragged into a murder in a strange city and among people we've never met before."

"I thought about that the second hour we were driving."

"Did you come up with anything?"

James shook his head. "It just doesn't make sense."

"You're right. Wait. What did you think about the first hour?"

His cheeks turned red, and he smiled.

"Oh, just fantasizing about what it would be like if we'd just gotten married for real."

Harriet's own cheeks felt hot, and she looked out the window to avoid having to acknowledge that she'd indulged in a few fantasies of her own.

✂ --- ✂ --- ✂

Mavis and Connie were waiting in one of the conversation areas of the hotel lobby when Harriet, James and Lauren returned.

"Don't you look nice," Connie said, surveying Harriet, who was still wearing her wedding dress.

"Walmart's finest," she said.

Lauren took the chair next to Mavis.

"So, what's happening here?"

"We went to class as usual," Mavis told them. "They collected our names and addresses last night. We put you both on the list."

"We told them you'd gone to the restroom," Connie interjected.

"But they haven't come back to talk to us," Mavis continued. "I think they've been busy with the wedding party. I heard from someone in my class that the groom arrived back at the hotel, very drunk, around midnight. She said he didn't seem to know his bride was dead, but he was so drunk it was hard to tell."

James cleared his throat, and the women all looked at him.

"If you're all okay here, I'm going to go back to the cooking school. I told them I'd been caught up in the investigation here, but if I'm gone much longer, they may start to doubt my story."

He took Harriet's left hand in both of his.

"I'll see you later. It's been fun."

Connie stood up.

"*Diós mio*. I can't believe you're married."

Harriet smiled.

"Me, either. Did you tell my teacher anything about where Lauren and I were?"

Mavis grimaced.

"I don't like to tell a fib, but I told your teacher that, all things considered, you weren't up to coming to class this morning. And I told her Lauren was helping you with your ice bags. At least that part was true. She probably was helping you, although your eye looks a little puffy."

"Both my eyes are puffy—we got almost no sleep last night."

Connie smiled.

"I think most brides lose sleep the night before their wedding."

Lauren laughed at that.

"We were awake trying to figure out how we found ourselves in such a mess."

Mavis waited for her to stop laughing.

"And? Did you come up with anything?"

Harriet told her about James seeing someone who looked like her and was addressed by her name being invited into the bride's room earlier last evening. They'd only given Mavis and Connie the minimal explanation the night before.

66

Mavis pressed her lips together.

"That explains why James thought marrying you was a good solution. If he told the police what he thought he saw, you'd be the number-one suspect for sure."

"Don't remind me," Harriet said. "What I can't figure out is whether this is a random coincidence, in which case, Who is the mystery woman who looks like me, and why did she want the bride dead? Or am I the target of someone, as evidenced by my bashed eye?"

Mavis's eyes narrowed as she thought.

"What possible connection could you have to these people?"

Harriet stood up and paced the small seating area.

"I can't imagine any connection. Apart from meeting the groom the first day we got here, I had no previous contact with these people."

"We did have cookies with the sister," Lauren pointed out. "She seems like she's as much a victim of the bride and her mother as we are. I imaging she'd rather be anywhere but here. And with her sister dead, her mom might start pressuring her to marry a prince and produce an heir."

Harriet stopped.

"Good point. I can imagine the groom not wanting to marry into that family. It sounds like his family needs the money, though. But maybe in the end, he just couldn't do it."

Mavis stood up.

"Well, it's not our problem to fix. Robin is arriving tonight, and her friend is meeting her here."

"Seems like overkill to me," Harriet said.

Lauren looked at her.

"You say that now, but we're not free of this place yet. The police are going to come and talk to you. Mark my word, they are going to hear about the bride's attack on you, and they're going to want to talk to you, and you'll be glad Robin's here when that happens."

Mavis put her arm around Harriet's shoulders and turned her toward the elevators.

"We have free time until our banquet. Why don't you get some ice for your eye and lie down for a while?"

"Sounds good to me," Harriet agreed as they moved to the elevators.

Lauren stopped and turned toward the lobby cafe.

"I'm going to get us some iced tea. All those hours in the car with the air conditioner on has me dried out, and I'm sure you are, too."

"That would be great. See you up there."

"And we'll meet both of you in the lobby across the street before the banquet," Mavis said as she pressed the up button on the elevator.

Chapter 9

Harriet grabbed her empty ice bag as soon as she and Lauren returned to their room.

"I've got to get some ice and do some serious eye chilling."

"I'm going to grab a fresh battery charger for my pad, and if you're okay for a while by yourself, I'm going to go to the upstairs restaurant and check my emails."

"Good reminder. I need to plug my phone in before I do anything else."

"Okay, I'll meet you back here in about an hour."

"I'll just be here chillin'."

Lauren shook her head and struggled not to smile.

The hallway was empty when Harriet went to the ice machine and back, which suited her fine. She had a lot to think about and wasn't in the mood for small talk with her classmates.

The hotel room's walk-in closet had a hinged door off the entry. As Harriet passed the door, she hesitated. She had abandoned her class project bag at the pajama party the night before—hopefully, Mavis or Connie had it—but she'd packed a hand-piecing project in a small bag in her suitcase. She considered it an emergency project. That usually meant something easy to work on when she was doing a project too big or too complicated to take with her to a group meeting.

She couldn't have imagined all that had happened so far on this trip, but sitting around putting ice on her injured eye certainly qualified as an emergency. Working with her hands always enabled her to focus on whatever the current problem was. And if she balanced her ice carefully, she could stitch one-eyed while she was sitting and thinking.

She carried her ice to the bathroom sink and returned to the closet. She was on her knees digging in her suitcase when the closet door behind her slammed shut.

"Hello?" she called out. She assumed the maid had entered the room with her cart and inadvertently pushed the door shut. "I'm in the closet. Can you open it please?"

She pressed her ear to the door and listened. She could hear the rustle of clothing. Someone was in the room.

"Hello?" she called again, her voice louder.

She heard the rustling noise again and then a door shut. She patted her pocket and realized two things—she was still wearing a dress that didn't have a pocket, and her phone was on the nightstand, plugged into its charger. She pounded on the door with her fist but knew there was no point. Whoever had locked her in was gone.

She felt the doorknob plate, hoping there would be a turn handle for the lock, but it didn't appear to have a locking mechanism at all. She discovered a switch on the wall next to the door and was happy a light came on when she flipped it.

If there was no lock, someone must have jammed something under the door to wedge it shut. She got on her hands and knees and leaned down to scan the bottom of the door. She yelped when she tilted her head below level as intense pain radiated from her eye. That wasn't going to work.

With a sigh, she sat back against her suitcase and hoped all of Lauren's clients hadn't filled her inbox with messages that needed immediate attention.

Harriet fought the urge to cry. She'd had a tough few months back in Foggy Point and had really hoped this retreat was going to be a true vacation. Now, all she wanted was to go home to her own house, her aunt Beth and her pets. She vowed never to leave them again.

After what seemed like an eternity, she heard the outer door rattle.

"Lauren, help, I'm locked in the closet." She pounded her fist on the door for good measure.

"Hang on."

Harriet heard a scraping noise, and then the closet door opened.

"Thank heaven you're back."

"Was that ever in question?" Lauren asked. "What were you doing in the closet?"

"I was inside it getting something from my suitcase when the door slammed shut, and I couldn't get it open."

Lauren held up a brown rubber triangle.

"This was wedged under the door. And that didn't happen by accident."

Harriet came out of the closet and went to the table holding the hotel phone.

"I think it's time to call my buddies in hotel security."

Lauren joined her.

"I'll call them while you do a little icing. You may not get another chance for a while."

Harriet grabbed her ice bag and sat on the bed, ice in one hand and her cell phone in the other. She tapped out a text message to Connie and Mavis.

"Are you okay?" Mavis asked as they rushed into the room a moment later.

"I'm fine. Just a little confused about what's going on."

Bruce from hotel security arrived before they could discuss the new development any further. He was followed by a slender man dressed in the same uniform; his name tag read *Cam*.

"Are you hurt?" Bruce asked.

"Nothing new," Harriet said dryly.

Bruce pulled a notebook from his pocket, and Harriet wondered if he was a former policeman.

"Tell me exactly what happened."

Harriet recited her short story.

"I really don't know anything except the door closed when my back was turned."

"Is anything missing from the room?"

Harriet glanced around, and her eyes landed on an instantly recognizable sky-blue jeweler's box sitting open on the coffee table. Cam followed the direction of her gaze and went to the table.

"Don't touch it," Bruce told him as he was about to do just that.

Cam sucked in his breath.

"I've never seen that before," Harriet said.

Bruce pressed his lips together and stared at her.

"We've been looking for this."

"What is it?" Lauren asked.

"If that holds what we've been told to look for in a box like that, it's the murdered bride's wedding ring."

Harriet gasped.

"How did it get in here?"

Bruce sighed and shook his head.

"I'd like to know that myself." He looked at Harriet. "I'm afraid I'm going to have to report this to the detectives."

Mavis put her hands on her hips.

"What about Harriet being locked in the closet?"

"If she *was* locked in the closet," Bruce said.

"I found this wedged under the door," Lauren said, handing him the rubber stopper.

"And you are?" he asked.

"Lauren Sawyer, Harriet's friend and current roommate."

"Exactly."

Bruce led Harriet to a conference room off the hallway opposite the check-in desk.

"The detectives will be here shortly."

Mavis, Connie and Lauren paused in the hall.

"We'll wait with her," Connie said in her teacher voice and brushed past Bruce before he could object. Mavis and Lauren slipped into the room while he was turned to Connie.

He glared at them.

"Fine, you can stay till the detectives get here."

He left as the hotel manager entered carrying a pitcher of iced tea and a stack of glasses.

"I'm sure this is all a misunderstanding," he said. "We'll get you ladies back to your conference in no time."

"At least somebody likes us," Lauren said when the door was closed again.

Harriet sat down at the table.

"He's just worried the appliqué group is going to give them a bad review."

Lauren poured a glass of tea and held it up.

"Tea, anyone?"

Harriet nodded, and Lauren handed her the glass then poured another for herself. Connie and Mavis declined.

Connie pulled out a chair and sat opposite Harriet.

"Why would someone lock you in your closet and then leave the bride's ring?"

Lauren sipped her tea.

"That's easy. Someone is doing a bang-up job of implicating Harriet in the murder of the bride."

Mavis finally pulled a chair out and sat down.

"Let's think about this a minute. Why Harriet? I mean, none of us knows any of those people. And what is with the jewelry? First, someone is caught 'returning' my necklace, and then someone puts the dead woman's ring in Harriet and Lauren's room. And what does that have to do with the murder?"

Harriet tapped her fingers on the table.

"I'm not sure the two things are connected."

The door opened, and two men with badges clipped to their belts came in. One had thinning hair and the trim physique of a runner. The second was shorter and stockier and had a full mane of black hair.

"I'm Detective Mike Settle," the thinner one said. "This is Detective Rob Grier. Which one of you is Harriet Truman?"

Harriet raised her hand.

Detective Settle looked at the other three women.

"I'm going to have to ask the rest of y'all to wait out in the hall."

Mavis glared at him, but Lauren took her by the arm and firmly guided her out of the room before she said anything. Connie followed.

"What happened to your eye?" Detective Grier asked when the room was cleared.

Harriet wondered if this was some sort of test. She was certain Bruce had given him the whole story. Nevertheless, she explained her encounter with the bride.

"And you're sure you'd had no contact with Ms. Johnson prior to meeting her and Mr. Williams in the bar?" Grier asked.

Harriet could see the skepticism written all over his face.

"I don't know how many different ways I can tell you; I've never met, seen, talked to or in any other way had anything to do with any of these people before I came here for the appliqué conference. And frankly, after being hit in the eye and locked in a closet, I'm ready to go home."

The two detectives looked at each other. Finally, Detective Settle spoke.

"That wouldn't be a good idea."

Detective Grier leaned back in his chair.

"So, we've got the Johnsons on one side of this thing—the daughter attacked you, now she's dead. On the other side, we have you—you were attacked, now your attacker is dead. From our perspective, neither of you is from around here so we have nothing to help us form an opinion about who did what to whom."

He pulled a smartphone from his pocket.

"Let's just see what Detective Google has to say about you both."

He tapped on the screen and, while he was waiting for the signal to connect and the data to download, pulled a pair of dark-rimmed reading glasses from his pocket.

"Okay, let's see here. Jennifer Johnson was presented at the Christmas Cotillion in Savannah, Georgia, last winter. Nothing too nefarious about that." He scrolled down the page. "She was on the Georgia Bulldogs cheerleading team." He read in silence for another minute. "I'm not seeing anything in her background that would suggest she's the type of gal who would attack a total stranger."

"And yet I'm the one with the broken eye socket. And a room full of witnesses to the attack."

Detective Grier tapped on his phone and waited again for a page to load. He read the first entry and looked over the top of his glasses at Harriet.

"Well, well, well. Now we're getting somewhere."

The door to the room banged open and Robin McLeod burst in before Harriet could say anything. She was dressed in a navy-blue pantsuit and looked more professional than Harriet had ever seen her.

"Don't say another word," she ordered Harriet and turned to the detectives. "Is she under arrest?"

"Who are you?" Settle asked.

"I'm her attorney," Robin shot back. "And since you haven't answered, I'll take that as a no. Come on, Harriet, we're out of here."

Robin hustled Harriet out of the conference room and then out of the hotel before she stopped.

"Is there somewhere away from here where we can talk?" she asked Harriet.

"Who are you and what happened to my friend Robin?"

Robin smiled finally.

"My friend Kirsten can't be here for another hour. She told me to get you away from the detectives and to be assertive enough they wouldn't stop to argue that I'm not licensed in Texas. My license or lack thereof isn't important at this point. We're not in court. You have a right to get up and walk out of what is essentially an interview. If you aren't arrested, you don't have to be there. We don't want to antagonize them, but you don't have to be intimidated or harassed by the local police at this point."

"Lauren found an old-time soda fountain-candy shop a block or two from here. We should be able to talk there."

When they were a block away, Robin finally stopped to let to let Lauren, Mavis and Connie, who had settled in one of the conversation areas in the lobby, catch up.

"Sorry to seem rude, but my friend said to get Harriet out of there before the police had a chance to twist her words or to decide she was an easy answer to their problem."

"She was awesome," Harriet told them. "Robin wants us to meet somewhere other than the hotel, so I suggested Lauren's candy place."

"Sounds good to me," Mavis said, and Connie agreed.

Lauren headed down the block.

"Follow me," she said over her shoulder.

Robin loosened her scarf and unbuttoned the collar of her white button-down shirt.

"I think this calls for ice cream all around."

Harriet leaned her head in her hands.

"If Robin is resorting to eating ice cream, I'm doomed."

Robin smiled at her.

"Just because I eat salads at our lunch meetings doesn't mean I never indulge in treats. Let's get our treats, and you can catch me up on the latest events."

✂ --- ✂ --- ✂

"I'm surprised Robin wants us to go to our banquet," Harriet said to Lauren as she iced her eye back in their hotel room.

Lauren sat on her bed tapping the face of her tablet.

"She probably wants us to seem normal compared to the bridal party," she replied without looking up.

"What are you doing?"

Lauren finally set her tablet in her lap and looked at Harriet.

"I'm researching the Johnson family. You said the detective looked them up. I thought we should fact-check him. So far, he's right. They have a disturbingly nonexistent digital footprint."

"What are they hiding?"

"Probably nothing. They live in a small town outside Savannah, Georgia. The bride was a Georgia Bulldog and on their cheer team."

"So I've heard."

"You want to explain that?"

"The detective found that. That was before Robin burst in. He said she had some sort of coming-out party, and I heard about her cheerleading from him but nothing else. He had just pulled up my name and read the first entry when Robin got there."

"Do you know which story he read about you?"

"Robin burst through the door before he said, but does it matter? Any rational person would ask themselves, *What is the common denominator in the*

74

recent crimes in Foggy Point? Oh yeah, that would be me. You don't have to be a detective to make that connection."

"I'll keep digging. I have some other sources I can tap in to, but I can't do that from my tablet. Their town newspaper went under two years ago, but if they digitized their archives maybe I can still find them."

Harriet took the now-warm ice bag off her eye.

"I guess it's possible the bride really was just stressed when she hit me, and maybe she walked in on someone stealing her ring, and they killed her. Two completely unrelated events."

"That would be quite the coincidence. And I don't believe in coincidence. Not like this."

Harriet's phone chimed, signaling a text message.

"Mavis and Connie want to know if we can meet downstairs before we go over to dinner. She says she heard something interesting."

"Works for me."

Mavis and Connie were in the lobby when Harriet and Lauren arrived.

"What's up?" Harriet asked.

Mavis leaned in and spoke in a whisper.

"I heard the two women sitting at the table in front of me in class talking. Apparently, the one named Nancy thought her necklace had been stolen. She was on a cruise the week before class and bought it on the ship. The clasp was stuck, so she was going to take it to a jeweler during lunch yesterday. Only, she went to her room, and it was gone."

"So, there's a jewelry theft ring in the hotel?" Lauren interrupted.

"Not exactly. She was going to report it to hotel security, but with all that was going on yesterday with the bride being murdered, she forgot about it. This morning, when she was getting dressed, she found it in her suitcase."

"Not where she'd left it," Connie added.

"Not only was it not where she'd left it," Mavis continued, "but the clasp was fixed."

"Are we sure it was ever broken?" Lauren asked. "Or missing, for that matter."

Mavis straightened her back.

"We can't know for certain, but she's convinced. And for the record, she wears sensible shoes."

Harriet laughed.

"What's that supposed to mean?"

"I've noticed that people who wear sensible shoes tend to be more practical in their thinking. You laugh, but when you think about it, you'll see I'm right."

Lauren turned toward the hotel doors.

"Let's go to the banquet, and you can point out the sensible shoe crew so Harriet and I can judge their credibility for ourselves."

Connie stepped closer to Harriet.

"Lauren may mock our source, but I believe them. Something bad is going on in this hotel involving that bride and her family and jewelry. I can't make sense of it yet, but you need to be careful."

"We all need to be careful," Harriet said and led the way out of the hotel.

Chapter 10

avis chose a table in the center of the room, and they settled into the four chairs that most directly faced the podium. Stephanie came into the banquet hall, looked around and smiled when she saw Harriet.

"Are these available?" she asked when she reached their table, gesturing at the empty seats.

Harriet smiled at her.

"Yes, join us, please."

"Thanks." She pulled a chair out and sat down. "I hope our keynote speaker is good. People in my class couldn't stop talking about the murder. One woman was talking about packing up and going home. We need something to distract us from all that and focus everyone back on quilting."

Mavis leaned forward so she could see past Connie and Harriet.

"I've heard Sue Garman is very good. She's a great pattern designer, and someone in my class has heard her speak before and said she was very inspiring."

Lauren laughed.

"I could use a little inspiration about now."

Harriet gave her a knowing look but didn't say anything.

Alice joined them and pulled out a chair.

"I hope you weren't saving this spot for anyone else."

"Now that you're here, everyone we know is present and accounted for," Connie said and then looked at Harriet. "Except for your husband, who is in a kitchen somewhere nearby cooking dinner for us, I hope."

Alice raised her eyebrows.

"I didn't realize your husband was here. I saw two other husbands in front of the hotel yesterday, but neither of them looked like they were cooks."

Harriet tried to sound casual, as if she'd been referring to James as her husband for years.

"My husband owns a restaurant back home and is in Galveston taking a Cajun cooking course. He's actually the one who told us about this conference when he found out he and his fellow students would be cooking the banquet dinner."

"It must be fun being married to a man who can cook. My husband burns water, and I get tired of cooking the same meals year after year."

Lauren smiled.

"Harriet loves it. They never eat the same meal twice."

Harriet gave her a glare then turned to Alice, her smile back in place.

"The unfortunate part is being married to someone who can make so many chocolate desserts. He's been experimenting with truffles, and they're so good I fear I'm going to have to become an ultra-marathoner to burn off all the extra calories."

"You could share more," Lauren pointed suggested.

"How's your eye doing?" Alice asked Harriet.

Harriet turned her head so the nurse could see it.

"I think it's getting better. With everything going on here, I haven't been able to ice it or to rest as much as they suggested. All things considered, it seems better."

"It still looks pretty puffy." Alice turned to Mavis. "She really does need to ice it and to lie down some every day. You don't want complications to develop."

"We'll make sure she does better," Mavis replied. "As she said, it's been a little difficult, what with classes and then the extracurricular problems at the hotel. Sort of makes me sorry we signed up for the extra tour days after the conference ends."

"I guess your eye puts you on the list of people they want to talk to about that girl's death," Alice said.

Harriet sighed.

"Unfortunately, it does. I tried to tell them I'd never met her before, but they aren't hearing me."

Alice unfolded her napkin and put it in her lap.

"Aren't you all from Washington state? Why would you know a college girl from Georgia, much less be angry enough at her to kill her?"

Mavis shook her head.

"As Harriet said, they don't want to hear it. Jennifer wasn't from here, and we're not from here, so that neatly ties it all up as far as the local police are concerned."

Alice leaned toward them so she could speak in a low voice.

"Who do you think did it?"

Harriet blew out a breath.

"I don't know, but I'd sure look at the reluctant groom."

"I heard someone in the bathroom say they'd seen him with another woman, someone in our group," Alice said.

Lauren and Harriet exchanged a glance but didn't say anything.

Uniformed servers began delivering baskets of bread and bowls of salad dressing to the tables, ending the speculations.

✂ --- ✂ --- ✂

Harriet pushed her chair back from the round banquet table.

"Wow, after that presentation, I'm ready to try to make an original quilt design."

Connie laughed.

"Sue Garman made it sound easy, but believe me, that woman is talented. I've tried designing my own quilt, and it was hard. And my result wasn't anywhere near as spectacular as hers are."

Mavis looked at her.

"Your quilt was real nice."

"Yeah, but no one is lining up to buy my design." Connie glanced across the room to where most of their fellow stitchers were crowded around baskets of Sue Garman's patterns.

Robin arrived with a young woman who could only be her lawyer friend.

"Hi, guys. This is my friend Kirsten Meyer. She'll be representing you while you're here."

Kirsten extended her hand to Harriet.

"Before we talk business, I have to say, your keynote speaker was incredible. The organizers were kind enough to let us sit in the foyer and listen in."

Harriet shook her hand.

"Thanks for coming on such short notice."

"No problem. Lucky for you, I'm just coming back from a maternity leave, so I haven't taken on any big cases yet."

Mavis looked at her.

"Let's hope that's still true after this week."

Kirsten smiled.

"Hopefully, a good strong defense will be all that's required to get the locals on the trail of the real killer."

Robin sat down beside Connie and leaned in, lowering her voice as she spoke.

"Kirsten and I have talked it over, and we think you need to make your…" She made air quotes with her fingers. "…marriage more visible to your classmates and the hotel staff."

Harriet wasn't naturally inclined to public displays of affection with her "husband"—or anyone else, for that matter. And she was still trying to accept the reality that she was married again herself. Selling it to the public was a tall order.

"Exactly how visible are we talking?"

Kirsten and Robin started to answer at the same time.

"Def—"

"You—"

They laughed.

"Go ahead," Kirsten said to Robin.

"You and James need to be sharing a room."

"And a few public displays of affection can't hurt," Kirsten added.

"We've already asked for a rollaway bed for Lauren in our room," Mavis informed them.

Connie smiled.

"And who knows? After all the close time together, maybe you and James will decide to make this a real marriage."

Harriet choked on the sip of water she'd taken.

"Not in this lifetime."

James had come into the banquet room from the lobby as they discussed him, smiling when he saw Harriet. He leaned over and kissed her gently, being careful not to touch the bruised side of her face.

"What's not in your lifetime?"

Harriet looked at him.

"Connie has a romantic notion that we are going to decide to stay married when all this is over. I was explaining to her that neither one of us wants to be married right now. But we've discussed all that already."

His smile disappeared as she continued.

"Robin was explaining that we need to stay in the same hotel room and have a few public displays of affection."

His smile returned.

"I can handle that. Speaking of which, I'm done if you are. Should we go over to *our* hotel and share some sparkling cider or something to celebrate our nuptials?"

"Good idea," Robin said, "But let's not let on that the marriage just happened. Of course, the police can check the public records, but no sense in calling attention to the situation."

Harriet got up and looped her arm through James's, and they headed back to the hotel bar.

Chapter 11

Robin drained the last drops of sparkling water from her glass and set it on the bar.

"I better go call home and see if the walls are still standing. I'll keep my cell phone on so you can reach me anytime if anything else happens."

Kirsten stood up as well.

"Remember, don't talk to anyone. If the police try to talk to you, call me." She looked at James. "That goes for you, too. If the police try to question you, call Robin or I." She handed business cards to everyone. "I wrote my cell number on the back." She looked sternly at Harriet again. "I mean it—call."

Harriet set her glass down.

"Don't worry. If they even look at me cross-eyed, I'm calling."

"Good," Kirsten said, and turned and left the hotel with Robin.

Lauren turned on her bar stool.

"I guess I better go pack my pillow and move down the hall."

"I'm sorry about that," James told her.

She laughed.

"Changing rooms is nothing compared to your shotgun wedding."

Harriet had opened her mouth to say something but closed it again when Sydney appeared.

"Whiskey sour," she said when the bartender came over.

"I'm so sorry for your loss," Harriet said when Sydney had settled her substantial bottom on the stool Robin had just vacated.

Sydney leaned her forehead on the edge of the bar.

"Thank you," she mumbled. 'It's kind of you to say so." The bartender slid her drink across the bar, and she sat back up and wrote her room number on the slip he handed her. "This is such a nightmare," She paused to sip her drink. "We should never have come here. Michael was marrying my sister for her money, and she didn't even care." A tear slid down her cheek. "And now my mother decided to have Jen's memorial service here. I mean, I guess I understand. Everyone is already flying here from everywhere, and it would be a huge hassle for them all to have to change their flights to Savannah on short notice. I just wish we could be home." She sipped her drink as more tears wet her cheek.

Connie handed her a tissue from her purse.

"Oh, honey, we're all so sorry for your loss. I can't imagine how painful it is to have something like this happen on what was to be such a happy occasion."

Sydney took the proffered tissue and dabbed her eyes.

"That's nice of you, especially considering what my sister did to your friend."

Connie patted her hand.

"It's all water under the bridge, now."

Sydney seemed to notice James for the first time. He reached his hand out to her.

"I'm James, Harriet's husband."

Sydney shook his hand but looked at Harriet.

"James is here taking Cajun cooking classes while I'm learning to appliqué," Harriet explained for what seemed like the hundredth time.

"We own a restaurant back home," James added.

Lauren choked on her drink.

James stood up.

"I would love to stay and chat with you ladies, but I better get back over to Gaido's. I left my knife set sitting out in the motel kitchen, and I can't trust those clowns I'm rooming with to keep their hands off them."

"He's been staying at Gaido's motel with the other students," Harriet hastened to explain before Sydney could ask about the odd living arrangements. "They have an apartment room that has a full kitchen and a washer and dryer so they can do homework assignments."

He leaned down and kissed her.

"See you later," he whispered and walked away.

Sydney tossed her drink back and stood up.

"Will you all be stitching down here again tonight?"

"I'll come for a little while," Harriet said with a sigh. "I'm behind on my class project."

Tears slid from Sydney's eyes.

"I guess I don't need to finish the double wedding ring quilt I was making."

Connie patted her hand.

"You could finish it and keep it as a remembrance."

"Even if you decide not to keep it, stitching will help soothe your nerves," Mavis added.

"I'm coming for the cookies," Lauren told them. "There's no chance I'll finish either one of my projects while we're here."

The young woman from the front desk came over to Mavis.

"We have the rollaway set up in your room."

"Thank you," Mavis told her.

"Thank you," Harriet told Lauren in a voice louder than necessary. "We didn't realize James's class was going to finish a day earlier than oursine when we made our reservations."

Lauren shook her head and took a long sip of her sparkling water.

"You can drop the act—no one's listening."

"You can't be too careful."

"Whatever," Lauren said and headed for the bank of elevators.

✄ --- ✄ --- ✄

Lauren and Harriet settled down at a table in the pajama party stitching room a half-hour later. Both were working on their wool appliqué projects. Harriet held hers up when she'd completed the leaf she'd been stitching.

"My blanket stitch looks like a zipper."

Mavis took the piece from her and looked at it.

"You just need to take a little bigger stitch and it'll be fine."

Sydney Johnson came in a few minutes later and took out one of her double wedding ring blocks. Connie moved her bag to make a space for her.

"I've never done that pattern as an appliqué," she said.

"It's easier than piecing all those curves," Sydney said, and began to appliqué a gray ring to her background fabric. "I've made several for my sister's friends."

Harriet finished sewing a second leaf to her background and set her piece on the table.

"I'm going to go upstairs and ice my eye."

Mavis reached over and, with a finger to Harriet's chin, turned her head so she had a better view of the injury.

"Your eye still looks puffy. How long are you supposed to keep icing it?"

84

Harriet sighed.

"They said it could take seven to ten days, but that probably assumed I was actually icing it every few hours. I better go get at it."

She crossed to the elevators without seeing anyone she knew. James opened the door to the room before she could use her key.

"Come in, said the spider to the fly," he said and batted his eyelashes.

He took her bag and set it on the floor before wrapping his arm around her shoulders and guiding her to the bed.

"Sit down and put your feet up." He went into the bathroom and came out with Harriet's ice bag. "I got ice after I got back, while you were still downstairs."

"Thanks," she said. "But I've got to get into something more comfortable. Stay right here." She headed for the bathroom. "I'll be out in a flash."

She'd decided not to wear pajamas to the stitching event after her previous hasty exit on her "wedding night." She came out of the bathroom dressed in the cotton pajama shorts Aunt Beth and Mavis had made her and an oversized tee-shirt. She sat down on the bed and took the proffered ice-bag.

James sat next to her and looked around the room.

"This is pretty deluxe. I mean, Gaido's Seaside Inn is cool in a beachey sort of way, but this is Old-World nice. And they have turn-down service."

"They do? Since when?"

"There were chocolates on the pillows when I came in."

"Where are they?"

"I was hungry."

Her eyes widened.

"You ate them all?"

He laughed and reached across her to the nightstand drawer. He nudged it open a crack, exposing four foil-wrapped chocolates.

Harriet relaxed.

"Good thing you didn't eat them, or we'd be getting a divorce before the ink's dry on our marriage license."

James took the ice bag from her and gently turned her toward him. He looked at her for a moment, all humor leaving his face. Then he leaned in and gently kissed her. When she didn't pull away, he deepened the kiss.

He finally pulled back.

"If you're divorcing me already, I've got to exercise as many of my conjugal rights as I can."

She plucked her ice bag from his hand and put it to her eye.

85

"If I remember right, this is a temporary situation."

James sighed.

"You're right. We shouldn't complicate things. But if we're being honest, earlier today, when you were talking to your friends…"

"When I reminded them that neither of us wanted to be married in real life?"

"Yeah, then. If I'm being honest, it sort of hurt my feelings when you said you didn't want to be married."

She turned to face him.

"James, you've said all along the restaurant is your mistress. And I certainly wasn't coming down here to husband-hunt."

"But you said it so quick. You didn't even pause."

"Are you saying you want our marriage to be real?"

"No…well, not like this, anyway. I mean, I wasn't looking to get married when I came down here, either, but then, while we were driving all those hours, thinking of our situation, I realized if I had to get married to someone under other than normal circumstances, I'm glad it's you."

Harriet smiled. She wasn't up to the serious discussion she knew they would have to have in the not-too-distant future.

"Why, James, that's the sweetest thing you've ever said to me. And if I had to have a shotgun wedding, I'm glad it's you, too."

He sighed and slid his arm around behind her and pulled her to him, leaning back against the pillows. She repositioned her ice bag and leaned her head against his chest.

"What a week," she said. "And it's not over yet."

James opened the nightstand drawer wider with his free hand and reached inside it.

"I hope this doesn't make it worse for you, but I got you something to commemorate our wedding. After what you said earlier, though, I'm not sure I should give it to you."

"What is it?"

He looked away.

"I don't want you to feel pressured. I'm not trying to make this more than it is. And we can talk about what to do with it after all this is over."

"Now I'm intrigued."

He slid the drawer shut.

"No, now that I think about it, this is a mistake."

"Oh, come on," she said and attempted to reach over him. "You can't give me that sort of set up and then not follow through."

"Well…" He paused. "It seemed like a good idea when I did it, but now I'm not so sure."

"How about this. Let me peek, and if I think it's over the top we'll stop right there and you keep it."

He hesitated a moment more then opened the drawer and pulled out a small velvet box. Harriet held her breath as he opened it. Then, she gasped and covered her mouth with her hand.

"Oh, my gosh," she finally said.

James misunderstood her reaction and snapped the box shut. She grabbed his hand as he started to return the box to the drawer.

"You bought me a wedding ring?" Her eyes filled with tears.

"I told you it was a mistake."

She took the box from his hand and opened it.

"It's gorgeous." She slid the Walmart wedding ring off and replaced it with the one in the box. She held her left hand out in front of her. "This must have cost a fortune."

"Do you like it?"

"What's not to like? It's fantastic."

James's shoulders relaxed. A brilliant-cut center diamond that was at least a carat in weight was surrounded by what had to be another carat of smaller brilliant-cut diamonds. He blushed.

"I know this wasn't the wedding of your dreams, but if we need to make a show of being married, I thought you should be wearing a ring we would have picked if we were really married."

Harriet laughed and turned to face him.

"You do realize we *are* really married, right?"

"You know what I mean."

She laughed again and turned her hand to one side then the other, watching the diamonds catch the light.

"Maybe I could keep it for a little while, and then you can return it."

"I'm not going to return it. Especially now that I've seen how good it looks on you. Even after our amicable divorce, I want you to keep it as a token of our brief but memorable marriage."

She sat up and looked at him.

"No. This ring is expensive—don't try to tell me it isn't. It's too expensive to be a token. I'll keep the Walmart version as a memento."

"Harriet. Listen to me. I'm not rich, by any means, but since I opened the restaurant, I haven't spent time or money on anything else; and now it's paid off, I can afford to buy a bobble for my main squeeze. Be honest. Even though we weren't planning on getting married, we *have* been going steady, haven't we?"

Harriet looked at her hand.

"It's a pretty fabulous go-steady ring."

James smiled.

"But you'll wear it?"

"I'll definitely wear it for as long as we're married. After that, we can talk."

James looked exasperated.

"I guess that'll have to do."

He swung his feet over the side of the bed and stood up.

"Since I didn't go to a banquet tonight and I left cooking class right at the end before we ate our project, I'm going to go down to the cafe and rustle up a snack. Can I bring you anything?"

"No, because I *did* go to a lavish banquet, and I ate cookies before I left the pajama party stitching session."

James leaned down and kissed her gently on the lips.

"Be right back."

"I'll be right here—icing."

Chapter 12

$\mathcal{H}$arriet was sitting on the bed playing with the television remote control when she heard pounding on the door. James hadn't been gone long enough to have gotten food. He must have forgotten something.

"Hang on," she said and went to the door. "What did you for—" she started to say as she swung the door open, but she stopped mid-sentence.

Detective Grier stood in the hallway with two uniformed officers a few steps behind him.

"Could you step out into the hall, please."

"What's this about?"

"Just step into the hall, please."

"My lawyer has instructed me not to talk to you without her being present."

"Go ahead and call her. That'll give us time for our search warrant to arrive. Keep the door open while you call her, or I'm going to assume you're destroying evidence, which will give me the right to search your room without the warrant."

Harriet looked up at the ceiling and took a deep breath before spinning around and going to call Kirsten.

"Don't say a word. Stand right where you are until I get there," Kirsten told her. "Robin and I will be there in a moment. Remember, say nothing."

It seemed like an eternity, but Kirsten and Robin were there in under ten minutes. Harriet was still standing in the middle of the room holding her cell phone when they arrived.

"Thank heaven you're here," she said and collapsed onto the edge of the bed.

"What's going on?" Robin asked. "I saw that detective standing in front of a room at the other end of the hall."

"I don't know. Detective Grier came to my room with two policemen and wanted me to step into the hall. When I told him I had to call you, he said that would give him time to get a warrant."

No one said anything for a moment.

"That's it?" Kirsten asked. "He didn't say what this is about?"

Harriet shook her head. Kirsten looked at Robin.

"You stay here with her. I'm going down the hall to see what's going on. Keep her in the room no matter what."

"Do you have any idea what this could be?" Robin asked Harriet when her friend was gone.

"I really don't have a clue."

James came through the open door before they could discuss it further.

"What's happened? Paramedics came running in when I got off the elevator. They were back a few minutes later with someone on the gurney and raced out of here with lights blazing. I didn't think too much of it until the detectives stormed in, and then Robin and Kirsten."

Harriet went to him, and he wrapped his arms around her, holding her close. *I* could get used to this, she thought. She was all for being independent, but still…

"The detectives came knocking on the door, and I told them I wasn't allowed to talk to them. Luckily, Robin and Kirsten were close by. They went to the other end of the hall, and now Kirsten is trying to find out what's happening."

He held her closer and leaned out into the hall.

"They're all still talking. I wonder if we could slip out and head for the airport?"

Robin gave him a grim smile.

"Unfortunately, the detective mentioned getting a search warrant. They have to state what they're looking for to get the warrant, so they must think Harriet is involved in whatever has happened down the hall. If we try to leave, they may take Harriet into custody for forty-eight hours to block that and give them time to gather more evidence."

Kirsten rejoined them.

"The mother of the bride was attacked in her room tonight. They're knocking on your door because the maid said she saw someone who looked like you in the hallway, and that the mom's door opened and she heard her say "Harriet?""

Harriet glared at her.

"That's nonsense. How would she even know my name? Besides, I haven't been alone until a few minutes before the detective beat on my door."

The door to their friends' room opened, and Lauren said, "I'm going to go call my client and see if I can find something salty to eat downstairs. All the sweets are starting to get to me."

She appeared in the hallway.

"Are we having a party?"

Mavis emerged behind her wearing her housecoat and slippers, and when she saw Robin standing with Harriet and James, she hurried past Lauren.

"What's happened?"

"There's been some sort of accident with the bride's mother," Robin told her. She recounted what they knew as Lauren and Connie joined them.

Other doors were starting to open.

"Please, go back to your rooms," one of the uniformed officers ordered the rubber-neckers. Harriet and James turned to lead the way back into their room.

Detective Grier pounded down the hall toward them.

"Stop! Not you people. Y'all need to stay out in the hall. We have a warrant to search your room."

They heard the elevator ding, and a detective disembarked and handed Grier a folded piece of paper. He scanned it then handed it to Kirsten, who did the same.

"It says they're looking for an orange linen shirt."

Robin followed the police into the room, holding up her cell phone.

"I'm going to do a video of the search."

Harriet's eyes widened.

"Why on earth do they want my shirt?"

"It doesn't say." Kirsten handed the warrant to her.

"Can I tell them where it is? It's on the floor of the closet in my pile of dirty clothes."

Kirsten put a hand on Harriet's arm.

"Stay as calm as you can. I don't want you to go in while they're searching, but let me see if they'll listen to me."

She followed Robin into the room.

"Let's go wait in our room," Connie suggested. "I'll make tea."

✂ --- ✂ --- ✂

Kirsten knocked on the door fifteen minutes later. She looked tired.

"They found the orange shirt they were looking for in the laundry pile, as you described."

"So, are they going to stop bothering Harriet?" Mavis asked.

Kirsten looked uncomfortable.

"Mavis, the shirt was soaked in blood."

James squeezed Harriet's hand.

"That can't be," he said.

"The detectives would like to talk to Harriet in her room," Kirsten said. "I can come with her, but the rest of you will have to wait here."

Harriet looked at James and then back to Kirsten.

"Now?"

"Yeah, let's get this over with. Robin will tape it for us."

Detective Grier and a uniformed officer were sitting on the small sofa in her room; She and Kirsten took the two chairs on the opposite side of the coffee table from them. Robin remained standing, her phone in hand, ready to record the interview. Kirsten nodded to her to start the video, then turned to Detective Grier.

"I'd like to note for the record that Harriet is speaking to you voluntarily and can terminate this interview whenever she wants. I am here as Harriet's counsel, and I also will terminate this interview if I feel it isn't in her best interest to continue talking to you."

Detective Grier sighed.

"Yeah, yeah, yeah, we get it. But you should get this. This whole thing will go a lot easier for your client if she'd start telling the truth."

Harriet could feel her face turning red.

"I don't know any other 'truth' to tell you," she finally said. "I didn't know the bride. I don't know why she hit me in the eye. I've never even met the bride's mother, much less done to her whatever you think I've done to her. I came to Galveston to learn how to do appliqué. No more, no less." She switched to French and repeated what she'd said just for good measure. "Would you understand if I told you in Italian? Or German? I don't know anything!"

Kirsten patted her hand.

"Take a deep breath."

"Can you account for your whereabouts today from…" He looked at his notebook "…three this afternoon until nine tonight?"

Harriet smiled.

"Fortunately for me, I was either in quilt group activities or with my husband this entire day."

Grier quickly riffled through his notebook then looked at her over the top of his glasses.

"Your husband is here? I don't seem to find any mention of your husband in our other conversation."

"I'm not surprised, since you don't seem to be interested in listening to anything I have to say."

Kirsten put a cautioning hand on Harriet's arm again. Harriet took another calming breath.

"My husband James owns a restaurant, and he's the reason we came to Galveston. He's taking a Cajun cooking class. Up until tonight, he's been staying at Gaido's Motel with the rest of the students so he has access to a kitchen." She was starting to feel like a broken record.

"So, what time did he come over to the Tremont?"

"After our banquet. Then he went back to get his knives while I was at the stitching group."

He made a note.

"I'm sure he talked to his roommates before he came back," Harriet told him. "In case you were thinking *his* time wasn't accounted for."

Kirsten nudged Harriet with her leg. A reminder to volunteer nothing.

"So, basically y'all are each other's alibi," Grier said finally.

Harriet sighed.

"We came here so he could learn Cajun cooking, and I came along to learn to appliqué. We don't know anyone except the people we came with and two women I met in class. This trip has been a total nightmare."

He asked her to recount her movements for the entire day—twice. She told him how there had been turndown service for the first time, and that she suspected that was when the blood was put on her shirt. He made a note of everyone who had been with her at each of her activities throughout the day.

Finally, he closed his notebook.

"You say you're an innocent bystander, caught up in someone else's problem. I'm sure Jennifer would say the same thing if she wasn't dead. I've got a boatload of evidence that says you made her that way. If, indeed, you did kill her and attack her mother, we will find out and then we will put you in jail and throw away the key."

Kirsten stood up.

"We intend to sit here while you threaten my client. I want you to leave—now."

She went to the door and held it open. When Grier didn't get up, Robin circled around and zoomed in on his face with her phone camera. He glared at her and got up.

"Come on," he said to the officer, who had remained silent throughout.

As soon as Grier had gone through the door, James rushed in, took Harriet's hands and pulled her up and into his arms.

Kristen patted her on the shoulder.

"Don't worry, we'll get you through this. He knows his evidence is a little too convenient. Hopefully, the mother will survive and wake up and be able to tell them who attacked her. Then you can put this behind you and get on with your life."

"Are you okay?" James asked finally.

Harriet stepped back from him.

"I'm fine. I just need to keep focused on the fact I haven't done anything wrong, so I don't need to worry." She looked at Kirsten. "Right?"

Kirsten was quiet for a moment then blew out a breath.

"In a perfect world, that would be true. But we live in the real world. In our world, the police sometimes follow the easiest answer instead of the correct answer. And so far, someone is doing a pretty good job of leading them straight to you. Whoever planted the blood on your shirt was expecting you to be alone in your room. Probably assuming you'd ice your eye at some point without anyone else being there."

Robin sat down on the end of the closest bed.

"I'm guessing Lauren goes off periodically to check her work email. Am I right?"

Harriet nodded and sat back down.

"So, whoever is doing this saw her doing that and assumed you'd be in your room alone long enough to create suspicion. What they didn't realize was James is now your roommate and he was here when you were."

"All we have to do is figure out who that could be," Harriet said.

There was a tap on the door, and Robin let Mavis, Connie and Lauren in. Lauren sat on the sofa.

"We've been thinking…" she started.

"Wait," Robin told her and pulled a legal pad and a pen from her purse. "I better write this down."

Connie sat next to Lauren and scooted close, patting the space beside her for Mavis.

"Since we know Harriet didn't do this…" She smiled at Harriet. "… we decided to make a list of possible suspects."

"We don't have any real evidence," Mavis interrupted.

Lauren laughed.

"What they're trying to say is, we were sitting in our room guessing who could have done the bride's murder and the mom's attack. We're starting with the assumption that the same person or persons did both crimes."

Robin made a note.

"We think the groom is the most likely suspect. He's been drinking like a fish since he's been here and was hitting on Harriet and probably other women," Connie told them.

Harriet covered her mouth with her hand and thought for a moment.

"I think the cleaning staff should be on the list. They have access to all the rooms, so they could have put the blood on my shirt. And then there's the weird jewelry stuff."

"Let's not complicate things with other crimes," Kirsten said.

Robin wrote it down anyway.

"We have to put everything on our first list," she said. "We can eliminate people after we *have* a list."

"What about the woman you saw with the groom when you and James went to Gaido's," Lauren asked.

"We should put the bride's sister Sydney on the list, for completeness' sake," Mavis said.

James was sitting in the chair next to Harriet, and she absently took hold of his hand.

"Sydney could possibly overpower her mother, but she'd be no match for her sister. She can barely walk up the six steps into the hotel without taking a break halfway up."

Lauren stood.

"What about the woman from our class who was invited to the wedding? She used to babysit the bride, I think she said. Maybe she has some grievance against the family."

"Sounds like a bit of a stretch," Robin said, but she wrote it down.

Harriet yawned.

"Don't forget the woman Lauren mentioned. We don't know her name, but James and I saw her with the groom when we went out to dinner the other night on the other side of the island."

Robin wrote "groom's other woman" on her list and put the pad and pen back in her bag.

"This is a good start, but we're just guessing at this point. Everyone keep your eyes and ears open, and don't go anywhere alone."

Lauren stood up.

"I've got to go check my email again and go to bed. One of my clients is having a little problem, and this has been a day and a half even without that."

"We could all use a good night's sleep," Connie agreed.

Mavis stood up and looked at James.

"And you—don't let this one out of your sight." She pointed at Harriet.

A flush crept up his neck.

"I don't plan to," he said with a sly grin.

✂ --- ✂ --- ✂

"Well, this is awkward," Harriet said when they were alone.

James came up behind her and wrapped his arms around her, his chin on her shoulder.

"We don't have to do anything that makes either of us uncomfortable."

"It's not that I don't want to…"

"I know, but this isn't the right time or place. If and when you and I become more than snuggle buddies, it's not going to be with the police breathing down our necks. And we are definitely not going to consummate this marriage unless we both decide we want it to be real. And if anyone here challenges the validity of our marriage, I'll swear till the end of time it's consummated."

Harriet turned in his arms and kissed him. He really was a good kisser, she thought.

"You are too good to be true" she told him. "There has to be some deep, dark secret you haven't told me yet, 'cause no one is this good."

He laughed.

"I am not perfect, by any means. Just ask Cyrano."

"Luckily, your dog can't tell tales."

He stepped away from her.

"How about this. We get ready for bed, watch a little mindless television, and then call it a night."

"Sounds good to me."

Chapter 13

James and Harriet were across the street at the breakfast buffet when Mavis and Connie joined them.

"Where's Lauren?" Harriet asked.

"She's talking to a client," Mavis said.

"She said she'd be along in a few minutes," Connie added and set her purse on a chair.

James stood up and took his empty dish to a bussing table.

"Now that you ladies are here, I'm going to take off. Two of the guys from my class are staying on an additional day, and we're going to ride the ferry across to Boliver to buy some shrimp fresh off the boat for lunch."

Harriet smiled at him.

"Stay out of trouble."

He laughed.

"You're the one that needs to stay out of trouble. And no more police."

Harriet did her best to look innocent.

"I'm going to class, to lunch and back to class again. No police, no bloody shirts, no trouble of any sort."

"I'll believe that when I see it," he said and turned to Mavis. "Keep an eye on this one." With that, he leaned down and kissed Harriet lightly before leaving the room.

✂ --- ✂ --- ✂

The wool appliqué teacher had placed a selection of her favorite thread in a variety of colors designed to match their projects on the back table. Harriet got up and carried a piece of fabric that was destined to be a flower

97

petal to review the thread and started setting spools of pink on her fabric, searching for the closest match. The woman she had seen out with The Groom earlier in the week came up beside her. She picked up a spool from the orange grouping and set it on Harriet's fabric.

"I think this one looks good."

Harriet held thread and fabric up to the light.

"You're right—thanks."

"You're welcome, but that's actually not why I came back here. I'm Kari Cruse, a friend of Michael Williams."

"Yeah, I recognized you from dinner on Monday."

Kari seemed taken aback for a moment but then recovered.

"Michael would like to talk to you."

Harriet laughed. "One meeting with him was enough for me. I'm pretty sure that's what led to my…" She paused. "…interaction with Jennifer. If memory serves, he's a drunken boor, so no thanks."

Lauren must have noticed what was happening and joined them.

"You two having a party back here?"

Kari held up a spool.

"Just getting some thread."

"This is the woman James and I saw with The Groom Monday night. She says he wants to talk to me."

"We're not interested in talking to anyone even remotely associated with that group," Lauren said.

"Please," Kari pleaded. "Someone is trying to frame Mike for Jen's murder."

Harriet barely managed not to gape at her.

"What do you mean?" She said it a little louder than she'd intended. The teacher looked up from the student she was helping and arched an eyebrow.

"I mean someone planted bloody clothes in his room. He found them and got rid of them before Jen's mom was found. He saw the police searching your room, too, and wants to talk to you."

Harriet wanted nothing to do with Michael Williams, but she was intrigued by the idea that someone was trying to implicate him in the attack on Jennifer's mother—if they were in fact doing that. If there was any possibility he was as much a victim of these people as she was, she owed to herself to find out, and to see if he knew anything that could help her situation.

"We're going to Star Drug for lunch," Harriet said in a quiet voice, "If he wants to walk along with us, I'll listen to what he has to say."

The teacher was now glaring at them.

"We're good," Harriet assured her.

Lauren stared at her.

"Are we?"

"I'm going to text Mavis and Connie so they're not surprised when he shows up."

Michael was waiting in the lobby when the group came downstairs from the classrooms. Mavis scanned him up and down then tipped her head at Harriet to come with her.

"Let's have a potty break before we go." She led the way without waiting for Harriet to agree.

"Are you sure this is a good idea?" she asked as soon as the door was closed.

"No," Harriet said and set her purse on the counter. She moved toward the nearest stall. "Kari said someone planted bloody clothes in his room, too, but he found them and got rid of them before the police came.

"If someone really did that, it's evident they're trying to make sure someone other than them is going to take the blame. In fact, they're making doubly sure."

Mavis frowned.

"That's only true if there really were bloody clothes planted in his room and if they were planted by someone other than him. He clearly didn't want to marry Jennifer. Maybe he put a permanent end to his arranged marriage."

Harriet came out of her stall and headed for the sinks.

"Didn't we hear he was penniless? If that's true, it would make more sense for him to go through with the wedding and *then* kill the bride after the marriage was official."

"Only if he didn't have to sign a pre-nup that kept him from inheriting."

Harriet dried her hands.

"One way to find out. Let's go see what he has to say."

Everyone had moved outside by the time they got back to the lobby; Michael stood some distance from Lauren and Connie. He fell into step beside Harriet as she started down the sidewalk. He looked different from the other times she'd seen him. For one thing, he didn't appear to be drunk. For another, he was wearing neatly pressed khaki pants and a white button-down shirt with the sleeves rolled up to the elbows.

"I'm sorry about our first meeting in the bar, but you have to understand…"

Harriet stopped.

"I don't have to understand anything. I don't *owe* you anything. I said I'd listen—no more, no less."

Lauren noticed they'd stopped and came back to joined them.

"Come on," she said. "You're the one who wanted to hear what he had to say, so let's hear what he has to say."

"Fine," Harriet said and started walking again.

Michael shoved his hands in his pockets and took a deep breath.

"Let me start at the beginning. My family owns an old plantation. It's been in the family for centuries, it's on the historic register, yada, yada, yada. Most of the plantations in our area have become tourist destinations, but my grandpa decided to try to return ours to being a farming operation. Unfortunately, when it was time for my dad to take over, he wasn't good at it. Now, he's trying to make it into a bed-and-breakfast, I guess. It has potential, but my parents don't have the money to do it right.

"Enter the Johnsons. Kevin Johnson founded a very successful custom jet manufacturing business in Savannah. He made bucket-loads of money and bought his wife and daughters everything their hearts desired. But they were *nouveau riche*, and no matter how many donations he made to whatever the charity of the moment was, he couldn't change that status.

"Judith Johnson is a social climber of the worst kind. Kevin couldn't make her Old Money, and that's what she wanted. Then, he got sick, and after about six months, he died, having been well insured. So, Judith was left with even more money, and she looked around for someone with an old family pedigree who needed some. Enter my daddy. Or my momma, really."

Harriet stopped again.

"Are you trying to tell me this was an arranged marriage?"

Michael looked at her.

"That's exactly what I'm telling you."

Lauren had again turned and come back in time to hear the last part of the conversation.

"Oh, come on. You can't tell me in this day and age anyone can be forced to marry anyone else, especially in this country."

Michael shook his head.

"I wish that were true. My sisters were wise enough to flee north as soon as they turned eighteen. Both of them got scholarships to good schools so it seemed sort of natural. I foolishly stayed in town to help my dad try to save the farm. I got an associate's degree in historic preservation and restoration on my own dime and have been working toward a bachelor's.

I figured I could help with the restoration. And then…" He held his hands out, palms up. "…all this happened."

"And drinking your way through the wedding seemed like the best way to handle it?" Harriet asked.

"Yes…I mean, no…I don't know, I was desperate. I said no right from the start, but the moms went on without me. They bought a ring, hid it in Jennifer's pudding after a dinner we were all invited to. Apparently, they'd told her she had a secret admirer. They'd been sending her flowers, candy, and who knows what else without me knowing anything about it."

It was Harriet's turn to shake her head.

"Do people really do stuff like that?"

Michael's shoulders sagged.

"It gets worse. My dad sat me down when we got home and said he was afraid we'd lose the place if I didn't go through with the marriage. I'm pretty sure that's not true, because we own it outright. And we're not behind on the taxes—yet. Fortunately, because of the historic status of the house, he's never been able to borrow money against it."

He sighed. "So, everyone was pressuring me, and meanwhile, Jennifer and her mom were planning this blowout wedding." He looked down at his feet. "And it gets worse."

Lauren laughed.

"Hard to imagine how."

Harriet looked up the block. Connie and Mavis had stopped, too, but were keeping their distance.

"Spit it out. Our friends are waiting."

"You met my friend Kari?"

They nodded.

"We've been together for five years. I have a room at the plantation, but basically, I've been living with her for the last three years."

"So, she doesn't want to give you up, I'm guessing," Lauren said.

"Worse."

"Oh, no," Harriet said.

"Oh, yes. Kari is pregnant. What should be the happiest time in our lives has turned into a living nightmare."

Lauren grinned.

"Bet it makes you wish you two kids had gotten married years ago instead of living in sin all this time."

Harriet glared at her.

"You're not helping."

She shrugged. "Just saying."

"I tried to talk to Jennifer, but she was so excited about getting married she didn't care who the groom was. I thought maybe I could scare her off if she thought I was a lush. That family cares a lot about appearances. I know the drinking plan wasn't a good one, but I couldn't think of what else to do. I thought maybe she'd want to call it off if I was obnoxious enough." He looked at Harriet's eye. "I'm really sorry about your eye. I had no idea she'd react the way she did to my little scene in the bar."

Harriet started walking again.

"I'm sorry for your trouble, but I'm not sure why you wanted to talk to us. I mean, your problem is solved, isn't it?"

He fell in beside her with Lauren bringing up the rear.

"I was hoping we could compare notes, since it seems like the cops suspect you almost as much as they suspect me. I know I didn't hurt anyone, and I can't imagine you'd kill Jennifer and then attack her mom just because she hit you in the eye. I mean, you don't even know these people, do you?"

"No, I don't."

"I think the housekeepers or someone else at the hotel has to be involved," he said.

"Why?"

"Think about it. Someone put blood on my shirt, and I heard they found Jen's ring in your room. Who else could get into both our rooms?"

Harriet thought for a moment.

"You're right about someone getting in our rooms, but it could be almost any of the employees."

"Do you know anything about jewelry weirdness at the hotel?" Lauren asked. "Did Jennifer have any jewelry disappear or go missing and then show up again but not in the same place?"

He gazed into the distance, considering the question.

"I was kind of out of it most of the time, but I think she did say something about a necklace. She was so neurotic, I didn't think anything about it. I don't remember what she said happened." He studied the pavement. "I feel bad. I didn't like her as a person, and I didn't want to marry her, but Jennifer didn't deserve to be killed."

Lauren stopped, and Harriet realized they'd reached Star Drugs.

"Do you have any idea who would have wanted her dead?" she asked.

"I've thought about that," he said. "And the only person I can think of is her ex-boyfriend. He was an older guy, and he treated her like his princess. I think he loved her, but I also think she had her eyes on a bigger fish."

Harriet rolled her eyes at him. He put his hands up and shook his head.

102

"Not me—that was all Mama's idea. She wanted to be like that blonde singer, Jessica somebody who always dated professional sports players. That's what Jen wanted. She'd been a cheerleader, and she wanted a football hero. Winston was a convenient date. He had enough money to take her nice places, places younger men tend not to go, like the opera and the ballet.

"When her mom hatched this scheme about me, she dropped him like a rock. Mama convinced her that marrying a historic local family was better that a pro football player. I think he was pretty upset. I think Jen told me that, but frankly, I tried to avoid spending time with her, and when we were together, she talked so much I tended to tune her out. But I think she said Winston had been a little hard to get rid of.

"And before you ask, I don't know what that means, 'cause I didn't ask."

Lauren smirked.

"Weren't you just a jerk."

He hung his head.

"I do feel bad. I'm not proud of my behavior, but I didn't want to marry her, and my focus was all on figuring a way out."

"Why didn't you and Kari take off for parts unknown?" Harriet asked. "No one can force you into a marriage if you're not physically there."

Michael ran his hands through his hair and sighed.

"It's more complicated than that. Jen's mom gave my dad a cash advance to solve his immediate problems. He's spent it already. My only out is—or was—if Jen backed out or, unfortunately, if she died. Hence, I'm at the top of the suspect list."

Harriet held the restaurant door for her friends. Michael came in with the group.

"Five for lunch?" the waitress asked him.

"Four—the gentleman is leaving," Harriet interrupted.

"No, he isn't," Michael countered. "Table for one."

Harriet turned to face him.

"What do you want from us?"

"Help, I guess. I mean, I thought since we're both suspects maybe, if we stick together, we can figure this thing out. It's clear the police aren't interested in the truth. They just want to arrest someone and lock them away so they can protect their precious tourism image."

"Look, we've heard your story. If anything happens that I think you need to know, I know where to find you. This didn't suddenly make us best friends. In my mind, you're still a suspect."

Mavis wedged herself between Harriet and Michael.

"Thank you for sharing. Harriet will take what you've said under advisement, but right now we need to eat and get back to class. We'd appreciate it if you would leave us be."

Michael blew out an exasperated breath. The waitress pointed to a seat at the U-shaped counter, and he slid onto the stool. She then led the four quilters to a table toward the back of the room.

Lauren and Harriet sat with their backs to the wall, Connie and Mavis opposite them. They ordered the hamburgers the diner was famous for and sat back to wait for their food.

"I could only hear part of what he was saying," Mavis said by way of starting the conversation.

Harriet, with interruptions and clarifications from Lauren, recited the bulk of what Michael had shared. Connie picked up her fork and tapped it on the table.

"Do you believe him?"

The waitress brought their lunch before Harriet could answer.

"I guess I believe most of it," she said when they were finally alone again. "I mean, James and I saw him out with Kari, so clearly he has a relationship with her."

"It's been pretty clear he was a very reluctant groom," Lauren added.

Connie ate a bite of her burger and set it down.

"It's interesting to hear the background, but I'm not sure how it helps Harriet."

Mavis wiped her mouth with her napkin.

"That's what I'm trying to figure out. Michael being a suspect, too, doesn't help Harriet unless they arrest him. So far, they seem more interested in her, and we only have his word that he's even on their radar. He says he is, but have we seen him being questioned?"

She looked at each of them. One-by-one, they shook their heads.

"Yeah, me, either."

"We need to tell Robin," Connie said.

Lauren made a note in her tablet computer.

"I'll check out this Winston character, see if there's anything to it."

Harriet chewed thoughtfully for a moment and swallowed.

"Let's just say for a moment that everything he says is true. Doesn't that make Kari a suspect? I mean, she's pregnant with Michael's baby and he was about to marry someone else. She had a vested interest in making sure the marriage didn't take place."

Lauren sipped her iced tea.

"I wonder if the police know any of this?"

"We need to tell Robin," Connie repeated. "Kirsten can make sure the police know about the baby and all."

Harriet picked up her burger again.

"Can we just eat lunch and go back to class? The more we talk, the more unanswered questions we come up with. Everyone has motive except me, but as long as I'm the only one they have evidence against, nothing has changed."

"How are you doing with your wool appliqué?" Mavis asked.

Harriet's and Lauren's eyes met, and they burst into laughter.

Chapter 14

Harriet sat on the hotel room sofa next to Lauren after class and pulled out her wool appliqué piece.

"Well, my last three stems don't look like zippers, so I guess that's progress."

Lauren took the piece and inspected it.

"You know, if you put a few extra leaves across the zipper-stems, it would prevent your eye from reading it as a zipper."

"This might be practice for my real wool appliqué pillow," Harriet said and laughed.

Lauren looked at her phone.

"I've got to go make a call. Is James coming back anytime soon?"

"James is going to dinner with the other chefs, and none of them have partners with them. He invited me, but I don't want to be a fifth wheel."

"This'll take a few minutes. Maybe you can ice your eye in my room with Mavis and Connie while I'm gone. If I'm not mistaken, you haven't iced at all today, and it looks a little puffy still."

"I think I'll see if either of them wants to come here. This room's closer to the ice machine, and my extra ice bucket and towels are here."

She called, and Mavis reported that Connie was in the shower, but she would be right down. Harriet then took a few minutes to text James and let him know what her plans were.

Mavis held up her electric water heating coil as she came in.

"I assume you have tea bags," she said. "If not, I can go back and get some from our room.

Harriet laughed.

"Of course I do. My aunt has trained me well, I never travel without tea. They're in a sandwich bag on the table over there." She pointed to the round table in the corner.

Mavis made a selection for each of them, put bags in their mugs and when the water was hot, poured it.

"Can you look at my piece and tell me what else I can do to make my stems look better," Harriet asked, handing her the wool felt piece.

"I believe I would reduce the number of strands of floss you're using. The thread is too dominant for the weave of the wool you're using. You don't want your stem to be heavier than the leaves and flower petals. That's my opinion, and your teacher probably has a good reason for having you use what you're using, but that's what I'd do."

"I'll try it. What I'm doing now isn't working at all. On a totally other subject, has Lauren said anything to you about this new client? When we left Foggy Point, she said all her clients were in a holding pattern, and now all of a sudden, she's on her phone constantly and she always says it's a client."

Mavis set Harriet's stitching down on the coffee table and picked up her cup of tea.

"She hasn't said anything to me about it."

"It just seems like she's on her phone or tablet more than usual."

"Hold on. I said she hasn't *said* anything. I didn't say I didn't *know* anything. I noticed two things when her phone rang in the restaurant. First, I couldn't read the name. Second, the prefix was the same as the place you got married. Did she connect with a client in Louisiana when you went to get married?"

"Not that I know of, but she got to the courthouse ahead of James and I, and she was working on the judge's computer. It sounded like he'd been hacked, but I got the impression Lauren had taken care of it."

Mavis shifted on the sofa.

"I guess it wasn't as simple as she thought."

Harriet picked up her wool piece and started to pick out the most recent buttonhole stitch she'd done.

"Aren't you supposed to be icing your eye, young lady?" Mavis asked.

"Arghh! I was just getting started again. You're right. I am supposed to be icing." She stood up and grabbed the ice bucket. "I'll be right back."

"Wait—you aren't supposed to go anywhere alone." Mavis started to wiggle to the edge of the sofa in preparation for standing up.

"Stay here. I'll leave the door open and scream bloody murder if anyone comes near me."

Mavis smiled and slid back into her seat.

"I'll be back in a flash," Harriet said and went out the door.

She was standing at the ice machine filling her bucket a few minutes later when she heard a commotion down the hall. Bucket in hand, she went to the hallway intersection to see what was going on.

A gurney was being wheeled from a room at the other end of the hall.

"Harriet!" a woman's weak voice called.

She tried to duck out of sight, but one of the emergency medical people called out to her.

"Miss, I think she's talking to you," he said.

She sighed, and walked slowly toward the gurney. As she got closer, she realized the patient was Sydney. The gurney was folded into a sitting position, and she was holding a gauze pack to her forehead. Rivulets of blood dripped down her face.

"Oh, Harriet, I'm so glad to see a friendly face." Tears filled the eye that wasn't covered by the compress.

"What happened?"

"I don't know. I mean, I was sitting in the chair watching television, and someone tried to strangle me." She pulled her teeshirt away from her neck, revealing an angry red welt on her throat. "I struggled, and whoever it was hit me in the head. I was able to grab my phone, and I couldn't see it, but I stabbed blindly at the emergency button and got lucky." She mimed pushing buttons with her free hand. "I managed to hit nine-one-one, and they answered. I was able to scream before the phone was knocked out of my hand and I guess whoever was trying to kill me got scared and left—the pressure released around my neck, and I could breathe."

"Ma'am, we need to get you to the hospital and get that cut stitched up."

Sydney gave Harriet a pleading look.

"Could you come with me?"

Harriet started to protest.

"Please! I don't have anyone left." Sydney started crying again.

Harriet hesitated for another moment, hoping someone else more appropriate would show up. She knew Sydney could see it on her face when she surrendered.

"Can she ride in the ambulance with me?" she asked the medical technician.

"I've got to let my friends know where I'm going," Harriet added. They'd continued pushing the gurney toward the elevator and were a few steps from her room. She stepped over to the open doorway and quickly explained the situation to Mavis.

"You go with Sydney. Connie and I will find Lauren, and then all three of us will come find you at the hospital."

With a plan in place, Harriet handed her the ice bucket and followed the gurney into the elevator.

✂ --- ✂ --- ✂

Harriet was sitting alone in the emergency room waiting area when the other three arrived.

"She's off getting her head scanned," she told them. "I couldn't deal with waiting in that little cubicle."

Lauren sat down beside her.

"So, why are we the ones waiting here? She must have other family."

"Her dad is dead, her sister is dead, and her mom is lying unconscious somewhere in this very hospital. She really doesn't have anyone else. She said her mom's sister is coming in tomorrow for the memorial service, but for now, we're the only ones she knows."

Mavis sat down on Harriet's other side.

"What have these people done that made someone want to wipe out their whole family?"

Lauren leaned back in her chair, legs stretched out in front of her.

"Who cares? Why do we have to be here for a total stranger the police will probably think you attacked?"

"What are you talking about?" Connie protested. "Is that detective here?"

She looked around the waiting room. Lauren put a hand on her arm.

"Relax, I was just speculating. Although Harriet *was* alone several times when Sydney was being attacked."

Mavis slid forward so she could look Lauren in the face.

"*You* were supposed to stay with her so she had an alibi at all times. I got there as fast as I could."

"Sorry, I had a client issue."

"I thought your clients were all taken care of before we left Foggy Point," Harriet said.

Lauren sighed.

"They were. This is a new one, and it's actually your fault."

"My fault? How could it be my fault?"

"It was at your wedding that I made the mistake of helping your judge fix his computer problem. Unfortunately, he now has a much bigger problem, and he needs my help to fix it."

Harriet smiled.

"And of course you can't tell us what it's about."

Lauren said nothing.

109

Mavis stood up.

"Since Lauren flunked at sticking with Harriet, I suggest she come with me to get some sort of takeout food. Connie, you can stay here with Harriet. I'm starting to really regret us having signed up for those extra days of after-conference touring."

Harriet stood up.

"You and me both."

Harriet stood up when Mavis and Lauren returned to the waiting room twenty minutes later. Lauren held a carry-out tray of cold drinks, and Mavis a large white paper bag with a Popeye's logo on it.

"We asked the cab driver for a suggestion, and he said Popeye's chicken, so we went with it," Mavis told them.

Harriet sat down again.

"Sydney's head scan was clear. Now she's in having her wound stitched."

Connie took a wad of napkins from the bag and handed them out.

"What I don't understand is, after her sister being murdered and her mom seriously injured, how did someone waltz into Sydney's room and attack her? Don't they have security in this hotel?"

"Very good point," Lauren said.

Harriet popped the final piece of her second chicken strip into her mouth.

"This is really good," she said when she'd swallowed and wiped her mouth with her napkin. "Why don't we have a Popeye's in Foggy Point?"

Lauren looked at her.

"Seriously? You haven't noticed Foggy Point has no fast food chain restaurants except for the McDonalds out on the highway?"

Harriet laughed.

"There is that."

Connie handed Harriet the empty bag that was now their garbage bag.

"Carla told me there's one in Bremerton. She and Terry found it when she was visiting him there."

The automatic doors opened, and detectives Grier and Settle came in. They stopped abruptly when they saw Harriet and her friends.

"What are you doing here?" Grier asked, looking directly at Harriet.

Harriet paused to choose her words.

"Sydney asked us to come with her," she said finally.

Connie stood up.

"The girl doesn't have anyone. She needed us."

"Unless you were the ones who did this to her," Settle said.

110

Connie's face turned red.

"Listen, young man—"

Mavis stood up and put a hand on Connie's arm.

"Let's not make this worse than it is." She turned to the two detectives. "Look, this is the last place we want to be, but Sydney has no one here in Galveston. As you well know, her sister is dead, and her mother is somewhere in this hospital. Her father passed away some time in the recent past, and her remaining family is presumably on their way here for the memorial service for her sister, but they aren't here yet.

"What would you have us do? She asked us to come with her. Are we supposed to tell that poor girl we couldn't provide her her comfort because it wouldn't look good to the police?

"I don't know how you do things here in Galveston, but in Foggy Point, we support each other. When someone is in need, we show up. We don't stop and think how it would look, or who might judge us. We come and ask 'What can I do?'"

Settle and Grier looked at each other, but neither man spoke.

The detectives were still toe-to-toe with Mavis and Connie when a doctor came through the doors to the patient area, saw Harriet and came over to give his report. He was tall, dark-haired and, in his scrubs, reminded her of Aiden. She was surprised to realize the thought didn't hurt quite as much as it would have a week ago.

He held his hand out, and they exchanged a brief handshake.

"I'm Dr. Hatcher. I'm happy to report that your friend is going to be just fine. Miss Johnson's wound has been stitched, and we've completed our tests and imaging, and fortunately, she has no damage other than the bump and cut on her head and the bruising around her neck. We'd like to keep her a few more hours—she's a little dehydrated, and of course, she's pretty upset. We're going to give her something to help calm her down, and she'll probably sleep a while."

He looked at his watch.

"She should be ready..." He paused. "She's not going to be ready to go until midnight or later." He paused again. "You know what? I'm going to go ahead and admit her. It's not going to help her for any of you to be driving around in the middle of the night, and I'd really like her to calm down before she goes back to the hotel. I understand she's had a rough week."

"You could say that," Harriet said.

Detective Grier stepped forward.

"We'd like to question her as soon as possible."

The doctor glared at him.

"Not tonight."

Harriet looked from the doctor to the detective and back again and wondered if the two men had a history.

"Okay, we'll be back in the morning. In the meantime…" He turned to Harriet. "I have a few questions for *you*."

The doctor cleared his throat.

"I'm afraid that's going to have to wait a few minutes. My patient wants to see Ms. Truman, and she won't let us sedate her until she has."

Grier started to protest, but Settle stepped in front of him.

"That'll be fine. We'll be out here waiting."

Dr. Hatcher led Harriet, with Lauren trailing her, through the doors into the treatment area.

"A part of me wants to sneak you out the back door," he said as soon as the door was shut. "But I'm sure that wouldn't help anyone."

"No, I've got enough problems without antagonizing the police."

Lauren chuckled.

"I take it you and Grier have a history?"

He laughed.

"You could say that."

He stopped in front of a glassed-in treatment room and slid the door open.

"Here we are. Keep it brief, okay?"

Sydney looked small as she sat upright against the pillows of the hospital bed, wrapped to the chin in warm cotton blankets. When she caught sight of Harriet and Lauren, tears began slipping down her cheeks. Her bottom lip quivered.

"I want my mother, but they won't let me see her."

"I'm sure they'll let you see her when they've got you patched up. In the meantime, is there anyone else we can call for you?"

Sydney let out a little sob, and Lauren handed her a tissue from a box on the bedside table.

"What's left of my family is on their way here." She dabbed at her eyes. "They're all going to arrive for Jen's memorial service, only I'm here instead of planning it." Her tears increased, dripping off her chin. "It's all a mess."

"Have you done anything about it yet?" Lauren asked.

Sydney sniffed.

"We still have the hotel ballroom reserved, 'cause that was where the wedding reception was going to be, but Mama had canceled the flowers and dinner because what she had planned for the wedding didn't seem right

112

for a memorial service. It doesn't feel right to have it with her in the hospital, either."

Lauren handed her another tissue.

"Can you postpone it?"

"Since everyone was coming already, Mama told them to come ahead and we'd do the memorial. I haven't even told all of them that she's in the hospital. It's just too much." She started crying in earnest.

Harriet took a small notepad and pen from her purse.

"Do you still have the minister?"

"One of Jen's friends got ordained on the internet for the occasion."

Need Speaker, Harriet wrote.

"I could ask my husband..." She felt her cheeks pink. "...about food. Maybe he and his cooking buddies could pull together some snacks. They did food for our quilt banquet, so they already have some sort of connection to the hotel."

Lauren pulled her tablet from her bag and began tapping its screen.

"If you want a religious person to perform the funeral service, I can probably find someone. There are several churches close by."

"We're Episcopalian now, but we used to be Lutheran. Either one is okay."

Harriet made a note. Lauren typed another search into her tablet.

"Ava's Flowers has same-day service and a free delivery special, so that could work."

Dr. Hatcher slid the glass door open and leaned his head in.

"We need to give Ms. Johnson her medication."

Harriet patted Sydney's arm.

"Don't worry. If you're okay with us working on this, I think with the help of our friends we can pull this together."

The relief was visible on Sydney's face.

"That would be so great. I don't know how to thank you enough."

"Don't worry," Harriet said. "Just get better. We'll talk to you tomorrow and let you know what we've done."

Sydney began crying again, and Lauren handed her the box of tissues before she and Harriet turned and left.

✄ --- ✄ --- ✄

Mavis sat beside Connie with her arms firmly crossed over her ample bosom. Detective Settle stood alone on the opposite side of the waiting room.

"How's Sydney?" Connie asked.

"Okay, I guess. They stitched her head, but it didn't look serious. She's more upset than anything." She gave them a sheepish smile. "Lauren and I sort of agreed to put together the memorial service for tomorrow."

Lauren stepped in front of her.

"She was crying," she added, "and she doesn't have anyone else."

Mavis frowned.

"I hate to point out the obvious, but she does have someone. Our errant groom. He should be helping with the memorial service—it was his fiancée, after all."

Lauren smirked.

"He's probably too busy celebrating."

Detective Settle had crossed the room and now joined them.

"Mrs. Garvin? Could I ask you a few questions?"

"It's Ms. Truman," she said reflexively. "And I think we both already know the answer to that. Let me remind you, in case you forgot. I'm unable to answer any questions without the presence of my attorney."

"Call her. I'll wait." Settle sat in a chair a few spaces away from Mavis. Harriet looked from Mavis to him and back to Mavis.

"Look, we can wait for my attorney, or you can just believe me when I say I don't know anything. I was stitching in my room with Mavis. I went out to get ice, leaving the door open so Mavis could hear me the whole time. The paramedics were with Sydney before I left my room. Sydney flagged me down as I was getting my ice. Like I told you before, she asked me to accompany her, and here we are."

Settle stood up with a sigh.

"Look, I know Grier's all over you guys, but we're getting a lot of pressure from above to close this case. Galveston only has about ten murders per year, but for some reason, a couple of years ago some journalist put us—not only Galveston but specifically the Strand area—on a list of the twenty-five most dangerous neighborhoods in the country. For crying out loud, we were number twenty-one. And the *Houston Chronicle* printed the article.

"We can't afford bad press. If the cruise ships decide we're not a safe place for their passengers to disembark, they could pull out, and our local economy would take a hit we might not be able to recover from.

"I don't think he really believes one of you did it, but it's equally unlikely that it was one of our local citizens. I don't know for sure, but I think he's hoping if he squeezes y'all hard enough you'll turn something up." He gave them a wry smile. "Y'all do have a bit of a reputation. At least, that's what the Foggy Point PD tells us."

Connie stood up and stepped in front of him.

"You are not making it easy for us to help. Your constant harassment of Harriet is inappropriate, and it has to stop. We did nothing but come to an appliqué conference hoping to enjoy your fair city and to learn a few new stitching tricks. Harriet has not only had her face broken but she's been locked in her closet and grilled repeatedly by you...you...goons! It has to stop," she repeated.

Mavis got up and stood beside her, glaring at Settle. He stared back at them for a moment and then put up both hands in surrender.

"Fine, go back to your hotel. Grier isn't going to like it, but I guess that's not your problem."

"Thanks for picking us up," Harriet said to Bruce as she climbed out of the hotel limo. Connie, Mavis and Lauren followed her out onto the sidewalk.

Mavis looked at her friends.

"We've got some planning to do," she reminded them.

"Let's get our stitching and go to the pajama party and see if Stephanie or Alice want to help us," Harriet suggested.

Connie shook her head as they got into the elevator.

"It's sad that we've had so much experience working together on memorial services."

Lauren snorted a laugh.

"Before I started hanging out with you people, I'd been to maybe four funerals in my life. Now I've been to that many in a year."

"It tends to happen more often as you get older," Mavis said and stepped off the elevator on their floor.

"Hey," Lauren said as she followed her. "I'm not even forty yet; "this isn't natural."

Chapter 15

Harriet came into the pajama party room still dressed in her day clothes, set her project on a table, and sat down.

"Stephanie, I'm glad you're here."

"I heard you went to the hospital with Sydney tonight. Is she all right?"

Lauren gathered a collection of cookies from the snack table and set them in front of Harriet.

"I brought a couple of everything, so help yourself."

Harriet picked a salted caramel bar and took a bite before answering Stephanie.

"Sydney's still at the hospital, but they'll let her out in the morning."

"What happened?"

Lauren looked at Harriet as she settled into her seat.

"Do we actually know what happened?"

Harriet set her cookie bar down and picked up her wool appliqué.

"All I know is what Sydney told me. She said she was in her room, and someone started strangling her from behind, and while she struggled with her attacker, she managed to dial nine-one-one, which made him or her mad. They hit her in the head and took off."

"Why would someone attack Sydney?" Stephanie wondered.

Mavis joined them juggling a plate of cookies and a cup of tea, while trying to keep her bag from slipping off her shoulder.

"That would be the question of the day," she said. "Someone appears to be bent on destroying that family."

"Where's Connie?" Harriet asked.

"She's talking to her family. She'll be down in a minute."

Lauren took a bite of chocolate chip cookie and frowned in thought.

"Do we know if anyone's told The Groom about Sydney?"

Harriet completed the buttonhole stitch she was making.

"Are we going to assume he isn't the one who attacked her?"

Mavis pulled her project from her bag and plucked the needle from the background fabric.

"Why would he want to hurt Sydney?"

"Because everybody lies," Harriet said and took a stitch. "We only have his word that he profits if his fiancée dies. His baby-mamma definitely benefits if Jen dies. Maybe she thinks Sydney knows something that will lead the police to her."

"Or maybe," Lauren suggested, "Sydney had to be out of the picture for him to get his money."

Stephanie took a sip from the teacup in front of her.

"I can't wrap my head around how Michael benefits from any of this, other than not having to marry Jen. I mean, Judith has to have known that giving money to Michael's dad was a donation and, no matter what, she was never going to see that money again. It certainly doesn't make sense for Michael to hurt Judith or Sydney."

Harriet snipped the thread on the backside of her project, cut a new length from her skein of green embroidery floss, and separated out two strands.

"What about the ex-boyfriend? Maybe he's out for revenge. This could be the old 'If I can't have her no one can'? Then he blames Mom for ruining everything and lumps Sydney in, too, mistakenly thinking she had something to do with Jennifer marrying Michael."

Lauren yawned.

"My money's on the pregnant also-ran. She's the one who gets everything she wants out of this."

Harriet threaded her needle and started to stitch on another leaf edge.

"On a whole other subject, Stephanie, would you like to help us plan a memorial service? Lauren and I sort of volunteered to pull together the one for Jen. With her mom in the hospital, Sydney hasn't gotten much done, and people are arriving tomorrow."

"Sure," Stephanie said immediately. "Anything."

"We know generally what we need to do, but since you know them, even if it's been a while, we were hoping you could help with some of the details."

"I have to say I'm amazed, considering what Jen did to you," Stephanie told her.

Harriet sighed.

"Just because she had a moment of bad behavior doesn't mean we shouldn't give her a decent memorial service. I mean, at this point, it's not really for her; it's for her family and close friends."

Stephanie turned her project in her hand so she could reach a flower petal.

"Well, I'm not sure I could be so gracious in your position."

Lauren went to the food table and returned with four glasses and a pitcher of water.

"Water, anyone?"

Her friends all nodded and she handed it out as she spoke.

"Did your hubby answer your text about the food?" she asked Harriet.

Harriet pulled her phone from her pocket and tapped the screen.

"He says it will be no problem, and after he consulted with his fellow chefs, they suggested building a menu around mini-muffulettas."

"What is a muffuletta?" Connie asked.

Harriet smiled.

"It's an Italian sandwich made on a round roll with salamis, cheeses and a green-olive relish. The story goes they were invented at an Italian grocery in New Orleans when some round buns were delivered in error. They didn't have time to replace them with the correct bread, so they invented a new sandwich featuring the buns. They were such a hit, they've been making them ever since. No trip to New Orleans is complete without one. I think James is going to try them at his restaurant later this year."

"That sounds good," Lauren said. "Somehow, I've been to New Orleans twice without having one. Back to the matter at hand, I ordered three big upright funeral sprays and two table arrangements online on the drive back from the hospital."

Stephanie sipped her tea.

"I can go to the Walmart and get paper goods before class, and if you want, I can ask the hotel if we can use their copier to print some sort of program. I can write something."

Alice, sitting at the next table, turned her chair so she could lean closer to them.

"I heard you talking about the memorial service for the woman who hit you. I hope I'm not speaking out of turn, but I sing in a female barbershop quartet, and my group is all here. We all sing at church, and if you don't have plans for music we could sing 'Amazing Grace' or something like that."

"I hadn't even thought about music," Harriet said.

"Sometimes it's helpful for us to do the music since we don't need any instruments, and in a venue this size, we won't really need a mic, either."

Mavis smiled at her.

"I think that would be just wonderful. Thank you."

"Do you have a minister or anyone like that?" Alice asked.

Lauren checked her phone screen.

"It's on our list. I was going to start dialing-for-dollars in the morning."

"I'm not one hundred-percent certain," Alice said after looking thoughtful a moment, "but I think I heard someone at the table next to ours at the get to-know-each-other say they were clergy of some sort. They were laughing about how many points that might be worth."

Stephanie stood up and addressed the stitchers.

"Is anyone here clergy? Or otherwise qualified to perform a funeral service?"

A tiny woman with white cotton-candy hair wearing a bright purple one-piece pajama stood up.

"I'm an Episcopal rector. I'm retired from my parish but still qualified to perform services."

"May we talk to you for a minute?" Stephanie asked.

"Certainly."

Stephanie sat back down as the rector made her way to their table.

"My name is Dorothy Tucker," the elderly rector said. "I assume this has to do with the young lady who was murdered. Am I correct?"

Harriet got up and pulled an additional chair from the next table over for her.

"The murder victim is a bride who was going to get married here at the hotel. Since her family was already on their way here, her mother decided to hold a memorial service instead. Unfortunately, *she* was attacked and is in the hospital, and tonight her other daughter was also attacked, although not as severely. She'll be released from the hospital in the morning, but that doesn't leave her any time to make arrangements."

Dorothy gestured at Harriet's eye.

"Isn't the murder victim the one who did that to your eye?"

"She is," Harriet answered. "Their family situation is complicated. You might have noticed Sydney stitching with us the last few evenings. She's all alone and now hurt on top of that. She asked me to go to the hospital with her tonight, and while we were there, she asked if we could help her with the service."

Dorothy looked at each person at the table in turn. Harriet and her friends held their breath.

"Of course. I'll do whatever I can."

119

Everyone collectively let out a breath.

"Check that one off your list," she said.

Lauren smiled and made a note on her tablet.

"Do you know what time Sydney will be back in the morning?" Dorothy asked.

"It didn't sound like they'd be keeping her very long," Harriet said. "The doctor was going to have us come back and get her in a few hours but changed his mind so we all wouldn't be driving around in the middle of the night."

"I've got my laptop in my room," Dorothy said. "I can pull some sample services off the internet to show her so she can get an idea of some possible structures. Once I have an idea what type program she wants, I can write it up. Do you have music?"

Alice explained her offer, and she and Dorothy talked about some of the songs her group could sing.

"That should do quite nicely," Dorothy said and stood up. "I better get my stitching and go upstairs to start organizing my materials."

She returned to her table and explained what had transpired to her friends. As she went out the door, James came in, scanned the room and, when he found Harriet, came over to the table. He kissed her, careful to stay away from her bruised cheek.

"I think we're okay on food for tomorrow. The hotel had a count for wedding guests, and we're assuming since they were all coming in from out of town, most of them will still come. We added a dozen or so more, since some of you will undoubtedly attend, too."

Lauren sipped her water and set her glass down with a thunk.

"Not to rain on the parade, but has anyone thought about how we're going to pay for this?"

James pulled a chair up and sat slightly behind and to one side of Harriet.

"Fortunately, Sydney had already talked to the hotel about turning the theme of the planned event around and had okayed using the credit card they had on file, so they were good with ordering the food on that."

Harriet smiled at him.

"That's good, I guess."

James looked at his watch.

"I don't know about you ladies, but I've had about as much fun as I can take for one day."

Harriet looked around the table.

"Do we have everything under control?"

Mavis ticked off their list on her fingers.

"Pastor, music, flowers, food, venue, program. I think that covers it."
Connie shook her head.

"It's too bad they're doing it on such short notice. With a little more time, they could have done a video of pictures from Jennifer's life."

Lauren picked up her tablet and danced her fingers across the face.

"I can get the florist to add a guestbook. I know it's not the same, but at least it will be something. Especially since her mother won't be able to attend."

Connie smiled at her.

"That's very thoughtful of you, dear."

"I do try," Lauren said, but suppressing a grin as she said it.

Harriet stood up.

"I think I'm going to turn in, too. See you all at breakfast?"

Lauren slid the tablet into her messenger bag and joined them.

"I'm going to go up, too. My rollaway is calling my name."

"Stay safe," Mavis said as they started for the door.

✂ --- ✂ --- ✂

James shut the door and came up behind Harriet, who was standing in the middle of their room.

"Are you sure you want to be point person on the memorial service for the woman who did this?" He reached around and ran his finger gently down her still-swollen cheek. She turned, and he wrapped his arms around her. She rested the undamaged side of her face against his chest.

"Truthfully? This is a nightmare that never ends. I want all of this to never have happened."

He reached down to take her left hand and raise it between them. She pressed her thumb against her third finger, pushing the ring up, and smiled.

"Maybe not all of it. I have grown pretty fond of this little sparkler."

He tilted her chin up and kissed her.

"We could go jump in the car and head west. The police can't stop you. They can bluster all they want about not leaving town, but if you're not charged with anything they can't stop you."

Harriet leaned back and looked him in the face.

"Are you secretly a lawyer?"

James laughed.

"Hey, Lauren isn't the only one who knows how to use a smartphone. I looked it up."

She settled in against his chest again.

"If you could have seen how pitiful Sydney looked at the hospital tonight, you would have agreed to anything, too. I mean, think about it. In less

121

than a year, she's lost her father, her sister, her mom's in the hospital with an uncertain future, and now she's been attacked. She asked me to help her, and I just couldn't say no."

He pulled her closer and kissed her again.

"Harriet Truman, you have a kind heart." He stepped away and took her by the hand, leading her to her bed. "Here, sit down and put your feet up. Let me get your ice bag filled, and we can watch more mindless TV while you chill."

Harriet smiled.

"You're too good to me."

"I'm trying for husband of the year. We may not be married long, so I've got to make every minute count."

She took the throw pillow off the bed and tossed it at him. He caught it and laughed.

"You think I'm kidding." He picked up her limp ice bag and headed for the door. "Do not open the door for anyone. I'll be right back."

Harriet settled back in her pillows and turned the television on. She caught sight of her ring and smiled. It really was spectacular.

Chapter 16

$\mathcal{H}$arriet and James were the first to arrive at breakfast the next morning. He took a bite of his croissant and made a face.

"Don't say it," she said with a laugh. "You could have done it better."

He grinned and took another bite.

"Okay, I won't," he said when he'd swallowed. "But I could have. On the other hand, it *is* free 'cause of your stitching thing. And I didn't have to cook anything to make it happen."

"You love to cook."

"I do, but not twenty-four-seven."

She sipped her orange juice and watched as Stephanie talked to the women at her table for a few more minutes then got up with two of them and approached Harriet's table.

"Sorry to interrupt your breakfast, but your friend Mavis was talking the other day about some strange stuff going on with jewelry in the hotel."

"Yeah. I encountered the hotel maid supposedly returning Mavis's necklace, which she claimed was accidentally scooped up with the dirty towels. It's a costume piece, so Mavis wasn't worried. And she is certain it was in her suitcase the last time she saw it. Then she and Connie heard some other classmates talking about a necklace that was temporarily missing and then showed up again with its broken clasp repaired. Once again, no crime, just weird."

One of the women, a slender blonde, said . "That sounds like what happened in our room. Kathy and I…" She looked at the third woman. "We both went on a cruise the week before this conference. You know how cruise ships always have great buys on jewelry?"

Harriet and James looked blank.

"Anyway, trust me, they have great deals, and on sea days they have all kinds of extra-special deals."

Kathy picked up the story..

"We both bought necklaces and were going to wear them out to dinner last night. They were very different pieces, but each was in the same kind of navy-blue box with the gold company logo on it. When we took out our boxes, the other person's necklace was in it."

"That's weird," James agreed.

Harriet set her glass down.

"It *is* strange, but since nothing was taken, I'm not sure what can be done."

"They could talk to your buddy Bruce," James suggested.

"Bruce is the hotel security guard I dealt with when I got hit in the eye," Harriet explained. "That's a good idea." She smiled at James. "I haven't found the police in this town to be very sensitive. James is right—Bruce will probably have a better idea about what you can do."

Lauren sat down at the table with a bowl of cereal.

"I didn't hear everything, but if you're talking about another jewelry problem-that-isn't-a-problem, I'd emphasize the fact that someone clearly made unauthorized entry into your room. Unless you assume it was the maid, in which case she wasn't unauthorized, merely digging through your possessions."

Harriet picked up her fork.

"Maybe the police should be looking at the cleaning staff for the attacks and murder, too. I mean, someone is coming and going from a lot of rooms without a problem. That almost has to be hotel staff."

"You could call your buddy Bruce for them," Lauren said as she opened the box of cereal and dumped it into her bowl. "Maybe he could meet them here."

"He's not my buddy," Harriet grumbled. Still, she was surprised. Lauren wasn't usually the first one in the bunch to offer help to strangers.

"Sure, I can do that. He still feels bad about my getting hit in the eye on his watch." She dialed the direct number to the security office Bruce had given her. He answered on the first ring; and when she explained what she wanted, he said he'd be right over.

✂ --- ✂ --- ✂

"What can I help you with?" Bruce said with a smile when he arrived.

Lauren finished her last bite of cereal and set her spoon down.

"Can you find out which of the cleaning staff were on our floor when each of the recent violent incidents happened? And some of our quilters have noticed some...shall we call them irregularities?...with their jewelry."

"Has anything been stolen?" Bruce was suddenly all business.

"No, Bruce, if someone's jewelry had been stolen, I'd have said 'some of us have had our jewelry stolen.' And I'm pretty sure they would have reported that immediately. Our jewelry is playing musical chairs. Like someone is gas-lighting us."

"Ma'am, I'm not sure what's been happening with your jewelry, but if nothing's been taken, I'm not sure exactly what we can do. As for your questions about our staff, we couldn't stay in business long if we hired people who stole from or otherwise harassed our paying guests. The hotel is very concerned about the unfortunate incidents that have happened this week, and we're working with the local police to figure out how someone was able to get into rooms without permission and commit these atrocities."

Harriet was impressed with Bruce's ability to avoid using words like *crime*, *murder*, or *attack*, given that one person was dead and two more had been injured, with one of those with her life hanging by a thread.

James stood up.

"Will you be all right here? I need to go check with the kitchen about the food for this afternoon. We asked them to order some stuff, and I'm sure they did, but I'd like to see what came."

"I'll be fine," she said with a smile. He leaned down and kissed her then hurried off.

"We've increased our security presence in the hotel since everything has happened," Bruce continued, "and... " He nodded to Lauren. "...we checked our staff assignments when each of the other events happened. While there were several people who were working during two of the times, there is no one who was on duty for all three incidents. Of course, it was one of the first things the police asked, and we were more than willing to help them however we could." He glared at Lauren for good measure before turning and striding out of the room.

Harriet waited until he was gone to laugh. Mavis and Connie joined them as she started to finish her breakfast.

"What's so funny?" Mavis asked.

Harriet wiped her mouth with her napkin.

"Oh, just Lauren making friends."

Stephanie smiled at Lauren.

"I'm with her. Bruce is definitely a company man. But I suppose he's right. The hotel can't really afford to have their reputation ruined by an errant employee. Everyone in this part of town seems pretty conscious of the cruise ship business and how not to do anything that might scare them off.

"Do you need me to do anything else for the memorial service?"

Thanks for asking," Harriet answered. "I think we've got the big stuff handled. You might help greet people at the door. I'm not sure how well the people coming to the memorial service know one another. From what you were saying, they may be newer friends who thought they were coming to a wedding and will now feel obligated to stay for the memorial."

"I think you've got that right. Our classes end at noon, so I'll just run upstairs and change clothes and come back over here to do whatever I can."

Stephanie's friend Kathy gave her a questioning look.

"I'll explain it all when we get to class." She turned and, with a little wave of her fingers, left the room.

Mavis set her bag down on the chair James had just vacated.

"Let me get my breakfast, and you can catch me up on what's been happening."

She and Connie went over to the buffet to make their selections. When they returned, Harriet explained the discussion with Kathy about the mobile jewelry and her summoning of Bruce.

Mavis cut her sandwich in half. It was made with a large croissant and was a bit unwieldy even in two pieces.

"At least he answered the question about the staff work schedules." She took a bite and chewed thoughtfully. "Not to overlook the obvious, but they must have a master key of some sort that allows them entry to all the rooms on their schedule. Maybe someone stole that."

"Possible," Lauren agreed, "but don't forget—even though our keys look like the old-fashioned kind, they all have a chip embedded in their end. If one was reported stolen, they could just reprogram it." She was quiet for a minute. "That would probably involve reprogramming all the keys on that person's schedule. None of us have been given new keys, or had our old keys taken and reprogrammed. I'm pretty sure these systems aren't sophisticated enough that they could remotely reprogram them."

Connie sipped her tea.

"So, that leaves us back at the beginning. Someone is getting into rooms, and we don't know how."

Harriet sighed.

"I can't believe our classes end today. I'd like to take that part sometime again when I can attend all of each session. I missed a lot bouncing in and out with this whole thing." She pointed to her eye.

Mavis reached over and patted her hand.

"Oh, honey, don't worry. Connie and I can show you what you missed when we get back home."

Lauren crumpled her napkin and set it on the table.

"Which can't come soon enough, if you ask me. I'm really regretting our decision to stay the extra days to tour Galveston. I've seen enough of this place."

Harriet drained her juice glass.

"I'm still looking forward to the ghost tour. It's away from here, and everything bad that's happened has been at the hotel. If we go someplace that's supposed to be bad, maybe it'll be the opposite."

Lauren chuckled.

"Or maybe it'll be that much worse."

"Oh, come on, where's your sense of adventure?"

Connie laughed.

"We've had more than enough adventure for one trip. I think we should spend the rest of our time together stitching in our room. Maybe that Bruce fellow can put a guard outside our door, too."

Mavis glanced at her watch and looked at Harriet.

"You should go ice your eye while we finish breakfast; class starts in thirty minutes."

"Yes, ma'am," Harriet said as she and Lauren got up. "I know," she added to Lauren, "you need to check your email."

✂ --- ✂ --- ✂

Harriet loaded her wool appliqué project into her canvas stitching bag and put the handles over her arm.

"Did you hear the teacher say how improved my stitching is?"

Lauren laughed.

"Yeah, I heard her say how far you'd come, but that may be because your 'zipper' stem left you lots of room for growth."

"Hey, I was impaired."

"Oh, so now you're going to play the black eye card?"

Harriet grinned at her.

"I'll use whatever I can."

"Have you figured out what you're going to wear to the service this afternoon?"

"Since I wore my 'wedding dress' to the banquet, I've still got my black pants. I don't have a dark top, but that'll have to do."

Lauren looked at her watch.

"If we hurry, we can run over to Tina's, and I can buy a pair of black pants. I noticed they had a whole rack of black clothes."

"Okay, let's drop our stitching bags across the street with the valets."

No one was at the desk when they entered the lobby, but Harriet saw Bruce in the hallway leading to the conference rooms. He offered to put their stuff in the secure room and took the bags.

"Wait here, and I'll bring you the tags for when you come back. Just give the yellow ticket to the valet, and he'll get them for you."

"Thanks," Harriet said.

Lauren turned sideways to face Harriet and murmured, "Don't stare, but isn't that Kari standing with Michael in the coffee shop?"

Harriet dropped her purse and bent to pick it up, moving to Lauren's other side so she had a sightline into the cafe.

"Wow. That head-to-toe black makes it look like she's planning on coming to the memorial service."

"Yeah, complete with small but noticeable baby bump."

"Takes 'stand by your man' to a whole new level."

Lauren took the tag from Bruce and dropped it into her messenger bag.

"I'd say it all depends on how Sydney feels about it. Mom's still unconscious in the hospital, so unless another relative shows up to object, maybe it will be okay. If her presence keeps Michael sober, it could be a good thing."

Harriet followed her down the stairs and out of the hotel.

"That's a big if."

✂ --- ✂ --- ✂

"You're back again," Boyce, the manager of Tina's on the Strand said as they walked up the interior stairs and into the clothing area of the shop. "Let me guess—one or both of you need something black to wear this afternoon."

Harriet looked at Lauren.

"There's always Walmart."

Boyce looked Lauren up and down.

"That won't be necessary. I think I have something that will work."

Lauren's eyes got big.

"I'm not wearing a dress or anything that makes me look like I just got off a cruise ship."

She laughed.

"I could see that about you. Wait here, I have a few pieces in the back room."

128

"I didn't realize that many people from our appliqué conference were going to the memorial service," Harriet said.

"They aren't," Boyce said as she brought out three tops and two pairs of pants on hangers. "I didn't mean to eavesdrop, but it's a small shop. We've had several groups of people who say they came early for a wedding only to have it turn into a funeral." She held up the first shirt. "Try this on."

Harriet held Lauren's messenger bag while she slipped the first shirt on over her teeshirt then turned side to side.

"Where's the mirror?"

Boyce led her to the back of the store, and Harriet followed.

"I'm surprised you two are going to the service," she said. "Isn't the dead girl the one that did that to you?" She gestured to Harriet's eye.

Harriet sighed.

"It's complicated."

"I'm just sorry this all has happened to you while you're visiting our city. Galveston really is a lovely place."

"This will work," Lauren said, coming out of the dressing room and handing back the top.

"Do you want to try the other two, just to compare?" Boyce asked.

"No, this works. And I'll take these." She took one of the hangers holding a plain pair of black linen elastic-waist pants.

Boyce turned to Harriet.

"How about you? Are you set?"

"I've got black pants and a white blouse."

"Come over here," Boyce led her to a display of scarves and began sorting through them. "I've got a large gray-and-black one you could drape over one shoulder. It'll tone down the white of your blouse." She found it and draped it over Harriet's shoulder.

"Of course it'll look better when it's not on a red teeshirt."

"I'll take it," Harriet agreed.

Boyce rang up their purchases, wrapped them in colorful tissue and put them in shopping bags.

"I really do hope you'll come back and see us again."

Lauren shook her head as they walked out of the shop.

"We're not even gone yet, and she wants us back ."

"We can't get out of this city fast enough, if you ask me. I think it's going to be a while before I feel good about coming back here."

Lauren chuckled.

"You mean you aren't coming back next year to celebrate your first anniversary."

Harriet rolled her eyes and led the way back to the hotel.

Mavis reached up and adjusted Harriet's scarf where it crossed her shoulder. She smoothed it into place when she had it where she wanted it.

"Is this new? I don't remember seeing it before."

"Lauren needed an outfit. We went back to Tina's, and the manager suggested this scarf to tone down my white shirt."

"She has a good eye. It's is perfect."

"Speaking of Lauren..." Harriet stopped mid-sentence as a balding man in an expensive charcoal-gray suit stormed into the lobby of the ballroom building.

"Where's Sydney?" he demanded.

Harriet and Mavis looked at each other but said nothing.

"Are you deaf?" he asked in a booming voice.

Mavis turned toward him.

"No, I'm ignoring you, though it's a bit hard, as loud as you're yelling. What is it that TV doctor is always saying? 'You teach people how to treat you.' Right now, I'm teaching you that yelling at me is not an acceptable way to communicate." She turned back to Harriet. "Is Lauren changing into her new outfit?"

The man dropped his chin to his chest and then looked up, his hands held in front of him.

"I'm sorry. You're right. I'm being horribly rude. My name is Winston Remington. I am....I was...a friend of Jennifer—Miss Johnson, that is. I really am sorry. I'm not usually so...." He stopped talking and let his hands fall to his sides, unable to find the words for what he wasn't.

"This whole thing is such a nightmare. I should have been the one marrying Jennifer. This whole charade..." He pronounced it "odd" not "aid." "...with Michael Williams was a joke. He was never going to stay with her just because their parents wanted it. I was the one who loved her. I know she didn't love me yet, but she liked me. And I could have given her the things she wanted. I know she would have seen it if we'd just had a little more time."

Harriet waited for him to finish.

"Didn't Jennifer break up with you?"

Mavis put a hand on Harriet's arm, but Harriet ignored her.

"How long had it been since you'd seen her?"

"Three months and fifteen days."

"I know you don't want to hear this, but it sounds like things were over between you two. I mean, three months is a long time."

"She called me two weeks ago," he said.

"What?"

His lip curled up like he was trying to smile but couldn't pull it off.

"I was surprised. I'm not proud of the fact I'd left her probably fifty messages in those first two months. But I'd finally given up. I had to accept she was going to go through with this craziness. For a couple of weeks, I went about my business, trying to put her out of my mind. Then, out of nowhere, Jennifer called."

The door thunked closed behind Lauren.

She passed Winston and joined Harriet and Mavis.

"Who's he?"

"Meet Winston Remington, Jennifer's former boyfriend. I'll catch you up later." She turned her attention back to Winston. "So, what did she say?"

He blew his breath out.

"She said she was confused. She was afraid she was making a mistake. We talked for hours. More than once, in fact. She invited me to the wedding. I believe she wanted me there so she could bail at the last minute."

"Did she say that?" Mavis asked.

"No, it was just the feeling I got from our hours of phone talk."

"Now we'll never know."

Lauren glanced up the sweeping staircase, looked pointedly at Harriet and glanced up again.

"I'm sorry for your loss," Harriet said. "Please excuse us, but we need to get upstairs and check on the floral arrangements."

She stopped when they reached the top landing and turned to Lauren.

"What's up?"

"What do you mean?"

"Unless I'm mistaken, you were signaling us to break it off with Mr. Remington."

"I spotted the happy couple across the street. It looked like they were headed this way."

Lauren looked down into the lobby.

"They must have been waylaid. I do not want to be present when that trio gets together."

Mavis headed into what had been the first classroom when they were stitching students. The center dividers had been compressed into their hiding places, resulting in one large room. The hotel had arranged rows of chairs with an aisle through the middle that lined up with a podium, complete with microphone, set at the front of the room. Matching standing floral sprays stood on either side of the center. A row of tables covered with black linens were arranged on the far side of the room. The third standing spray

131

stood to one side. A framed picture of Jennifer was on one table; a guest-book open in front of it, a smaller vase of roses in various shades of pink to one side.

"*Diós mío,*" Connie said. "The florist did a wonderful job for such short notice. And the hotel transformed this place."

Mavis came up beside her.

"It's just so sad. That poor girl may have been spoiled, but no matter how ill-behaved she was, she didn't deserve to have her wedding turned into this."

Harriet rubbed her finger absently over her injured cheekbone.

"I wish we knew who killed her. Chances are, they'll be one of our funeral guests."

"That's a happy thought," Lauren said. "Do we know if our friends on the Galveston PD are going to be in attendance?"

"Don't they always go to the victim's funeral?" Harriet answered.

Mavis led the way to a pair of tables set up at the back of the room with pitchers of ice water and glasses.

"I called Robin. She and Kirsten will be here any minute. They're assuming the detectives will be here and want to be sure they don't try to ambush you."

Harriet poured a glass of water and held it up.

"Anyone?" When her friends declined, she took a sip. "I'll just be glad when this is over. I don't think I can take another grilling by that pair."

Chapter 17

*H*arriet heard the elevator bell, and a moment later, Dorothy Tucker came in, a leather-bound Bible under her arm and a sheaf of papers in her hands. She watched the retired pastor cross the room and joined them at the water table.

"How's Sydney doing?" Harriet asked her.

Dorothy shook her head.

"Hard to say. She's had a lot of loss to deal with. And her momma took a turn for the worse early this morning. Sydney stopped by to see her before she checked out, but she said her momma's monitors started going off. The doctor got her stabilized and she wasn't any worse for the wear, but it was very hard on Sydney. I don't know how much more that girl can take."

Mavis held up a glass, and Dorothy nodded. She filled it with water and handed it to her.

"Have any of her family showed up yet?"

"Her aunt was supposed to arrive a couple of hours ago," Dorothy said. "I just hope she's the sort of relative who can provide some comfort to that poor girl. She told me she was close to her father and it's pretty clear from talking to her that she's still grieving for him. This trouble with her sister and mother would be enough to put anyone over the top even if they hadn't just lost their father. Someone's going to need to keep an eye on her when she gets home. Especially if her mother doesn't make it."

Alice arrived, followed by three other women from the appliqué conference.

"Is it okay if we run through our songs. We need to get a feel for the acoustics in here."

"Sure, it'll be a while before the guests start showing up," Harriet told her

Alice led her quartet to the far side of the podium, and they lined up, then began singing notes and clearing their throats.

Harriet headed for the door.

"I'm going down to the restroom. Anyone else want to come?"

Lauren joined her, and they headed for the door.

"Do you think we should see if Bruce has anyone who could act as an usher?" Harriet wondered.

"Don't you think we could get one of the stitchers to do that?"

They reached the bottom of the stairs and crossed the lobby.

"I was just thinking that Winston seems pretty tightly wound. When he sees Michael and Kari, he may go ballistic. A burly security guy standing by the door ready to step in at any moment might be a good deterrent."

Lauren opened the door to the ladies room, and Harriet went in.

"I suppose we can go across the street and ask him," Lauren said. "If he says no, we can figure out a plan B, but I bet he'll say yes."

✂ --- ✂ --- ✂

"Hey, Bruce," a young, muscular blond man Harriet had never seen before called back into the bellmen's storage room. "That hot chick with the black eye needs to talk to you." He turned back to her and grinned.

Harriet smiled back at him.

"If you're trying to score points with me, it's working."

His grin got bigger.

"My momma didn't raise a fool. The boss lady told us to give you the VIP treatment. How're we doing so far?"

Lauren stepped between them.

"Over the top and heading toward really annoying. Could you actually go into that room and get Bruce?"

The blond disappeared, and Bruce appeared a moment later.

"I know you're busy," Harriet explained, "but we may have World War Three brewing across the street. In a nutshell, Jennifer's ex-boyfriend showed up, and he's pretty angry with her fiancé. In addition, Michael, the fiancé, has his pregnant girlfriend with him."

"All three plan to be at the memorial service," Lauren added, just to be sure Bruce got the picture.

"That doesn't sound good." He looked at the floor and thought for a moment. "One of my guys called in sick, so I'm shorthanded. Tyrone!" The blond came to the door of the storage room. "You up for a trial run in security?" He looked at Harriet. "He's been bugging me about joining the security staff for months."

"Yes, sir! I'll do anything."

"Hopefully, you won't *have* to do anything except be present. Go back to the security office and ask Meg to find you a coat and print you a badge. "When does the service start?" he asked.

Harriet glanced at her phone.

"Thirty-five minutes."

"And the ex is already in the room," Lauren added.

"Get going," Bruce said to Tyrone. "And have Meg issue you a radio, too."

Harriet moved toward the door.

"Thanks."

"Thank you for warning us," Bruce said. "Prevention is usually the best approach in situations like these. And don't worry about Tyrone. He's worked security before in the bar scene."

"You mean he was a bouncer?" Lauren asked.

Bruce smiled.

"Basically, yeah. He's studying criminology and would like to eventually go into law enforcement. I think he'll be able to handle whatever happens with your warring parties."

Harriet looked across the street.

"We better go—looks like people are starting to arrive. Thanks again."

"Good luck," Bruce told her and headed back into the storage room.

Lauren led the way back across the street.

"That Tyrone is a hottie," she murmured to Harriet.

"I've never been into the muscular, body-builder type."

"That's because you have two or more men throwing themselves at you at any given moment. I can't afford to be picky."

"If you consider my ex-boyfriend, who currently resides in Africa, and my shotgun husband as multiple men 'throwing themselves' at me, then okay, fine, I'm drowning in men. But, seriously, Tyrone has to be at least ten years younger than us."

Lauren laughed.

"I could get into being a cougar. Besides, need I remind you of Aiden's age?"

Harriet shook her head.

"Right."

Mavis opened the door just as they reached the ballroom building.

"Where have you been? Connie and I came downstairs to the restroom to see if you'd fallen in, and you were nowhere to be found."

Harriet explained their mission across the street with Bruce.

"Good thinking," Connie said with a nod of approval.

"Has anyone important showed up yet?" Lauren asked.

Mavis shook her head.

"The ex is the only one of note. We introduced ourselves to the only other group that arrived and went in, but it sounds like they hardly knew the female Johnsons. They were employees of the father's business."

Lauren sighed.

"That's really pathetic. I could almost feel sorry for the bride if she hadn't tried to kill you before she died."

"Come on, she didn't try to kill me. She just didn't know her own strength when she slapped me," Harriet said and looked past Lauren. "Hey, Robin, glad you're here."

"Has something happened?"

Harriet laughed.

"No, just the safety-in-numbers thing. We met the bride's ex, who turned up for the event. There may be fireworks when the groom arrives."

Robin surveyed the room.

"Then we're going to sit near the exit, and if fireworks break out, we're leaving. All of us, understood?"

She stared at each of them in turn until they'd all agreed.

Harriet saw two cars pull up to the valet parking space across the street.

"Looks like people are starting to arrive. I was just thinking—assuming there aren't fireworks to the point that we have to leave, we need to circulate and see what we can find out from the guests."

"Would it do any good if I said we need to stay out of it?" Robin asked.

Mavis shook her head.

"Harriet's past the point of being able to stay out of it. The police want to pin Jennifer's death on her. If we can find something out that will help clear her name, I think we should at least try. Of course, we'll be careful, but a little talk can't hurt anything."

Harriet chewed her lip.

"Jennifer's bridesmaids will undoubtedly be here. Why don't Lauren and I talk to them. I think Sydney said something about an aunt. Connie, why don't you and Mavis see if you can chat her up. And, Robin, since the ex-boyfriend hasn't met you, maybe you can take a run at him."

Robin stared at her for a moment.

"Assuming nothing has happened prior to that, I guess I could ask a few questions. And if Kirsten gets here in time, she could talk to the fiancé."

A trio of young women wearing pink dresses and black shoes, gloves and headbands, came through the door.

"Where do we go for the memorial?" the middle one, a thin girl with long auburn hair, asked.

Lauren gestured up the stairs. Mavis stared at the pink dresses.

"These were our bridesmaid's dresses," a shorter, dark-haired girl offered. Tears filled her eyes. "Jen loved these." She held out a handful of skirt. "They had pale-green sashes, but we replaced them with black out of respect."

Connie patted the dark-haired girl's arm.

"Oh, honey, I'm sure Jennifer would have liked that."

The thin girl handed her friend a tissue.

"Come on, Taylor, I want to be sure we can sit at the front."

Lauren slid her phone out of her pocket and took a picture of the three as they ascended the stairs. Harriet chuckled.

"What?" Lauren said.

"Come on, let's go upstairs." Harriet turned and led the way up the stairs.

✂ --- ✂ --- ✂

The ballroom was nearly full when Sydney made her entrance, followed by Michael. They sat in the front row. Harriet was relieved to see that Kari came after them and took a seat at the back of the room. Winston, unfortunately, chose to sit in the second row, on the opposite side of the center aisle from Sydney.

Harriet held her breath as Michael sat down, but Alice and her group began singing 'Nearer My God to Thee' and everyone settled back in their chairs, the occasional sniffle the only interruption to the program.

Dorothy delivered a moving service. She had obviously spoken to Jennifer's friends prior to the service and worked in stories about her serving meals to the homeless and creating a spa day at home for a young cousin who had a life-threatening illness.

James and his classmates started bringing in trays of muffulettas and setting them on tables at the back of the room as Dorothy finished and Alice and company sang "Amazing Grace."

Kirsten arrived after the service had started and slid into the spot Robin had saved for her. Robin had texted her with her assignment, and as soon as the final note had been sung, she got up and headed for the front and

137

Winston. The rest of the attendees made their way to the back of the room where James, with the help of the hotel staff, had coffee and tea laid out along with the spicy muffuletta sandwiches.

Harriet nudged Lauren and nodded to the front of the room.

"Sydney doesn't look very happy."

"That gathered skirt makes her look bigger than she usually does, and she's no feather under the best of circumstances."

"Lauren!" Harriet scolded her.

"Hey, I'm just saying she can't feel very good about herself on top of everything else."

"That older woman she's talking to must be the aunt. Kind of looks like she's lecturing Sydney about something. If I'm reading the family dynamic right, Sydney was blamed for anything that went wrong in that group."

"Have you been reading 'Cinderella'?" Just because Sydney is chunky and plain, and Jennifer was thin and pretty, doesn't mean Mom treated them differently."

"Yeah, right."

Lauren stood up.

"Let's go see what we can find out from the bridesmaids. Connie and Mavis should be able to get a sense of the family from the aunt."

Harriet stepped into the center aisle.

"At least Tyrone is taking his job seriously."

Lauren turned and looked. The newly minted security guard was talking to Winston and had positioned himself between the red-faced ex-boyfriend and the rest of the room.

The three forlorn bridesmaids were clustered around the coffee service. Taylor's mascara had run down her cheeks.

"That was such a beautiful program. Sydney told us you put it together." She reached her hand out. "I'm Taylor, and this is Dixie." She gestured to the thin, auburn-haired girl. "And this is Megan."

Harriet took the girls' hands in a brief shake.

"It was the least we could do. With Sydney in the hospital and all the wedding guests already on their way, we thought she could use some help. And it wasn't all us. The singers and the pastor are all from our quilting conference."

"This is all such a shock," Dixie said. "Jen was so excited to be getting married."

"Was she?" Lauren asked.

"Of course!" Dixie snapped.

Taylor dabbed her eyes with a crumpled tissue. She shook her head.

"Jen was making the best of a difficult situation."

When Taylor didn't say anything else, Harriet glanced at Lauren. She gave a small shrug.

"We met her ex-boyfriend Winston earlier."

Dixie gave a harsh laugh.

"That was a joke. She may have gone to the opera with him a time or two, but it was a convenience thing, encouraged by her mother. They were never going together."

Megan spoke for the first time.

"Her ex-boyfriend is a football player—DeWitt Williams. He's on the practice squad for the Miami Dolphins."

"Do you know why they broke up?" Harriet asked.

"Mama," the three young women said at the same time.

Lauren poured herself a glass of iced tea.

"So, what about Michael, the groom?"

"That was all her mother, too," Taylor said.

Harriet tilted her head.

"Help me understand this. Jennifer has the boyfriend of her dreams, and her mother hatches a scheme for her to marry a penniless stranger just to acquire his good family name, and she just goes along with it?"

"It wasn't *that* simple," Dixie said. She picked up a glass. "Mama controlled the purse strings," she continued as she filled her glass with tea. "She told Jen she'd disown her. No more designer bags, no spa dates, and no luxury sports car."

Lauren sipped her tea.

"She has a college education, doesn't she?"

Dixie rolled her eyes.

"The salary she could earn as a kindergarten teacher wasn't going to pay for the lifestyle she was used to."

"And her relationship with DeWitt wasn't far enough along for her to go live with him," Megan added. Tears filled her eyes. Harriet handed her a napkin from the food table.

"You three knew her pretty well, I assume." They all nodded. "What do you think happened to her?"

"It has to be Michael, doesn't it?" Taylor said.

Dixie shook her head.

"My money's on his baby-momma."

Harriet looked at her.

"What makes you think it's her?"

"Well," Dixie said, "she's here flaunting her baby bump in front of the world, and Jen not even cold in her grave."

"And him, trying to pretend he cared about Jen," Megan added.

Lauren set her glass down.

"If one of them killed Jen, why would they go after Jen's mother."

"Have you met the woman?" Dixie asked.

Megan put a quelling hand on Dixie's arm and frowned at her.

"Now, Dixie…"

"I'm not kidding. Jen's mother is an unbearable social climber. She treated everyone around her like they'd been put on earth just to serve her every whim." She shivered. "I can't say I'm sorry she was injured. She probably annoyed someone one too many times."

"It seems pretty unlikely someone hurt her after her daughter was killed and the two events aren't related," Lauren said.

Taylor stepped closer to the table, picked up a muffuletta and took a bite.

"These are heavenly," she said.

Harriet smiled.

"My husband made them."

"Wow," Megan said, "a man that can cook."

It was Lauren's turn to roll her eyes.

"We're very sorry for your loss." With that, she led Harriet away from the trio to the far end of the table.

Stephanie joined them and grabbed a sandwich, then turned to Harriet.

"That was lovely, all things considered."

Harriet scanned the room.

"I'm sure these people would rather have been at a wedding, but I guess it was okay, given everything."

Stephanie ate a bite of muffuletta before speaking again.

"There's definitely a little tension in the air. I feel sorry for Michael. I know he didn't want to marry Jen, but I'm sure he didn't want her dead."

"Are you?" Harriet said.

Stephanie hesitated a long moment.

"I guess I don't really know," she admitted. "Did I hear your husband made these delicious mini-sandwiches?" Alice asked as she arrived and set one on a napkin.

Harriet's cheeks pinked slightly.

"He did. I'll be sure and tell him how much you liked them." She put a sandwich on a napkin and picked it up. "You and your friends did a great job with the music."

Alice blushed.

"We were happy to do it. It's so sad when someone so young dies."

"Well, we appreciated your songs."

Harriet took a bite of her muffuletta.

"These really are good."

"Don't sound so surprised," James said from behind her. He slid his arm around her waist.

"I was just telling your wife how delicious these are," Alice told him.

"Well, your music was beautiful. I was bringing food in, but I stopped and listened when you did 'Amazing Grace.' Do you perform professionally?"

The conversation continued until Harriet noticed Robin talking with Kirsten in the center aisle; they appeared to have just left their interview targets. She located Winston and Michael and gasped when she found them. James turned to see what had caught her attention.

Winston was striding toward Michael, who was standing in front of the podium, his back turned to the larger man. She opened her mouth to shout a warning to the would be-groom.

Tyrone dropped his radio into its belt holster and took off after Winston, but it was clear he wasn't going to reach him in time. Winston was moving too fast.

"Arghhh!" he yelled as he swung a powerful roundhouse punch into the side of Michael's head. Michael dropped to the floor with a soft "Ooff!"

Kari screamed and started to run to her boyfriend. She was pushed aside by Detective Settle, who had been standing in the hallway observing.

Tyrone reached Winston and tackled him to the floor, splitting the rear seam of his own dress slacks in the process. Winston had been in the act of punching Michael again when Tyrone rolled him off to the side.

Winston landed a good pop to Tyrone's eye but in the end was no match for the younger man. He continued to struggle until Detective Settle reached them and pulled his hands behind his back, clamping handcuffs on as he went.

Michael wasn't moving.

"I need backup and a bus at the Tremont," Settle said into his cell.

Alice hurried over to Michael's side and knelt.

"I'm a nurse," she told Settle as she started assessing Michael and making sure he had a clear airway.

Sydney reached the food table, where James, Harriet, Alice, Stephanie and Lauren still clustered. Sydney's face was pale, and she looked like she might faint. Harriet considered fetching her a chair.

"This is Jane Wilson, Sydney's aunt," Connie told the group as she and Mavis led the older woman over.

"Would anyone like a cup of coffee or some iced tea?" James asked, breaking the silence.

"Coffee, please," Jane said.

Sydney stood watching in silence, her lips trembling. James handed a cup of coffee to her aunt and poured another for Sydney.

"Here, drink this."

She looked up at him, and when she didn't move, Harriet took it then put her hand on Sydney's arm.

"Come on, this will help."

Jane put her arm awkwardly around her niece's shoulder.

"It's going to be okay, Sydney. Sip your coffee and have a sandwich. Have you eaten anything today?"

Sydney shook her head, and James placed a muffuletta on a napkin and handed it to her. She finally relented and took a bite, and then another. The color started returning to her face as she ate and then drank the coffee.

"I just wanted a nice memorial service…for Jen. Now, instead of thinking about her, everyone is talking about Winston and Michael. And Jen didn't like either one of them."

Lauren put her glass down.

"Winston told us Jen had been calling him the last few days."

Mavis tugged on Lauren's sleeve, and when Lauren turned to her, she gave her a stern look and shook her head.

"She wasn't talking to Winston," Sydney said. "I'd have known. He may have tried to call her. He didn't really want to take no for an answer."

Connie rolled her napkin edge in her fingers, ignoring the shreds that fell to the floor.

"I hope Michael will be okay."

Sydney glared over at the group of people clustered around him.

"He deserves whatever he got. Winston is a controlling jerk, but Michael is no better. His whole drink-till-you-pass-out routine since he's been here wasn't fair to my sister. She wasn't excited about marrying him, but once she agreed to it and put that ring on her finger, she was trying to make the best of it."

Alice rejoined the group when the paramedics loaded Michael onto a gurney and wheeled him out of the room.

"He's going to have a headache," she announced to the group.

Harriet handed her a glass of tea.

"Was he still unconscious?"

"No, he had come around, but he was a little confused. They strapped him down to be sure he doesn't have a spinal injury. He probably has a burst eardrum on the side where the punch connected."

"That's terrible," Connie said. "He may not have been a wonderful fiancé, but surely he didn't deserve this."

Alice sipped her tea.

"He's lucky he woke up. A roundhouse swing like Winston gave him is much more damaging to the brain than a straight jab would be. Especially given that Winston outweighs Michael by a good fifty pounds."

James slid his arm around Harriet's waist and squeezed.

"I'm going to go downstairs and get the last tray of sandwiches. Looks like people are going to be hanging around for a while longer. Don't go anywhere, okay?"

She smiled.

"I'll be right here."

Mavis followed James with her gaze and then turned to Harriet and lowered her voice so only she could hear.

"Seems like things are going well with you and your chef."

Harriet shrugged, but her smile didn't fade.

"What's not to like about a man who can cook?"

Chapter 18

G iven that everyone's going to be here until the police finish questioning them," James said when he returned a few minutes later with the sandwiches, "I'm going to go over to the hotel and see if they can cough up some cookies or something to keep the crowd tame."

"We'll just be here," Harriet told him, and he leaned in for a quick kiss.

Lauren caught Harriet's eye and made a finger in her throat gagging gesture. Harriet grinned.

You're just jealous, she mouthed.

Mavis nudged her as Detective Settle approached their group.

He made eye contact with Sydney first.

"I'm so sorry for your loss. And I'm sorry your memorial service had to end like this. Unfortunately, since Mr. Williams was injured and taken to the hospital, Mr. Remington has been arrested, and I need to ask you all some questions."

Harriet pulled her phone from her pocket to check for messages. She assumed Sydney and her aunt would be the first interviews.

"Ms. Truman, would you come with me?"

✂ --- ✂ --- ✂

He led her down the hall to another of the large rooms. This one was still divided into two smaller classrooms. He gestured for her to sit down at the closest table and pulled out his spiral notepad.

"I'm guessing you're surprised that I'm talking to you first." He waited a beat for her to confirm his assumption. When she nodded, he continued. "With everything that's been going on, I decided to call a Detective Morse in Foggy…" He looked at his notes. "…Foggy Point. From what I found on the internet, it looks like she's been the investigating officer when you've been mixed up in local crimes." He glanced up at her.

"That's right."

"She tells me that despite her admonitions to run the other way, through no fault of your own, you and your friends have found yourselves in the middle of some pretty messy situations." He looked at his notes. "Did someone really blow up cars in your driveway?"

Harriet sighed.

"Unfortunately, yes."

"According to Morse, you've provided some useful insights in solving several of these situations."

She shrugged but didn't say anything. He flipped his pad to a new page.

"What have you got for me?"

"I know it may be hard to believe, but I honestly have nothing. As I've been saying all along, I don't know these people."

"You misunderstand. Like I told you the other day, I don't think you killed Miss Johnson or attacked Mrs. Johnson. In spite of what my partner may have implied, I believe you when you say you didn't know them before you came here. But Morse tells me you and your friends are pretty perceptive. That's all I'm asking. Given no prior knowledge of these people, what do you think is going on?"

Harriet leaned back in her chair.

"I *have* learned some things, but none of it makes sense yet. At the center of all this is the arranged marriage between Michael Williams, poor but from an old Savannah family, and Jennifer Johnson, from a new-money family lacking in pedigree. Apparently, Mrs. Johnson is behind it all, but due to some financial considerations between the elder Williamses and Johnsons, the kids felt compelled to go through with a marriage neither one of them wanted."

Settle was scribbling furiously in his notebook.

"Michael had a steady girlfriend before all this came about, and she is currently pregnant with his child."

"So, he was still having relations with his ex?"

"Not according to them."

Settle raised his eyebrow at this.

"Hey, people tell me things. Believe me, I didn't solicit the information. Anyway, I think this whole marriage plan came about recently, and Mrs. Johnson was moving forward before anyone could stray."

145

"So Michael has his baby-mama, who doesn't want the marriage to happen. On the other side, Jennifer had a boyfriend who is apparently a Miami Dolphins football player. Additionally, she has Winston. I've heard several different versions as to what his relationship with Jen was, but as you could see today, he feels passionate about the situation."

She waited while he finished writing.

"Apart from that, Jennifer's bridesmaids have been here all week. They seem like they were good friends to her, but I only met them today, so I don't really know. Her aunt arrived today, so unless she's really sneaky, she's probably not involved.

"Sydney's been coming to our evening stitching group at the hotel, so we've gotten to know her a little. As I told you last night, I was out in the hallway when the paramedics were taking her to the hospital, and she asked me to go with her since she has no one else here. At the hospital, she told me she had a bunch of people arriving and nothing planned. All the people were originally coming for the wedding, so she and her mother had decided to turn it into a memorial. Once her mother was injured, the planning fell by the wayside."

"So, you and your friends stepped in?"

"The pastor and the singers are quilters who met Sydney during the stitching sessions, and my husband James is a chef who was in Galveston to attend a cooking class that included serving our banquet dinner. That's how I came to be here, actually. Anyway, he took care of the food for the memorial. The hotel is anxious to appear helpful, so all things considered, it wasn't too difficult to pull it together. And it was real nice until Winston decided to attack Michael."

Settle smiled.

"The big security guy told me it was you who asked to have hotel security come and keep an eye on Remington."

"After talking to him, I was worried he might try to pull something. I was expecting it to be a verbal attack. I was as shocked as anyone when he punched Michael."

"Sounds like Morse is right—you do have good instincts. If the guard hadn't gotten to Winston as quickly as he did, Williams might not be with us."

"Do you really think he meant to kill Michael?"

"I'm not sure he formed the intent before he came here, but he ended up in a rage that wouldn't have stopped until Williams was dead." He put his pen down. "Kind of makes him sound like a good candidate for Mrs. and Miss Johnsons' attacks."

"It *would* be interesting to find out when he actually got to Galveston."

The detective smiled.

"That will be one of the first things I find out when I get back to the station. See, you do have good instincts."

She smiled.

"You know," he went on, "when we first talked to you and your group, I thought something was off. Every time someone mentioned your husband...I can't put my finger on it, but your friends exchanged glances that seemed significant. Just to satisfy Grier, I tracked down your marriage license."

Harriet felt the blood drain from her face. Her legs felt like rubber.

"Now, see, you're going all pasty on me. Only being married a couple of weeks is nothing to be ashamed of."

Heat rushed back into her face.

"My wife and I got married in a civil ceremony, too. It saves a lot of money." He took out a business card and wrote a number on the back then handed it to her.

"Call me if you think of anything else. Any time." He put his pad back in his pocket. "Okay, I better get on with this. It's going to be a long day."

He walked Harriet back to the big room and summoned Sydney to the hallway.

James was arranging cookies on a large black serving plate when Harriet returned. He put his tray down and came to her side.

"What was that all about?" he asked. "They can't think you had anything to do with this." He gestured toward the center of the room.

She put her arm around his waist and rubbed her hand up and down on his back.

"Everything's fine." She caught sight of Lauren. "I think. Detective Settle called Detective Morse to check up on me and probably the rest of you. She vouched for us and apparently convinced him we sometimes hear things the police don't. He also did a background check on me and commented on my wedding—two weeks ago. Perhaps Lauren can explain that to us."

Lauren grinned.

"Ahh, that would be my new client."

"Are you going to tell us who this client is?" Mavis asked.

She thought a moment.

"I'm not sure, given client confidentiality."

Harriet tensed and wondered what her friend had done. If she'd bribed someone to fake the dates, would that invalidate their marriage? She wasn't sure how she'd feel if, after all this. it turned out she and James weren't really married.

"Clearly, if Detective Settle was not mistaken, someone changed the date on James's and my marriage certificate. We're the ones who will be liable if things go sideways."

Lauren frowned.

"You're no fun. If you must know, your judge's computer problem was a little more complicated than I first thought. It involved other employees and would have been embarrassing if it had become public. He was very, very grateful. He said backdating your marriage license would pose no problem."

Harriet shook her head, but she couldn't help grinning.

"It's not even clear James was going to be questioned. Now we have a counterfeit marriage license on top of everything."

"It's not counterfeit," Lauren protested. "They were keeping a temporary log because of their computer problem. Until that was fixed, they couldn't assign permanent registration numbers or enter documents into their searchable data base. If anyone were able to prove the date is wrong, they'd just blame it on a data entry error related to the other problem they were having."

Harriet sighed.

"This better not come back to bite me or James."

"Hey, I was just trying to look out for you. Anyway, if you stay married for forty years, it will be a funny little footnote. If you get annulled when we get back to Foggy Point, it won't matter anyway."

Connie patted Lauren on the shoulder.

"I think that was very nice of you."

Mavis also seemed to be holding back a smile but didn't say anything.

James went back to arranging cookies, putting one on a napkin and handing it to Harriet.

"Have some chocolate."

She gave him a grateful look and took a bite of the double chocolate cookie while he handed some to the rest of the group.

"Did you learn anything from the aunt?" she asked Mavis.

"Not really. She's worried about her sister. I guess Mrs. Johnson almost died this morning, and the doctors aren't sure why. She doesn't know the state of Jennifer's relationships with Winston or Michael, and she didn't even know about DeWitt."

Connie swallowed her last bite of cookie and brushed the crumbs from her mouth with her napkin.

"We didn't talk about Michael's girlfriend, but after the ceremony here and before the fight, I ran into *her* in the ladies room."

"Did you talk to her?" Harriet asked.

Connie laughed.

"I'm not sure I'd say I talked to her. It was more like I absorbed her rant. I made a neutral comment about the situation being tragic all the way around, and that was all it took. She hates Jennifer, her mother, her sister, and everyone associated with them. She's very fearful about what's going to happen to her and her baby. As we all know, fear can be a very powerful motive."

Mavis finished her cookie and crumpled her napkin.

"I'm just glad we don't have to deal with this now that the police seem to have figured out Harriet didn't have anything to do with it."

Harriet selected a second cookie.

"I wouldn't go that far. Detective Settle believes I'm not involved, but his partner isn't there yet."

"We've only got to get through one more day, and then we can go home," Robin commented as she and Kirsten joined them. "In spite of what you see on TV, they can't stop you from going home if they haven't charged you with anything. Once we're back in Foggy Point, I think you'll be a lot less interesting to them. They know they don't have a bit of evidence tying you to their crime."

Kirsten brushed crumbs from her blazer.

"I have to believe you were only a suspect because of their wishful thinking."

Mavis took a deep breath and blew it out.

"I say we go back to the hotel, put our feet up, and do a little stitching. We've got several hours before we go on our ghost tour."

"Good idea," Connie concurred.

✂ --- ✂ --- ✂

"Are you sure you don't mind if I go to Katie's Seafood with the guys?" James asked Harriet when they were back in their room. "I've heard they can get red snapper to me while it's still red. It would be a nice addition to my menu."

Harriet rifled around in her stitching bag to be sure she had what she needed for her wool felt project.

"That's important—we can't have red snapper that isn't red. Besides, you don't need to hover. I'm going to be with the whole group until time to go to dinner."

He came behind her and wrapped his arms around her.

"Somehow that's not as comforting as it once was. I mean, you did get clubbed in the eye with them sitting all around you."

149

"Even you couldn't have stopped that," she said and laughed. She turned around so she was facing him, and he held her close.

"I would have if I could have," he said in a soft voice. "As long as we're married, and even if we aren't when we go back, I'm going to do everything I can to make sure nothing bad ever happens to you again."

Harriet tilted her head up and smiled, and he bent his down and kissed her. Things were just starting to get interesting when there was a tap on the door.

They separated, and Harriet straightened her teeshirt as she went to answer the door. Bruce was the last person she expected to see when she opened it.

"Sorry to bother you," he said. "I just wanted to thank you for the heads-up about the security problem across the street this afternoon. Tyrone tells me that guy Remington would have killed the other guy if he hadn't been there."

"I'm glad he *was* there. As near as I can tell, it's all a big mess in that family."

"Well, thanks again. It would have been terrible if that man had died. Also, I wanted to let you know...I think I've figured out how someone locked you in your closet."

"I assumed it was the maid."

"I hope not. I'd like to think we don't employ people who would do something like that. Anyway, we discovered one of our master keys is missing. The maids all have them to get into rooms to clean. One of them left hers on her cart when she was in a room, and when she came out it was gone. They're supposed to keep it in their pocket, but she had a cold and didn't want to put it in with her handkerchief."

"Somehow, that's not comforting. I think I liked it better when I thought it was the maid."

Bruce smiled sheepishly.

"And I was hoping it was one of your friends playing a practical joke on you."

"I'm afraid neither one of our scenarios is likely. Thanks for telling me...I guess."

He sighed.

"I thought you should know, and I do appreciate the heads-up . Be careful."

"Don't worry. I'm not going anywhere alone till I get back to Foggy Point."

Bruce turned and went back down the hall. Harriet watched until he turned the corner, then went back into her room.

150

"Who was that?" James asked.

"Bruce was telling me he's discovered a master key was stolen. He thinks someone used it to come in here and lock me in the closet while they planted the bride's ring."

"Did that detective ever mention that ring again?"

"No, and they've never asked me about the bloody shirt they found here. I guess I'm assuming they've figured out someone was trying to set me up for killing the bride and attacking the mother. I can't imagine why a complete stranger would want to do that to me."

"Maybe it's someone who saw Jennifer whack you in the eye. Someone who did her harm and figured you'd be an easy scapegoat."

"Great, that's only a hundred or so people and all the people they told about it."

He put his arm around her shoulders.

"No one, including those two detectives, could possible believe you'd kill that young woman and attack her mother for no reason."

She slid her arm around his waist. She couldn't help noticing how perfectly she fit, there by his side, and wondered if she'd feel this way if they weren't married...or if there wasn't a murder accusation hanging over her head.

"You're sweet to say that, but they can think that about me or anyone else. They have a dead woman on their hands. It's their job to think people killed her."

She pulled away and picked her bag up from the sofa.

"Are you going to meet us for dinner before the ghost tour?"

"Sure, where are you going?"

"One of Mavis's classmates told her about a place called Rudy and Paco. It's Mexican or South American or something."

"Wow, that's supposed to be a nice place. And they're supposed to be good with fish. I'm there."

"I'll text you when I find out that the plan is."

James picked his keys up from the table and slid them into his pocket.

"I'll walk you to Mavis's door. You can't be too safe."

She smiled at him and led the way out of the room.

Chapter 19

$\mathcal{H}$arriet sat on the couch between Mavis and Connie.

"My stitches are so uneven," she lamented.

Mavis looked at Harriet's project over the top of her half-moon reading glasses.

"They aren't so bad. You're doing much better than you were the first day of class."

Connie turned her piece and smoothed it over her lap.

"If I stitch on the plane on our way home, I might get this done before we get back to Foggy Point."

Harriet checked on Lauren, who was sitting on Connie's bed typing on her laptop .

"What are you doing that's more important than stitching?"

Lauren stopped typing and rubbed her hands together, cracking her knuckles at the end.

"I've been trying to dig deeper into the Johnson and Williams families."

"Have you found anything?"

"There's a lot about the Johnson father's rise in the business world. There are a lot of pictures of Mom in the society pages, mostly for giving money. And it's sort of curious…"

She clicked a couple of keys and turned her screen toward Harriet.

"What am I looking at?"

"See the two little girls?"

Harriet got up to have a closer look at the screen.

"Is that Jennifer? And a twin?"

"That's what it looks like to me."

Mavis and Connie stopped stitching and paid attention to the conversation.

"If Jennifer has a twin, where is she?" Harriet asked.

Lauren turned her computer back around and tapped some keys.

"I can't find a death report for a child named Johnson anywhere near the right age range. These people were pretty careful about keeping their kids out of the public view. Mom and Dad are all over the society pages and business pages, but not so much the girls."

Harriet came over beside Lauren and looked at the screen.

"What about Sydney? Is she in any of the pictures?"

Lauren hit another series of keys and pointed at a picture that opened.

"It's not very clear, but here she is in a group photo of her junior high science fair."

"You're right. It's hard to tell much about her."

"If the caption didn't say her name, I'd have never picked her out."

Harriet crossed to sit back down between Connie and Mavis.

"So, what do you two think?"

Mavis blew out a breath.

"I think we're missing something. I can't tell if it's something they brought with them from Georgia or if it's something right in front of our faces. But we're definitely missing something."

"I agree," Connie said. "There's a piece of the puzzle that fell off the table. We don't have enough information to make sense of this."

She looked at Harriet as she spoke and then made a close inspection of Harriet's injury.

"Have you iced your eye lately? It looks puffy."

Harriet reached up and touched her cheekbone.

"I sort of forgot about it."

Mavis tucked her project into her bag .

"Let's get you some ice right now. You can wrap it in a towel."

"I saw the maid's cart at the other end of the hall when James walked me down here. It's on the way to the ice machine. I'll get an ice bucket liner and a hand towel from her on my way there."

Lauren clicked her laptop off and shut the lid.

"I'll come with you. I need to stretch my legs, and you aren't supposed to walk the halls alone."

Harriet glanced at her phone There was still plenty of time before dinner. She was looking forward to the ghost tour tonight but wanted to be sure they had time for James to enjoy the restaurant before they had to meet their tour guide.

"Let's get going, then."

153

She led the way into the hallway.

"Oh, good, she's still there."

The maid's cart was outside an open room door.

"Hello?" Harriet called out. She could hear a vacuum running, but it was making a steady hum, like it was sitting in one place. "I don't think she can hear me over her vacuum."

"You could just help yourself. I mean, it's not like they count every little bag."

"I'm not stealing supplies. That's all Detective Grier would need to throw me in the slammer."

Lauren laughed.

"Have you been watching old gangster movies again?"

Harriet didn't answer, just went into the room.

"What are you doing?"

The uniformed woman stood at the lamp table in the corner of the room. She had an open navy-blue necklace box in her left hand. A second blue box lay open on the table.

"Lauren, get in here, quick." Harriet called.

She pulled her phone from her pocket and dialed the front desk.

"This is Harriet Truman. Tell Bruce we need security in room three-fifteen, now."

She listened a moment then ended the call.

Lauren stepped beside her so they blocked the door, which she'd shut when she came in.

"Do you want to explain what you're doing with that jewelry? Or shall we wait for hotel security to arrive?" Harriet asked.

"Oh, *s'il vous plaît. Je veux mon père.*"

Lauren looked at Harriet.

"Your father can't help you now." Harriet said in French. "And I'm pretty sure you speak English better than I do, so drop the act," she continued in English.

"I still need my father," the woman said.

The door opened, and Bruce came in.

"What's going on here?" he asked Harriet.

"I wanted to ask the maid for another towel and an ice bucket liner. Her vacuum was running, so she couldn't hear me, and I came in here and found her with two open jeweler's boxes and a necklace in her hands."

"We're pretty sure she wasn't cleaning them," Lauren added.

Bruce took a good look at the young woman.

"Odette? What's going on here?"

The girl started crying.

154

"Is your dad here?" He asked her.

Harriet looked at him.

"What's with her dad? What does he have to do with anything? Does he own the hotel or something?"

"Sit down," he ordered Odette then told Harriet, "Odette's whole family works at the hotel. Her dad has been here for years." He pulled out his cell phone and called the front desk.

"It's Bruce. Find Juste Comeaux and send him up to room three-fifteen."

Bruce's phone chirped an instant after he ended the call, and he pressed the answer button.

"Is Enola here? ....None of them? ...Okay, bye."

He turned back to Odette.

"This isn't looking good. The rest of your family seems to have gone home unexpectedly, and without you."

The door opened again before she could answer.

"Hello!" Kathy called out. "What's going on?"

"Ma'am, I'm with hotel security." Bruce said by way of introduction. "I'm not sure what's going on, but Ms. Truman and her friend came to your room to ask the maid for a towel and found her with your jewelry box in her hands."

"Well, thank heaven," Kathy said and plopped down in the chair beside the table.

Bruce, Harriet and Lauren stared at the her.

She looked back at them and laughed nervously.

"Not about her hands in the goods. I thought I was going crazy with all that talk about my necklace being switched with my roommate's. I was afraid it was a sign of dementia."

She sat up straight and pulled herself together.

"So, what do we do now?"

"Odette?" Bruce asked. "Can you explain what's going on here?"

Harriet noticed Odette's hand was fisted in her pocket.

"Ask her what's in her hand."

"Show me what's in your pocket, Odette," Bruce directed.

"I think I'd like a lawyer," she said.

Bruce sighed.

"Are you sure you want to go that route?"

She nodded silently.

"I still need you to empty your pockets."

She didn't move.

He shook his head.

"Okay, we'll do it by the book, then." He stepped away from the group and tapped a number into his phone. After a brief conversation, he hung up and rejoined them.

"A detective will be here in a few minutes."

Lauren texted Mavis; and moments later, there was a tap on the door.

Kathy opened it, and Mavis rushed over to Harriet and Lauren.

"Oh, honey, are you okay?" She looked at Harriet's eye.

"I'm fine," Harriet assured her.

"We may have solved the musical-chairs-with-the-jewelry problem," Lauren added.

Detective Settle arrived after they'd spent an uncomfortable ten minutes, Harriet and Lauren staring at Odette, and the young woman staring at her shoes. He was with a younger man they hadn't seen before.

"Okay, Bruce, what do we have here?"

Bruce explained Harriet and Lauren's inadvertent discovery.

"All right." He turned to Odette. "Empty your pockets."

The girl pulled two necklaces from her pocket. They were identical to the two in the open blue boxes.

Settle gestured with a tilt of his head toward Odette to the other man.

"Cuff her and read her her rights, Nelson."

He looked at Harriet.

"Do you have anything to add?"

Harriet sent a questioning look to Lauren and, when she didn't say anything, shook her head.

"No, it was just like Bruce said. Lauren and I came in here to ask for an extra towel. When we found her with the necklace box in her hand, I called Bruce."

"Thanks. You ladies can go back to your rooms." He smiled at Harriet. "I'm sure Bruce will agree that you can help yourself to a towel on your way past the cart." He turned to Kathy. "I'm afraid we're going to need you to stay out of this room for a few hours. I'm sure Bruce can arrange with the hotel for another one for the duration. We're going to have to bring the forensic people in here."

Mavis cleared her throat, and Detective Settle looked at her.

"If it would be okay, Kathy and her roommate could come to our room. We're stitching for a while, and then going out to dinner before the ghost tour. That all will keep them out of your way for several hours."

He turned back to Kathy with an inquiring expression.

"That would be real nice," she said. "Can I take my stitching bag?"

"Where is it?" Settle asked.

"In the closet," she replied.

"Did your jewelry box come from that closet?"

She shook her head.

"Both of us kept our jewelry in our suitcases by our beds."

"That should be fine, then. Nelson will open the door for you." He looked at Nelson, who snapped on a pair of latex gloves and followed Kathy to the closet. "Can you give me your full name and a phone number I can call you at when we're done? We'll need to take a full statement from you then, too. I need the same from your roommate as well. And could you call her and let her know your room is off-limits for the time being?"

Kathy nodded then accompanied Mavis, Harriet and Lauren out into the hall.

Bruce accompanied them as far as the door.

"I'll call downstairs and let them know you can order whatever you want from the restaurant on the house."

"So, what do you think was really going on there? I mean, she obviously was doing some sort of jewelry switcheroo, but she couldn't have been working alone," Harriet said.

"Let's wait till we get back to our room," Mavis said.

Lauren smiled and pulled her phone from her pocket as they went down the hall.

"I'm ordering tea from room service."

Harriet grinned.

"Ask for some of those chocolates, too."

✂ --- ✂ --- ✂

Harriet finally managed to put some ice in a plastic bag, wrapped it in a towel and applied it to her black eye. She and Lauren reclined on the two double beds while Connie and Mavis sat on the sofa opposite Kathy and her roommate, Ruth. They were sitting on the two side chairs. A glass-topped coffee table in the middle of the seating area now held two pitchers of iced tea, a tray of cookies and a plate of chocolates.

Ruth set her needle-turn appliqué flower project aside and picked up her tea glass.

"Can anyone explain to me what's going on in our room?"

Harriet lowered her ice pack to her lap and prepared to tell her.

"You can talk with the ice on your eye," Mavis scolded her.

She put the towel-wrapped ice back on her eye.

"Tell me something, Ruth. Did both you and Kathy go on a cruise and buy jewelry?"

The woman looked surprised.

157

"We did. So did Nancy and several other people who were in our classes. The jewelry is good quality at a very affordable price."

"And they were all gemstones, right?" Harriet asked.

Kathy took a cookie.

"They better be. The jewelry is affordable, but they don't give it away."

Mavis looked at Harriet.

"What are you thinking?"

Harriet picked up her own glass of tea and took a sip.

"I could be completely wrong, but I've been trying to figure out why someone would move the necklaces around but not remove them. And in the one case, the necklace had a broken clasp, and then it didn't.

"What if the necklaces from the ship's jewelry store have been stolen and replaced with copies that are nice costume pieces but made with glass, not gemstones? I mean, people look carefully at the stone when they purchase a necklace, but not so much after they take it home. They put it on and enjoy it, but don't really scrutinize it."

Lauren set her stitching down in her lap.

"How would they know what the necklaces looked like in order to have copies ready?"

Mavis popped a chocolate into her mouth and chewed it thoughtfully.

"I can think of several ways. First, they probably don't change the jewelry designs every time a ship comes and goes. The thieves could have a stock of the common styles. Second, they could have a jeweler in their group who gets a picture from the maid when people check in and then creates the copy before they check out. Or third, depending on how elaborate their operation is, they could have someone on the ship, maybe even in the jewelry shop. That person could send pictures to the shore team for fabrication."

Lauren sat up straighter, getting into the spirit of the discussion.

"If they were really tricky, they could send pictures of people when they make their purchase. That way, the hotel team could not only fabricate the copy but would know what copy to take to what room."

Kathy took another bite of her cookie.

"That sounds pretty elaborate. Do people really do stuff like that?"

Harriet and Lauren looked at each other and laughed.

"What?" Kathy asked.

Connie set her tea glass down on the table.

"We've seen a few strange things in our hometown."

Mavis brushed a few crumbs from her lap.

"No point in speculating. I'm sure the detectives will get to the bottom of it."

158

Lauren started stitching again.

"I hope they took her cell phone from her. Bruce seemed surprised that her family had all gone home. Her dad must have caught wind of what was going on. He's probably destroying evidence as we speak."

Harriet shifted her ice compress.

"As long as we're hoping, let's hope Detective Settle is smarter than you're giving him credit for. If we can think of all this stuff, I'm sure the detectives can, too."

Kathy shook her head.

"It's so unbelievable. Stuff like this doesn't happen where we live."

Lauren laughed.

"Crime happens everywhere. Some of my work involves internet security, and I never cease to be amazed by the schemes people dream up. I think a lot of petty crime goes unnoticed. In some cases, the thieves have a profitable scam going, but they get greedy and escalate. Eventually, a business will suffer a big enough loss that someone notices. In our case, we were lucky Harriet caught the thief red-handed. If we hadn't had several people talking about jewelry problems within our group, she might not have paid attention to what the maid was doing. Or at least would have believed whatever story the maid made up to explain her having hands on the necklaces."

Harriet set her ice pack down again.

"And if I hadn't been whacked in the eye and my attacker murdered, I wouldn't be acquainted with hotel security. I'm not sure what I would have done if none of that had happened and I noticed a hotel maid with a jewelry box in her hand. Maybe reported it to the front desk? Hard to say."

Mavis stabbed her needle into her project.

"The hotel is lucky you wandered into that room. If it turns out they've been stealing gems, who knows how many people have been robbed and how many more would have been."

Harriet picked up a chocolate from a napkin full of snacks on the nightstand between the two beds.

"It makes you wonder whether Jennifer came into her room while a jewelry exchange was being made. We'll have to ask Sydney if her sister and her bridesmaids went on a cruise last week."

Connie set her stitching down on the coffee table.

"I think I'll call the restaurant and see if we can get a reservation. How many of us will there be?"

Mavis looked around the room.

"There are six of us here." She looked at Harriet. "I'm assuming James will be joining us."

"I can text him if you want, just to be sure, but I think he's planning on it."

Connie searched her phone for the restaurant's phone number.

"We'll assume he's coming. I'm going to see if they can seat us at six forty-five. That should give us time to eat and walk to the meeting spot before the tour starts at nine."

Harriet pulled her phone from her pocket and texted the information to James.

"James says he'll meet us here at six-thirty."

"Sounds like a plan," Lauren said as she picked up her wool table mat and resumed stitching.

Chapter 20

So, who-all are we having dinner with?" James asked Harriet as they waited in the lobby for the rest of their group to arrive.

She stepped closer to him, and he slid his arm around her waist.

"Kathy and Ruth, who are the women from our conference who were banned from their room while the jewelry investigation continues; Connie and Mavis and Lauren and, I think, Robin. Her friend Kirsten has a new baby at home, so she isn't able to join us."

James smiled.

"Am I the token male again?"

She laughed.

"Sorry, there didn't seem to be a lot of men at our conference."

He squeezed her closer to him.

"By that, I take it you mean less than one."

"Pretty much." She twisted so she could put her hand on his chest. "You could have invited a friend, you know."

Lauren came out of the elevator.

"Aren't you two just looking like the cute newlyweds."

This time it was James who laughed.

"We *are* the cute newlyweds."

Lauren rolled her eyes.

"I'm going to be diabetic by the time we go home if this sugary phase keeps up."

"Hey, Robin told us to sell it," James reminded her. "We're just following instructions."

Lauren put her hands in her pants pockets and rocked back on her heels.

161

"I think that directive expired a while ago."

James smiled.

"No one told *us*."

Nevertheless, Harriet stepped away from him, and he frowned. If she was truthful with herself, she liked being a couple again, even if it hadn't come about in the conventional way. She had to keep reminding herself that it wasn't real and to pretend otherwise was opening herself up for a lot of hurt when they got home and went their separate ways.

"Is everyone hungry?" Connie asked as she emerged from the elevator. "I've been looking at the menu online, and it all sounds fabulous."

"I'm not eating too much, though, in case we have to hotfoot it out of any of the haunted buildings we're touring," Mavis added.

James leaned around Harriet to make eye contact with Mavis.

"You don't really believe all that ghost stuff, do you?"

Mavis laughed.

"You never know."

Kathy and Ruth appeared from the hotel office side of the lobby.

"Any news?" Mavis asked.

"The security people said we can return to our room after the ghost tour. As for the rest, they're still investigating. They need to keep all the jewelry and have a jeweler see which are real and which are fake," Kathy reported.

"I'm just glad we can get back in our room," was Ruth's opinion.

✂ --- ✂ --- ✂

Harriet could tell James was going to like the restaurant the minute they walked through the door. It shared the same dark-wood table, white-linen tablecloth esthetic as his restaurant. He smiled as he surveyed the room. A well-stocked bar took up the back wall of the long narrow space, and bottles of wine were displayed in cabinets that covered half of one of the side walls. They were shown to their table after only a brief wait, and water was poured as soon as they were seated.

Lauren picked up her menu but didn't open it.

"Anyone want to share *antojitos?*"

Mavis arranged her napkin on her lap.

"If I knew what an anti-hee-to was I might be interested."

Connie smiled.

"It's Spanish for 'appetizer.' There's a list in your menu."

Lauren sipped her water while Mavis looked.

"How do you all feel about empanadas mixtas or Paco calamars?" Connie asked them. "That's beef, chicken and shrimp empanadas and pan-fried calamari," She explained to Mavis.

Mavis continued to study the menu page.

162

"I can see that. With as many as we are, we could get both of those and one more, at least."

Kathy and Ruth deferred to Lauren and Connie, and the selections were made.

A stout, round-faced man in a blue blazer and blue-and-yellow stripped tie came to their table.

"I understand from one of my waiters we have a visiting chef dining with us tonight. I'm Paco, welcome to my restaurant."

James stood up.

"It's an honor to meet you, sir."

"What sort of restaurant do you cook for?"

"It's a small place in a smaller town in…"

Connie began speaking to Paco in rapid-fire Spanish, and Harriet smiled. Paco asked a question, and Connie answered.

Lauren leaned over to Harriet.

"What are they saying?" she whispered.

"Connie told Paco that James was being much too humble, and that he was not only the chef but the owner of a very highly rated restaurant in the Puget Sound area."

Paco turned back to James.

"Your friend here…"

"Connie," she supplied with a smile.

"Your shy friend Connie tells me you own a successful restaurant in Washington. I'm honored that you choose to visit my humble establishment."

James's cheeks turned red.

"The honor is mine. According to the reservation apps, you're the top-ranked place in the whole Houston area."

Lauren cleared her throat and tipped her head at the waiter, who stood patiently behind Paco.

"Could I interrupt this love fest and order our appetizers?"

Paco gave a slight bow and made room for the waiter forward.

"Would you like to come to the kitchen?" he asked James.

"Boy, would I. I mean, yes, sir, it would be a privilege."

Paco smiled at Lauren.

"Enjoy your dinner."

James took a step toward Paco then hesitated.

"Go, tour the kitchen and talk food," Harriet told him. "We'll try to save you a snack."

Lauren ordered their first course, and the waiter returned a few minutes later with the plates they'd ordered and two additional items he said were "compliments of Paco." Harriet took a bite of calamari and closed her eyes as she chewed.

"I can see being married to a chef is going to have more perks than I first thought."

Lauren gave her a wicked grin.

"It's going to have lots of—" She stopped mid-sentence. "Look who just arrived."

Harriet reached for an empanada to mask stealing a glance.

"I guess hanging out in the hospital cafeteria isn't Aunt Jane's style. I wonder who the other people are? The girls all have the same narrow face all the Johnson women have."

Aunt Jane stood beside Sydney, her arm entwined with her niece's. Two more women and a man hovered nearby, along with three teenagers. All were dressed in black. The wait staff hustled to place an additional table with a pair that had already been set up. Clearly, the group had showed up with extra diners.

Sydney noticed Harriet and her group and gave a small wave of her fingers in acknowledgment. Harriet got up and walked to their table, stopping behind Sydney. She put a hand on her shoulder, and the woman turned to her.

"How are you feeling? Have you had a chance to rest a little?"

Sydney gave a wan smile.

"We went to the hospital to see my mom."

"Is there any change?"

"No, and they don't know what happened earlier today, either. They told us not to expect much if and when she wakes up."

"I'm sorry to hear that."

Sydney lowered her voice, and Harriet leaned closer to hear her.

"My aunt went crazy when they told us, and my mom's doctor ended up having to give her a Valium to calm her down. They suggested we go get something to eat. I'm pretty sure they just wanted my aunt to leave, but anyway, here we are."

Harriet decided Sydney had enough on her plate without hearing about the excitement at the hotel.

"I wish you could have been with us. We stitched on our class projects and had cookies and tea.""Thank you for saying that. Are you still going on the ghost tour tonight?"

"We are, right after this."

"I'm thinking of joining you, if that's okay. I'd rather be resting, but…" She glanced pointedly at her aunt. "I think the fresh air would do me good."

"Sure. We'll meet you outside after we all finish dinner."

Harriet returned to her table. Lauren wiped her mouth on her napkin. "What was that all about?"

Harriet sat down and scooted her chair in.

"Nothing, really. I asked how she was doing, and she asked if she could come on the tour with us. Seems like she's getting tired of her aunt."

Mavis put her fork down.

"If she's anything like the mother, I can see why. I feel sorry for Mrs. Johnson being in the hospital and all, but I can't help but think her arranged marriage scheme set a lot of the trouble we're seeing in motion."

Harriet and Lauren both glanced over at Sydney's table. James returned from the kitchen, trailed by their waiter.

"If it's agreeable to you all, Paco would like to have us served family-style so we can sample a number of the house specialties."

Harriet looked at Mavis and Connie, who nodded, and then turned to Kathy, Ruth and Robin, who had arrived while she was talking with Sydney.

"That sounds lovely," Kathy said.

James looked at Lauren.

"Okay with you?"

She grinned.

"Hey, I'll never turn down an opportunity for great food."

He turned to the waiter.

"Let's go for it," he said, and followed the man back to the kitchen. He returned a moment later and sat down beside Harriet.

"This operation is amazing. The staff told me everyone loves working here so much they have almost no turnover. I know their boss was in the kitchen, but I think they really meant it."

Two waiters appeared, one carrying salad plates and the second carrying two big bowls of salad.

"We have a traditional Caesar salad here," He set the first bowl down in front of Connie. "And a house salad featuring mixed greens, tomatoes, julienne vegetables, croutons and tossed with a creamy Italian dressing." He put this one at the opposite end of the table in front of James. "Enjoy."

The salads were followed by Filete de Pargo Enchilado—a red snapper dish, Sea Scallops Granada, Ojo de Costilla—a rib-eye steak that for this presentation had been cut into smaller pieces to allow for sampling. Their last dish was Pollo Empanizado, a plantain-encrusted chicken served over a black bean sauce and drizzled with queso blanco. James explained the details of each dish as it arrived at the table, and none of them disappointed.

Harriet took a last bite of scallop.

"Wow," she said when she could speak. "That was fantastic."

James smiled.

"This is definitely the high point of the trip for me." He smiled at Harriet. "Besides our wedding, of course."

Lauren smirked.

"Of course."

Paco came to the table again to see how his feast had been received. Harriet glanced around the room and leaned over to Lauren.

"Did you notice who came in while we were in food heaven?"

She nodded toward the front of the restaurant. Michael's girlfriend had come in with Megan, one of the three bridesmaids they'd met at the memorial service.

"Now, that's interesting. Are we to assume Kari had a fox in the hen-house?"

Harriet wiped her hands on her napkin and set it on the table.

"I'm going to the ladies room. Want to come with?"

Lauren got up and followed her. Once they were inside, she bent and looked for feet under the bathroom doors to be sure they were alone.

"I wouldn't have thought Savannah was that small of a place, and Kari didn't strike me as the sorority-sister type, either."

Harriet leaned against the counter.

"It definitely adds another wrinkle. If Kari's had a spy in Jen's camp the whole time, she could keep track of which room she was in and when she'd be alone."

Lauren turned water on at the sink and washed the food residue from her fingertips

"And let's not forget her baby gives her motive.

"And—" Harriet was interrupted as Sydney stormed into the room.

"What is that woman doing here?" she shouted. "Is she following me around just to torment me?"

Harriet put her hand on Sydney's arm. She didn't need to ask who Sydney meant.

"I'm sure it's a terrible coincidence. I mean, Galveston is not that big."

The other woman sighed, and her anger seemed to deflate.

"I just want to go home. My aunt is driving me nuts. I'm sure she cares about Mama because they're sisters, but she is also very aware that the supplemental income Mama provides for her could be in jeopardy. She also mentioned Mama promised she was in her will. Hard to tell which eventuality she's pulling for."

Lauren stared at her.

"Your aunt is in your mom's will?"

Sydney leaned against the counter beside Harriet, arms crossed over her chest.

"I'm sure she's in the will. How much she might benefit, who knows? I think Mama added and subtracted people depending on her mood. I don't know for sure. She was pretty secretive about it."

"I'm sorry you're having to go through this. Are you sure you're up for the ghost tour? You've had a pretty rough few days."

Sydney turned to the sink and splashed water on her face then dried it with a towel.

"I'll be fine. Besides, I can always drop out and go back to the hotel if I get tired. The Strand isn't that big of an area."

She headed for the door.

"Make sure you eat," Harriet said as she left.

"Make sure you eat?" Lauren repeated. "That was the best you could come up with?"

"You know I'm not good at this comforting stuff."

Lauren went into one of the stalls.

"I guess we should add the aunt to our list of suspects if what Sydney says is true."

"Yeah, it didn't sound like Mama Johnson came from money, and if she's been providing an income for her sister, sister could have motive. I mean, what if Mama was cutting her off?"

Harriet went into another stall.

"Or what if she's in the will for more than her stipend, and she wanted to collect before Mama changed her mind again?"

"Sounds like motive to me," Lauren said.

"I feel sorry for Sydney," Harriet said when she came out and went to wash her hands. "Think about it. Even apart from the recent violence, it seems like everyone in that family had a scheme. Mama wants to buy an old-money name for her daughter. Auntie wants to protect her income stream. Winston wanted Jennifer to be his arm-candy. Jennifer wanted her professional athlete so she could be famous for being famous. Michael just wanted to be left alone to lead his life. Where does Sydney fit? Is she the glue that tries to hold the whole mess together?"

Lauren joined Harriet at the sink.

"Not our problem, but I hear you. It does seem kinda sad."

The door opened, and the three teen-aged girls from Sydney's table came in and began fluffing their hair in front of the mirror. Lauren pulled the tablet from her bag and clicked it on.

"Hi! Are you three with the Johnson group?"

The girls stopped talking and stared at her.

"I'm a journalist for a web newspaper. I'm writing an obituary for Jennifer. Are you related?"

The oldest-looking one of the three took a step forward.

"We're her cousins. I'm Miranda, and this is Trish and LeAnn. Our mom is Jane, Aunt Judith's sister." Her cheeks turned pink. "Our mama is a country-western fan."

Lauren gave them a blank look.

"I'll explain later," Harriet said in a quiet tone.

Lauren asked them to spell their first and last names and typed them into her tablet.

"I have another question. I was doing some background research this morning, and I came across a picture of Jennifer and another little girl that looked like she might be a twin sister. Is that possible? Did Jennifer have a twin?"

LeAnn held a hank of her long blond hair in one hand and a brush she'd pulled from her purse in the other. She started brushing as she spoke.

"Not that I've ever heard." The three sisters shared a look. "We would have heard if there had been a sister who died or ran away or something."

"Our moms talked—a lot," Trish added.

Miranda spread gloss from a purple-colored ball onto her full lips.

"I wouldn't put it past Aunt Judith to try to buy a child if it had a better pedigree than us."

The girls gave each other a knowing look and laughed.

Lauren read what she'd typed.

"Did Jennifer work?"

Trish laughed.

"Aunt Judith wouldn't let her. She wanted to be a preschool teacher, but Aunt Judith told her that her job was to marry well and produce an heir."

"What about you guys?" Harriet asked. "Are you expected to marry well, too."

Miranda laughed.

"We don't matter."

Harriet frowned.

"Everybody matters."

"I didn't mean it that way. I just mean our dad manages the YMCA in our small town. It puts food on the table, and people like him, but we'll never be high society like the Johnsons. It won't really matter who we marry or even *if* we marry."

Lauren tapped a few more notes into her tablet.

"Good for you," she said as she turned it off. "This whole arranged marriage thing doesn't seem to be working for the Johnsons."

Harriet nudged her arm.

"We need to get back to the table before they send a search party after us."

"You okay?" James asked when Harriet slid into her chair beside him. She reached over and took his hand, resting it on his leg.

"Lauren and I were gathering information."

"We noticed Sydney and then those girls all went to the ladies' room while you were in there."

"We added another suspect to our ever-growing list and got mixed information from the younger crowd. I'm afraid we aren't ever going to know what happened here."

James squeezed Harriet's hand.

"I'm okay with never knowing. How about you?"

She smiled.

"I'm good."

Connie slid her chair back.

"I'm ready to go home."

"We didn't learn anything while you two were gone," Mavis said, setting her napkin on the table, "but we were entertained."

"Oh?" Harriet said.

"Auntie decided to have it out with Kari about her distinct lack of taste in showing up for the memorial service, given her relationship to Jennifer's intended."

Connie picked up her purse.

"It wasn't lost on Auntie that Kari is now getting everything she wants."

"And Sydney looked like she was mortified," Mavis added.

"I'd like to go the back to the hotel and change into my jeans and running shoes for the ghost tour," Harriet said as she got to her feet.

"I'll let Sydney know we're stopping back at the hotel before we leave on the tour," Lauren added as she headed toward the other tables.

James picked up the leather folder that held the bill. He got a curious look on his face as he read it, folded it and put it in his pocket. He snapped the folder shut and smiled.

"What's going on?" Harriet asked.

"Paco left a note in lieu of a bill." He took the note from his pocket and read it aloud. "'Dinner's on me tonight. You can pay me back when I come visit your restaurant.'"

169

He glanced to the back of the restaurant where Paco was charming the socks off another table of customers. He looked up and nodded at James, a broad smile creasing his face. James gave him a small wave, and he turned back to his other guests.

Robin took her phone from her purse and checked her messages.

"I think I'll pass on the tour. I need to call home and help my husband navigate the kids' schedule. He has a busy driving day coming up tomorrow with me not there."

"I'm sorry we dragged you away," Harriet said.

"Oh, not to worry." Robin smiled. "He owes me for the golf trip he and his buddies took. They were gone a for a week and came back all tan and rested. I was home with the kids and a nasty norovirus."

Lauren rejoined them.

"She'll meet us in the hotel lobby in twenty minutes."

Chapter 21

Is this a regular thing?" James asked Harriet.

"Mavis and Connie are usually pretty prompt, but I suspect this trip has worn them down. Plus, with Lauren staying in their room, and now Kathy and Ruth, you have five women sharing one bathroom."

He put his hands in his pockets and rocked back on his heels.

"It's nice of them to give us our privacy for our honeymoon."

Harriet's cheeks turned pink.

"I hope you don't think this counts as a honeymoon under any circumstances. Real marriage or not, this is not a honeymoon."

James smiled, put one arm around her, and held the other hand up, three fingers together, his thumb holding his pinkie down.

"I promise I will take you on a proper honeymoon no matter what happens after this. Scout's honor."

She smiled. He really was a good person. He was smart and successful and being with him was so uncomplicated compared to her previous relationship.

He noticed her studying him.

"Was that smile because you're planning our honeymoon?"

"Something like that."

"I hope the ghosts aren't involved in what's been going on here. I was reading up on our tour, and the Tremont House is one of the most haunted locations on the island."

Harriet's brows knitted together.

"You're kidding, right?"

He smiled.

"Kind of. The hotel ghosts are known for unpacking people's suitcases and moving things around. They supposedly turn the fans on and off and pound on doors."

She shook her head.

"The solution to this mystery is going to turn out to be a living, breathing person. I just don't know who."

Lauren joined them, holding her tablet in one hand, and she frowned as she finished reading a page before clicking it off.

"I feel like I'm missing something. I keep going over the articles about the Johnson family." She held the tablet up. "The answer is right here in front of us, but I just can't see it."

Sydney emerged from the hallway to the office area.

"Did I hear you say you have the answer to all this?"

Lauren gave a harsh laugh.

"No. I wish. I said I feel like the answers are here staring me in the face. I just can't quite put my finger on them."

Sydney sighed.

"Well, if you figure this mess out, let me know."

Lauren slid the tablet into her messenger bag.

"Believe me, you'll be the first to know."

Connie and Mavis got off the elevator together as a young man with a *Ghost Tours* teeshirt came in from the street. He held a clipboard in one hand and a pen in the other.

"Are you here for the tour?"

"We are," Harriet told him, and he began calling out names and marking them off.

More people from their class arrived and got checked in.

"My name is Jordan, and I'll be your guide for tonight's tour," he announced. "Since you're a larger group, I'll be joined by my assistant Emma.

"This is usually a walking tour, but your conference organizers have arranged a custom tour for you, which will include some short walks but also two bus rides in place of the longer walks. We've divided you into two groups. The first will walk with me, and the second will take a bus to another location. We will all end up back here, as the Tremont Hotel is the final stop on our tour."

Harriet, James, and their friends were in the first group.

"Are you sure you're up for walking?" Harriet asked Sydney.

"I can ask Jordan if you can ride the bus," James added.

Sydney dipped her head down and blushed.

"Thank you, but I'll do fine. I think the walk might be good for me." She rolled her shoulders. "With all the tension these last few days, my shoulders are stiff as boards."

172

Jordan waited until the bus riders were loaded before he led his group out to the street.

"Okay, people, how are we tonight?"

Several members of the group called out "great."

"Good, good. The first stop on our tour is just a few blocks from here. The Mayfield Manor is a commercial haunted house…"

A few people groaned.

"…having said that, it is also a true haunted house. It was owned by Doctor Horace Mayfield around the turn of the twentieth century. Dr. Mayfield was a public physician, which is what they called general practitioner in those days , but he also studied the impact of fearful situations on the individual. It is believed he conducted experiments on his unwitting patients. So, he maybe wasn't a great guy right from the get-go. Then, when the big hurricane of nineteen-hundred struck, he lost his wife and parents and, so the legend goes, his mind.

"There will be actors portraying Dr. Mayfield and his family, staff and patients. Don't let that fool you. You'll be getting a great haunted history lesson along with the entertainment. Let's go ahead and start walking."

✂ --- ✂ --- ✂

Sydney led the way up the stairs when they'd walked the three blocks to the haunted house.

"The walk seems to have done someone some good," Lauren said to Harriet and James.

Sydney heard her and turned to face them.

"It feels good to stretch my legs."

Mavis patted her arm when she reached the top of the stairs.

"I'm glad you're feeling a little better."

The tour of the Mayfield Manor took a half-hour and lived up to its billing. The actors stopped just short of over-the-top, and the history was detailed and interesting. The house had been used as a quarantine clinic in the aftermath of the terrible hurricane of 1900, and they learned that the event continues to be considered the deadliest event in North American history with between six thousand and twelve thousand lives lost.

Harriet took the bottle of water Jordan handed her when she and James came back out onto the porch.

"That was interesting, but sort of a downer."

James unscrewed the top on her water bottle when she was unable to dislodge it.

173

"The hurricane was a terrible tragedy," he said. "One of the guys in my class was telling me how they raised the whole city up after they built the sea wall."

Lauren had come out with them, but she was studying her tablet.

"Did you know about the hurricane?" Harriet asked her.

She looked up.

"Huh?"

"I was asking about the hurricane, but obviously, you're engrossed in something."

"I'm going back through all the info I've found about the Johnson family. It's got to relate back to Jennifer's twin or purchased sister or whatever she is. I've tried every database I can think of to find out what happened."

"One more day, and it won't matter."

She clicked the tablet off and stowed it in her bag.

"It'll bug me until I figure it out."

Sydney sat down on a bench on the porch, and Harriet stepped closer.

"Are you okay?"

"I think I may have overestimated how good this would feel." She leaned her head back against the house.

Jordan came over when he saw everyone clustered around Sydney.

"Everything okay over here?"

"Our friend isn't feeling well," Harriet told him.

"Would you like me to call a car to come get you?" he asked.

Sydney sighed, hesitated, but then nodded.

"I hate to be a bother, but maybe that would be best."

Harriet touched her arm.

"Would you like me to go back to the hotel with you?"

Sydney gave her a weak smile.

"I don't want to spoil your fun. I'll be fine. I just need to lie down for a while."

"Oh, honey, are you sure you don't want one of us to go with you?" Connie asked.

"I'm sure. I'll be okay, and my aunt and cousins are at the hotel. I can call them if I need anything."

"I hope she's going to be okay," Harriet said as they watched Jordan's driver pull away from the curb, Sydney tucked safely in the back seat.

Jordan clapped his hands when the car was out of sight.

"Okay, is everyone else here?" He took a quick count. "Our next stop is about ten blocks away. Are we all good with that?"

The group indicated they were, indeed, good to go, and he led them toward their next stop.

"The Mayfield Manor is the only commercial operation on our route. Our next spot is the exact opposite. In fact, the University of Texas Medical Branch—UTMB to the locals—discourages people from coming on their campus to observe their haunted building, but we've made special arrangements. I have to ask you to line up by twos when we enter the campus and follow the exact path I take. Do not go into any of the buildings or spread out into the parking lots."

James took Harriet's hand.

"Can I be your partner?"

She smiled.

"Always."

Lauren was once again poring over her tablet as they walked, three abreast.

"Don't worry about me, I'm good by myself."

Harriet nudged her with her shoulder.

"Come on. You would have had a partner if Sydney hadn't left. Besides, there might be someone else who needs a partner."

"I'm good. Besides, I think I might be on to something."

"What?" Mavis asked from behind them.

"Not sure. I need to check a couple of more places, then I'll reveal all," she told them.

Harriet tried to see what Lauren was reading on the tablet, but her friend moved it away before she could.

"Patience is a virtue," Lauren said and smirked.

Jordan began talking as they walked.

"Our destination is Ewing Hall, or Building Seventy-one on campus maps." He was wearing a wireless microphone setup that allowed the whole group to hear him. "There are two conflicting stories about this one. The first story says it's haunted by the former owner of the land. No one knew the name of this owner. He wanted his family to keep the property forever, but when he died they sold it.

"The second story is much more likely, as there are names and dates that can be verified. Supposedly, William A. A. Wallace was promised a piece of land in return for his service in the Texas Army of the Republic before Texas was a state. He filled out the paperwork for a piece of property on Galveston Island that was large and included the area where UTMB now sits. His paperwork was signed by President Sam Houston, and he was granted his request.

"Soon after," he continued. "Texas became a state, and the State of Texas refused to turn the property over in spite of efforts that continued over the rest of his lifetime."

Harriet leaned in to James and whispered, "Has he said what form the haunting takes?"

"Not yet," he whispered back.

Jordan regaled them with exploits attributed to "Big Foot Wallace" until they reached campus.

"Okay, two-by-two from here on," he instructed, and then led them through the cluster of buildings. It was starting to get dark, but Jordan had a strong flashlight in his hand. He stopped when they reached the correct building and waited for the group to form a semi-circle around him. Then, he flashed his light on a stone siding panel to the right of the building entrance, revealing the image of a man's face etched into the stone.

Several people gasped.

"This image appeared sometime after the completion of the building. It first became visible on the fourth-floor panel." He flashed his light to the top panel of the wall.

"The university didn't like the attention it was drawing, so they ordered their maintenance department to sandblast the panel until the image was removed. They did as they were told, but were dismayed to discover the image had reappeared, only this time on the third-floor stone panel.

"Not to be outwitted by an apparition, they sandblasted the third-floor panel. And...yes, you guessed it. The image appeared on the second-floor panel where, as you can see, it remains. The school is not proud of their ghost, and they try to avoid letting people see it, but as I said, we were able to make special arrangements to allow you to see this amazing vision."

Jordan reached into his pack and pulled out a laminated picture.

"Pass this around, please," he said and handed the picture to Harriet. "As you can see from this actual picture of William 'Big Foot' Wallace, the image is a very good likeness."

Harriet turned to Lauren.

"Amazing, right?" But Lauren only had eyes for her tablet.

Jordan turned his flashlight off.

"Listen up, everyone. The shuttle bus is across the street if you want a ride to our next stop. Stay here if you want to walk with me."

Lauren moved up between Harriet and James.

"Hey, if you guys don't mind, I'm going to go on the bus with Connie and Mavis so I can work on this search. I'm about to find some answers."

"Are you willing to reveal what you're finding yet?" Harriet asked.

Lauren smiled and headed toward the shuttle bus.

"All in good time, all in good time," she said as she walked away.

Harriet and James stayed with the walking group, which headed back to the Strand. Jordan came up beside them.

"Are you enjoying the tour so far?"

James looked at Harriet, and they both laughed.

"Can I take that as a yes?" Jordan asked.

Harriet smiled at him.

"Yes, you can. I'd heard about the nineteen-hundred hurricane before, and I knew it was the greatest disaster in American history as far a loss of life, but somehow, being down here really brings it home."

"Most people like the Mayfield Manor because of the actors and all the embellishments, but the place I'm about to show you is my personal favorite."

"Which one is that?" James wanted to know.

"We're about to go to Hendley Row. It's the oldest remaining commercial building in Galveston. Actually, it's four attached brick buildings. Even apart from all her ghosts, she has a colorful history. It was originally constructed to be business offices for two brothers, but during the Civil War it was used as a watchtower, since it was the tallest building on the island and afforded views of both the Gulf of Mexico and Galveston Bay.

"The building was hit by a shell from the *USS Owasco* during the Battle of Galveston on January first, eighteen sixty-three. They've preserved the damage as a feature ever since."

Jordan flashed his bright light on as they approached the curb.

"Watch the steep curb," he warned, then continued.

"Hendley Row was used as a morgue after the hurricane of nineteen-hundred. All of that has resulted in a lot of paranormal activity."

James put his arm around Harriet.

"Are we going to see a ghost?"

Jordan laughed.

"I can't guarantee anything, but there are at least four ghosts I know of in various parts of the building. We have The Lady in White around the back side of the building, the Confederate Soldier, who walks up and down stairs and across his unit. We often see a shadow or white mist when he's about. In the shops and residences, we have the Little Boy, a wet, disheveled child who probably lost his life in the hurricane. We also have a little girl who appears to be four or five years old. She hangs out on the second floor and is also believed to be a hurricane victim.

"Last but not least, is the teenager or young man. It's believed he was a child laborer who was killed in the cotton factory at a different location that was owned by the Hendleys. Their headquarters were in Hendley Row, so he comes there to haunt them. The legend says if someone sees the young man, who is wearing a white shirt covered in blood, with cuts on his face and missing an arm, it foretells something dire happening to them."

Harriet snuggled closer to James.

"I hope I don't see him." He gave her a squeeze.

"Don't worry, I'll protect you."

Jordan smiled.

"We don't usually see any of the ghosts while we're on the tour. They *have* been sighted when we've taken paranormal investigators to study the building. A few people have captured images on film, and several have recorded the little girl crying out for her mother, and also the little boy."

"I hope I get a picture," a woman said from behind them. Jordan let Harriet and James continue on without him and went back to explain the rules about photography to her.

"So, do you believe in ghosts?" James asked. "I feel as though I should know this about my blushing bride."

"I try to keep an open mind about things, but do I believe there are a bunch of spirits hanging around Galveston and performing for the tourists? No, not really. How about you?"

"I believe that at least some of the people who report ghost sightings truly believe they saw something. Maybe they did, maybe they didn't but I'm with you, it seems a bit convenient they would all hang around here and appear for the tourists."

"I heard Jordan say we were going to be meeting the others at the Hendley Market, which is apparently a fantastic gift shop. He said the owners are keeping it open just for us, and I need to bring something home for Aunt Beth."

"Lead the way," James said as they approached the building.

Inside, Harriet looked around the store. People from their tour group were spread out in twos and threes throughout the space.

"Do you see Mavis anywhere? Or Lauren? Or Connie?"

James slowly turned around scanning the room as he did.

"Maybe they're in the ladies' room?"

"Can I have my tour group over here?" Jordan called, using his microphone so everyone in the store could hear. He stood by the checkout counter. "We'll still have time to shop when I'm done introducing our store manager. Cheryl has managed the Hendley Market since nineteen seventy-nine, when it opened. The business has been owned by her family since its inception."

He continued regaling them with information about the artists and wares available in the market, and then described the various ghosts and apparitions he'd already told Harriet and James about.

Harriet kept looking for her friends.

"As I mentioned before," Jordan continued, "Hendley Row is actually four connected buildings. One quarter of the building has been turned into condos; the market, of course, takes up the section we're in; and the rest is being renovated into retail space and probably more apartments. We have permission to enter the area that's being renovated as well as a couple of the hallways in the undeveloped space. I'll take you in small groups into those areas. Please do not attempt to enter these areas by yourself. The first group can meet me outside."

Harriet turned toward the door.

"Let's go look outside. Maybe they went out for air or something."

Mavis appeared just before they reached the door. Her lips were clamped together, and her face was devoid of color.

"What's wrong?" Harriet asked her.

Connie was right behind Mavis.

"*Diós mio.*" She twisted her hands together. "We can't find Lauren, and she's not answering her phone."

Mavis held up Lauren's tablet; a visible crack ran diagonally across the screen.

"We found this inside the open door to the space they're renovating. We've looked everywhere we can get to."

Harriet pulled her cell phone from her pocket.

"I'll call the hotel."

She dialed the hotel room but got no answer.

"She's not in your room," she reported. "Let me see if Bruce can send someone up to check in person." She dialed again, and Bruce agreed it sounded suspicious and said he'd check and call back in a few minutes.

"Lauren would never go anywhere without her tablet," Harriet said. A pain formed at the back of her head and started pounding its way to her temples. She knew something was wrong; she could feel it.

James took her hand and squeezed.

"I'm sure there's an innocent explanation. She probably got a call from a client, and when she tried to put the tablet away it fell without her noticing."

Harriet felt a warm glow in her chest. She didn't believe what he was saying, but she loved that he was trying to make her feel better. Her phone buzzed in her pocket, and she answered.

"Thanks," she said after hearing the report and ended the call.

179

"Bruce says she's not in the room—he went inside to see for himself—and no one at the front desk saw her come back."

James tugged on her hand gently.

"Let's go see if the store manager remembers seeing her."

Cheryl Jenkines was behind the checkout counter ringing up a notebook for one of their fellow tourists.

"Hi," Harriet said when she'd finished with the customer. "We came in with the walking part of the tour, and our friend rode the bus, and now we can't find her. Have you by any chance seen a tall slender woman with long, straight blond hair? She would probably have been carrying a tablet computer."

Cheryl thought for a moment.

"I think did see her earlier—she asked me where the restrooms are. I told her, and she went off in that direction. I think I saw her later standing out front with a dark-haired woman. I didn't get a good look, since I was inside and they were outside, but I think it might have been her."

"Which way are the restrooms?" Harriet asked.

Cheryl pointed to the back of the store.

"I'll go check the ladies room," Harriet told James. "Could you check the men's room, just for completeness' sake?"

"Sure."

They came out of their respective rooms a few moments later, neither having found Lauren. They went back outside, where Jordan was gathering their group to continue the tour. Mavis still clutched Lauren's tablet to her chest.

"I think we should do the tour in case Lauren is inside somewhere. She may have gone into the area that's only available to the tour group. You know if she got an idea she would pursue it, whether she was supposed go into an area or not."

Connie twisted the edges of her cardigan in her hands.

"Do you think we should call the police?"

Harriet chewed on her lip.

"If we don't find her back at the hotel after the tour, we probably should. I'm not sure they'll do anything this soon, but given everything else, I'm guessing Detective Settle will be interested."

James pulled his phone out.

"Shall I call Robin?"

"Good idea," Mavis said. "Tell her we'll meet her at the hotel as soon as our tour is over. Probably thirty minutes or less."

Jordan led them into the construction area.

180

"I've drawn chalk lines to define a pathway for us to follow. Please do not stray outside the lines. Now…"

He continued talking, but Harriet didn't hear what he said. She was too busy thinking about Lauren. She knew her friend could get distracted by her work, but she wouldn't have left without saying anything to Mavis or Connie.

James nudged her.

"Hello? Where did you go?" He pointed to the back of their group.

Jordan had moved down the hall into another area. He stopped, and the group assembled around him.

"We're now at the back of the building. When I finish speaking, please be quiet and listen. You might hear the Lady in White moaning and crying, or you could hear the Little Boy thumping and bumping."

Everyone was quiet, straining to hear something—anything.

Harriet jumped along with the rest of the group when they heard a muffled but still loud sound.

"That must have been the Little Boy," Jordan said.

James was standing beside him, and when the rest of the group had moved on, he held the guide back..

"You seemed a little surprised by the ghostly noise."

Jordan gave a forced laugh.

"He usually doesn't perform on cue like that. I mean, we always do the moment of silence, but…"

"What's on the other side of this wall?" Harriet demanded.

Jordan thought a minute, frowning.

"I think there was a teak-paneled hallway that went to the cotton merchants' offices. If I remember the floor plan of the old building right, I think there was a set of utility stairs at the end of it. They would be servant's stairs in a house. The contractor said something about the stairs not being up to code, so for now they just sealed the whole area up."

"And the ghost hangs out in there?" Harriet asked.

Jordan smiled.

"I think the ghosts can be anywhere. They aren't bound by the same rules and structures we in the earthly plane are."

"Right," she said, drawing the word out.

The ghosts were quiet for the remainder of their time in Hendley Row.

Jordan led the group out to the sidewalk.

"Our last stop is your hotel, the Tremont House. I'm sure they didn't tell you when you checked in that your hotel is one of the more haunted locations in Galveston."

Connie came up beside Harriet.

181

"Maybe that's been our problem."

Harriet laughed.

"I don't think ghosts go around killing people."

Connie frowned.

"You don't know that. Maybe ghosts can control other people. La Llorona kidnaps children in Mexico."

Jordan counted noses and then looked a question at Harriet

"Our friend Lauren seems to have left early," she told him. "I take it she didn't say anything to you about leaving?"

He shook his head.

"We think she got a work email or something," she added.

He wrote something on his clipboard list and moved to the front of the group.

"When we go into the lobby of your hotel, you'll notice a brick facade. This is from the former Belmont Boarding House, where a salesman is rumored to have had a good night gambling only to be murdered when he returned to his room. He is now referred to as 'Lucky Man Sam.' He's supposed to have had a bad leg, which he dragged. The fourth floor, where he lived, experiences pounding on the doors and, especially since the reconstruction of the hotel after Hurricane Ike, strange one-footed stomping in the hallway."

James slipped his arm around Harriet's waist.

"Don't worry, I'll protect you."

She smiled.

Mavis came up beside them.

"Let's meet in our room when we're done here," she murmured, then fell back into line.

Chapter 22

C an Ruth and I do anything to help?" Kathy asked Mavis when the group had returned to the hotel.

"Could you go check on Sydney?" Harriet asked her. "She said she was going back to her room when she left the tour. She's probably fine, but I'd feel better if we knew that for sure."

She and James then went to the reception desk.

"Is Bruce available?" she asked the woman behind the counter, who called the security office. Moments later, he came down the hallway.

"Any news?" he asked.

"Not yet."

Mavis joined them, holding out Lauren's tablet.

"She wouldn't leave this behind. Some had to have pried it from her fingers. Something is very wrong."

Bruce pulled his phone from his pocket.

"Have you called the police yet?"

Harriet shook her head.

"We wanted to check back here first, just to be sure she wasn't holed up in the restaurant dealing with a client problem or something."

"I've had Tyrone searching this place since you called. Your friend isn't anywhere that we can find. I have him driving a grid pattern between here and Hendley Row, but I don't think he'll find anything. There are too many people out and about in this area for her to be lying on the sidewalk or anything like that. I think it's time to call the police." He hit a button on his phone and turned away as he spoke.

Connie got her cell phone from her purse.

"I'm going to call the hospital and see if they've admitted her."

"Before you do that, can you call Robin?" Harriet asked.

Mavis fidgeted with Lauren's tablet.

"Don't you think we'd have noticed if Lauren had passed out or been hit by a car or something? She was with us when we arrived at the Hendley Market. She disappeared into thin air."

Bruce returned just as Kathy and Ruth came out of the elevator and crossed the lobby.

"We couldn't get an answer at Sydney's door, and we ran into her aunt in the hallway." Kathy said.

"And they thought she was on the tour with us," Ruth finished.

Harriet looked at Bruce.

"Are you allowed to do welfare checks on guests?"

He grimaced.

"Not normally, but given the murder and the attack on her mother…"

Detective Settle came through the street doors up the stairs straight to Harriet and Bruce.

"When did you last see your friend?" he asked without preamble.

"I saw her last when we got off the shuttle bus in front of the Hendley Market," Mavis said. "I went to find the restroom, and she stayed out on the sidewalk to continue a search she was doing on her tablet." She held up the device. "We found this inside the construction area in the marked pathway."

Settle slipped on plastic gloves and took the tablet. Harriet searched the lobby. A couple at the bar was staring at their group.

"Is there a meeting room down here where we can continue this? We're starting to attract attention."

Bruce spread his arms as if to herd the group, ushering them into the hallway that went past the reception desk toward a conference room. A large table dominated the room, and they sat down around it—James, Harriet, Connie and Mavis on one side, Kathy, Ruth, Bruce and Settle opposite.

Settle pressed the open button on Lauren's tablet.

"Okay, does anyone know her password?"

"Try one-one-oh-one-nine-seven-nine," Mavis suggested.

He tapped the numbers in, but the tablet didn't wake up.

Harriet looked at Mavis and Connie.

"What else would she use? Her birthday didn't work."

James turned to Harriet.

"Do you think she'd use her home address?"

Harriet recited Lauren's address numbers, and Settle tapped them in.

"Nothing," he said. "I suppose I could call in the forensic people and have them dust the surface with fingerprint powder to see if there's pattern of use in the area where the keypad shows up."

"Try it," Harriet said.

She drummed her fingers on the table until James put his hand over hers. Her lips curved into a half-smile, and they shared a glance. Finally, she turned to Bruce.

"What about Sydney?"

Settle sighed and slumped a little in his chair.

"Sydney Johnson? What about her?"

"She left our ghost tour early. She said she wasn't feeling well," Harriet told him.

"We decided we should check on her, given everything else that's happened," Mavis added.

"And?"

Bruce got up and started pacing.

"We can't locate *her* at the moment, either."

Settle ran both of his hands through his short hair.

"So, what are you thinking? Maybe she's the real target, and your friend Lauren is collateral damage?"

Harriet winced.

"You say you can't locate her," he pressed. "Where have you checked? And are you sure she isn't off with some of her out-of-town guests?"

Bruce stopped.

"We don't really know anything. Those two ladies…" he nodded at Kathy and Ruth. "…knocked on her door and also talked to her aunt. The aunt doesn't know where she is."

Robin arrived, out of breath, her normally neat hair plastered to her forehead, as if she'd run here in the heat.

"What's going on? Have you found Lauren?"

Settle turned to Harriet.

"You called your lawyer?"

Connie, Mavis, and Harriet all started to speak at once. Settle held his hands up.

"One at a time please."

Harriet and Connie looked at Mavis. She cleared her throat.

"Robin is not only a lawyer, but a member of our quilting group and our friend. Of course we called her."

He gave the ceiling a *Why me?* glance.

"Bruce, could you go check Ms. Johnson's room? Go inside and see if she's there?" He turned back to Harriet. "Has you friend Lauren ever gone missing before?"

185

Harriet and her friends exchanged a look.

"No, not on purpose."

"What's that supposed to mean?" Settle pressed, then apparently thought better of it. "Never mind, I don't want to know. You said she was at the tour with you and just…what? Walked off?"

Connie tugged on the hem of her sweater.

"We were on the shuttle bus to the Hendley Market. Lauren was fixated on her tablet and said she thought she was on to something. Mavis and I went into the building, but she stayed out on the sidewalk."

"We asked the store manager if she had seen Lauren, and we described her. The manager said she thought she'd seen her by the restrooms and again out on the sidewalk," Harriet told him.

Settle pulled his spiral notebook from his pocket and made a note.

"And where did you find her tablet?"

"We found it on the sidewalk near the entrance to the construction area," Mavis said.

He sighed.

"That's not much to go on." He closed his notebook and tapped his pen on its cover. "I think that building is owned by Mitchel Historic Properties. They're going to be hard to get hold of tonight."

Robin pulled her own pen and a legal pad from her bag. She made a note.

"Do we know what sort of arrangement the tour company has with the building owner? Could they let you in to have a look?"

Settle turned his attention to her.

"Good idea. Let me see what I can find out." He stood, taking out his phone, and went into the hallway to make the call.

Before the door closed behind him, Detective Grier came in. Harriet rolled her eyes at James.

"My day is complete."

He took her hand under the table and gave it a squeeze.

Grier set a box on the table.

"Where's the tablet?" he asked.

Nobody moved. He opened the box and focused on Harriet.

"The forensic crew are busy at an arson fire on the other end of the island. I was in doing paperwork, and believe it or not, I worked for three years as a criminalist in Houston."

Mavis handed Lauren's tablet to the detective when he had his gloves on. He held it up at eye level and peered at the glass surface.

"Does it still turn on?"

Harriet nodded.

"The white button on the top."

He turned it on.

"Fortunately, it doesn't look like she's wiped the glass lately."

He took a soft brush from his case and poured powder from a small jar into its lid. He dipped the brush in the powder, tapped it on the edge of his case and then gently brushed powder onto the surface of the tablet. Like magic, it defined areas that had previously been mere smudges.

Grier held the tablet by its edges and tilted it one way and another, letting the light reflect off the surface.

"Looks like the two, three, seven and eight get more use than the others."

He took his own phone and took a picture of the dusted surface and then gently pressed two, three, seven, and eight. It was clear the device expected two more digits. He pressed two and three again but nothing happened.

Harriet pulled out her own phone and pulled up the keypad.

"Can I have a piece of paper?" she asked Robin.

Robin tore a page from her pad and handed it over. Harriet wrote the word *Carter*, the name of Lauren's dog, on the page and then wrote the corresponding keypad numbers.

"Try two, two, seven, eight, three, seven."

Grier tapped the numbers, and Lauren's tablet lit up to show a picture of Carter.

He smiled at Harriet.

"Well, I'll be."

"She does love that little dog."

Grier opened the browser and tapped the history button.

"Here we go," he said.

Harriet, James and Robin all got up and clustered around as Detective Settle came back into the room.

"Hey," he said to Grier.

Grier grinned at him.

"The forensic team is all out at an arson fire at Jamaica Beach."

"I didn't realize this was one of your talents."

Grier smiled.

"I am a man of mystery." He tapped the link to the most recent site Lauren had looked at. "Here we go."

Settle came to look over Harriet's shoulder. Grier covered his mouth with one hand and leaned his elbow on the table, clicking through pages on the tablet with the other.

"Looks like she was interested in Agnes Scott College in Atlanta. That mean anything to any of you?"

"The Johnsons are from Georgia," Mavis said.

Grier leaned back.

"The dead bride went to Georgia."

Settle straightened.

"She might have gone to Agnes Scott, too."

Harriet stared at the tablet screen.

"Could you scroll through the page again, only slower this time?"

Grier tapped the screen, and a page displayed. It was the first of several with the Agnes Scott heading. He displayed the next page and the next.

"Stop."

There was a photo of a group of women in martial arts clothing.

"Can you make it bigger?"

"What are you looking at?" Grier asked.

James stepped aside so Harriet could get closer. She leaned in.

"Make the names under the picture bigger."

Grier did as she asked. She pointed.

"Look at the third person from the left."

"'Jennilee Johnson,'" Grier read. "Is that the bride?"

Settle studied the screen.

"Her name was Jennifer, not Jennilee. Kind of looks like her, though."

Harriet blew her breath out.

"The mysterious twin again."

Settle started to say something, but Bruce burst into the room before he could.

"Detective, I think you need to come upstairs."

Grier turned around.

"What's going on?"

Bruce put his hands up like he was going to run them through his hair, but stopped short and dropped them.

"I went upstairs to check on Ms. Johnson, like Detective Settle asked me to."

"Did you find her?" Harriet asked.

Bruce looked at her.

"No. But I did find some weird…stuff."

Both detectives now focused their attention on him.

"Define weird," Grier demanded.

"I went to her room, and once again, no one answered, so I went in. The maids had been inside, and everything looked tidy." He paused and looked at the floor.

Grier stood up.

"What else?"

188

Bruce raised his hands again.

"I know I probably shouldn't have, but I opened the closet. There were some really weird-looking...I guess they were undergarments...and a suitcase with blond hair sticking out of it."

Connie covered her mouth with her hand and gasped.

"*Diós mío!*"

"Did you touch anything besides the closet door?" Grier asked.

Bruce shook his head then pulled his phone out and made a call. Both detectives headed for the door; Bruce ended his call and joined them. Harriet got up to follow, but Settle turned back.

"You all wait right here. If we need you, we'll call."

Robin got up and started pacing.

"How could Lauren have ended up in Sydney's room?"

The conference room door opened, and a woman wearing a hotel vest and nametag came in with a tray of cookies followed by another employee with a carafe of coffee and a tray of mugs.

Mavis sat wringing her hands, the color drained from her face.

"She wouldn't. She was on the tour. She wouldn't just leave."

Harriet and James took cookies from the tray. She slid Lauren's tablet closer and started paging through what Lauren had most recently looked at. Robin came up behind them.

"Are you finding anything?"

Harriet sat back and blew her breath out in a huff.

"Yes and no. She looked at a lot of stuff. Unfortunately, I'm not sure which of these things is the one that was leading her somewhere." She scrolled through a few pages with Robin leaning over her shoulder.

"What's that?" Robin asked.

"She'd done a search on Michael, the groom." Harriet read the first few lines of the article. "This is about his family home being on the Historic Register." She swiped another page open. "This one is about his dad turning the place into a bed-and-breakfast. It mentions Michael getting an associate's degree in historic preservation to help his father's plan to make it a destination for history buffs."

"So, at least that's true," Mavis said from across the table.

Harriet kept scrolling.

"She looked up the other guy—Winston Remington. There's a lot about his business interests." She swiped another page. "Here's a picture from last spring of Jennifer and Winston at an opera benefit."

Robin took a cookie and started slowly pacing the length of the room again.

"So, which one of those two would benefit if the whole Johnson family was wiped out?"

Harriet put her hands in her lap and thought a minute.

"Unless Winston was written into someone's will, I can't see how he benefits from any of this."

James poured himself a cup of coffee.

"Maybe he's just that mad about losing Jennifer."

Connie took a bite of her chocolate cookie.

"With the family gone, Michael is free to be with his real girlfriend."

Harriet took a cup from the tray and held it out for James to fill with coffee.

"Thanks," she said with a little smile. "I think the aunt may have as much motive as anyone. With the dad dead already, if Mom and both girls are out of the picture, Auntie may be in line to get some if not all of the money."

"Don't forget the mystery twin...or sister...or adoptee," Mavis reminded them.

Harriet sighed. "Yeah, there's that." She put her face in her hands. Then, she scrolled back to the page with the mystery sister.

"I can't help but think the answer is in these last two pages Lauren was looking at." She read the page again. The rest of the group sat in brooding silence.

Bruce came through the door, followed by Detective Settle. Harriet and her friends stopped what they were doing and collectively held their breaths.

"We didn't find your friend," Settle told them.

"What was the blond hair?" Harriet asked him, somewhat relieved.

"It was a wig. Actually, it was several wigs. A couple of different styles, mostly blond."

Connie wiped her hands on a paper napkin.

"That sounds more like Jennifer."

"There were...prosthetic devices hanging in the closet," Settle continued.

"What do you mean?" James asked. "Like a wooden leg or something?"

Settle's cheeks turned pink, and he put his hands up like he was holding two softballs.

Mavis stiffened.

"You mean falsies?"

James laughed.

"You don't hear that term very often."

Settle looked confused.

"Chest enhancements?" Harriet suggested.

He pointed at her.

"Yes! Chest enhancements."

Mavis relaxed.

"That makes a little sense. What little we saw of the bride, she wasn't well endowed. Maybe she wanted a little shape to fill out her dress."

"This would definitely do that."

Robin stopped in front of him.

"What about Lauren?"

"Unfortunately, we didn't find anything that helps us locate your friend."

"So, what's your plan?" Robin demanded.

It was his turn to sigh.

"We're sending patrolmen over to search Hendley Row, and we're still working on getting permission to get into the construction area. Give me your cell phone numbers, and I'll call if we find anything."

He looked down, then opened his mouth as though to say something. Harriet held her breath, afraid he was going to tell them they needed to prepare themselves for the worst. Instead he picked up a cookie from the tray on the table and took a bite.

Chapter 23

Grier turned to Settle.

"Check and see if Remington made bail and then see if Williams is out of the hospital. It doesn't seem like he could have done much, as bad as he was beaten, but have someone check on his whereabouts anyway."

Settle turned away and started his phone calls.

"Do you people know anything about the aunt?" Grier asked.

"She told us she was coming to the service," Harriet said, "and we met her briefly, but that was just the usual 'sorry for your loss' conversation."

Mavis tore the edge of her paper napkin into a fringe as if her fingers didn't know what to do if they weren't holding a needle and thread.

"What about those three girls—the cousins. Maybe they inherit."

Connie's eyes filled with tears.

"If Lauren was here she'd be able to look them up."

Robin stopped behind Connie and put her hands on her shoulders.

"Come on, I'm sure Lauren's fine. She's smart and tough. She'll find a way to tell us where she is, and then we'll go get her. I'm sure there's a reasonable explanation."

Settle ended his last call and came back.

"Williams is still in the hospital, so he's out. The other guy, Remington—he made bail two hours after he was arrested. Apparently, he has friends in high places to go along with his deep pockets." He turned to Harriet and James. "You all should go back to your rooms and stay there. We'll let you know when we find your friend."

No one said anything. No one moved, either.

Settle sighed.

"Stay away from the Johnson family and friends."

Not waiting for a response, he and Grier turned and left the room.

"So, what are we going to do?" Mavis asked when the door had closed.

Harriet studied the images on Lauren's tablet again before turning it off.

"Before we do anything else, I'd like to go back to the Hendley Market. It's late enough it should be quiet on the street. I want to call her phone and listen so see if we can hear it ringing."

Robin steepled her index fingers and pressed her lips against them.

"You think she's still in that building somewhere?"

"I'm not sure, but we have absolutely no evidence she ever left that location. The police have probably already checked with the taxi company."

"Do they have those ride-sharing services around here?" Mavis asked.

Robin pulled her smartphone from her purse and checked.

"No. Apparently, they ordered them to follow the same rules as the taxis so they left town."

"Why don't Harriet and Robin and I go to the market and do the phone experiment," James suggested. "The rest of you can wait here in case Lauren shows up. We'll let you know what, if anything, we've found as soon as we're done."

Connie slumped in her chair.

"Call us as soon as you know."

"You'll know when we know," Harriet assured her as she, Robin, and James started for the door.

✄ --- ✄ --- ✄

They stood in front of the Hendley Market; a lone car drove by, and they waited until it was in the next block.

"Okay," Harriet said. "Here goes nothing." She hit the speed-dial button for Lauren's phone and strained to listen as it rang on her end. "Did you hear that?"

Robin stepped closer to the building and all but pressed her ear against the exterior wall.

"I don't hear anything."

Harriet's call went to Lauren's voicemail.

"Lauren, if you can hear this and can answer, let us know where you are."

"Try again," James said, and Harriet ended the call and hit the button again. This time she didn't hear anything.

"Let's walk around to the back side of the building."

Before they could move, a beige sedan followed by a large white pickup with a metal rack on its back pulled up to the curb. Detective Settle climbed out of the sedan, and his shoulders slumped when he saw the trio standing on the sidewalk.

"Why did I think you'd stay at the hotel and wait to hear from us?"

Harriet shrugged.

"Mavis and Connie are there."

"Please tell me you weren't going to break in here."

Harriet's eye's widened with feigned innocence.

"Of course not."

James stepped closer to her.

"We thought we would try ringing Lauren's phone. We figured it would be quiet enough this time of night we could hear if it was ringing inside."

"And did you hear anything?"

"I think I heard *something*," Harriet told him.

Settle looked at Robin and James.

"Did the rest of you hear it?"

James looked

apologetically at Harriet before he shook his head.

"I didn't hear anything, either," Robin concurred.

Settle studied the front of the building.

"It's possible her battery died when it started ringing."

"I know it was her phone," Harriet insisted. "She uses this crazy song for my ringtone. I'd recognize that first note anywhere."

A man in jeans and an orange teeshirt with rolled-up sleeves got out of the truck and joined them on the sidewalk.

"You ready to go inside?"

Settle glared at his would-be helpers.

"You people wait here until I check it out."

The other man, who must have been with the construction company, opened a temporary door fashioned from plywood and led Settle inside. He returned a moment later.

"There's not much to see, but come look, if you want."

He wasn't exaggerating. They entered the area they'd been in earlier during the tour, but now an unlocked interior door in the plywood wall stood open. The construction workers had built a barricade to protect the existing interior wall, which was polished teak and went from floor to ceiling between the former cotton company offices in this building and the Hendley Market next door.

Robin dialed Lauren's number again, and they all listened. Try as they might to hear something…anything…the silence stretched on.

Harriet turned around to leave.

"We're getting nowhere here. I say we go back to the hotel."

"You're right," Robin agreed. "Whatever happened, there isn't anything I can see to point us in the right direction."

James opened the door for them.

"I want to go look at Lauren's pad again," Harriet decided as they started back to the hotel. "She told me she thought she was on to something. If she figured out what's going on here and said or did something in front of the wrong person or people, they could be trying to keep her from telling the rest of us."

"Hopefully, they just stashed her somewhere while they make their getaway," Robin said.

Harriet couldn't help thinking that anyone who was willing to kill Jennifer, badly beat her mother and attack her sister wasn't likely to take a chance on letting Lauren talk to anyone, now or ever.

Connie opened their hotel room door before Harriet could knock.

"Did you find her?"

Harriet shook her head.

"I thought I heard her phone, but only the first note. Detective Settle came with the contractor, but the door off that hallway only went into a narrow space that was built to protect a floor-to-ceiling teak wall."

Robin went to a vacant chair and sat down.

"There was nothing to see. And I mean, nothing."

Harriet picked Lauren's tablet up off the coffee table.

"I thought we could go through the pages Lauren looked at one more time and see if we can figure out what she'd put together."

Robin pulled her ever-present yellow legal pad and pen from her bag.

"Okay, as you go through the pages on the tablet, I'll make notes of whatever we think is important. Maybe when we see it compiled in one place, something will jump out at us."

After fifteen minutes, she had a page full of notes and Harriet had reviewed all the history she could open on Lauren's tablet.

"Shall I read what we've got?" Robin asked.

Connie and Mavis nodded. Harriet turned the tablet off.

"Go for it."

Robin stood up to pace as she read.

"Okay, I've divided it into categories. First, she looked at a lot of stuff about both the bride's and the groom's families. They're rich, he's poor. We know from what he said that the families arranged the marriage, but we don't know what the terms were. Although it appears Lauren was trying to find out if Michael benefited from his bride's death before they married, it doesn't seem like she found anything, and from a legal point of view that doesn't make sense."

She flipped the page.

"Now, Lauren was also working on the twin, or extra-unknown-sibling, theory. She found pictures of a Jennilee Johnson who bears a striking resemblance to Jennifer and attended Agnes Scott University while Jennifer, we know, attended Georgia. If I had to hazard a guess, I'd say this is where Lauren found something. I'm not seeing it, but I think this is where something popped for her."

Harriet crossed her arms and leaned back in her chair.

"So, if there's a twin or adoptee, where is she? And if she looks like Jennifer, why was one chosen as the target of the arranged marriage and the other never even mentioned, much less invited to the wedding?"

Mavis bit her lower lip.

"Wasn't Lauren checking some death and birth records?"

Harriet thought for a moment.

"She said she found no record of a twin coming or going, but I don't know if she checked the name 'Jennilee.' If she did, those pages weren't in her history. Of course, she might have done that on her phone, or maybe some of those databases she's able to access because of her clients don't leave anything behind in her history."

James pulled out his phone.

"I can try to look up Jennilee Johnson on the Social Security birth, death and marriage record database."

"Go for it," Harriet urged him.

Someone tapped softly on the door, and Robin strode over and opened it.

"Hello?"

"Is Sydney here?" Harriet heard Sydney's Aunt Jane ask. She got up and joined Robin at the door.

Jane Wilson had changed out of her drab charcoal memorial service outfit and into a bright-yellow off-the-shoulder dress and matching designer shoes. She had clearly benefited in a big way from her sister's good fortune and generosity.

"We've looked all over for her and our friend Lauren, and we can't find either one," Robin informed her.

"Where are they?" the aunt demanded.

Harriet moved in front of Robin, holding on to the doorknob and blocking the doorway.

"We just told you—we don't know. And to be clear, we have no reason to believe your niece is with our friend. Sydney left the ghost tour to

196

go back to the hotel before our friend went missing. Have you checked the hospital? She wasn't looking well when we last saw her."

"We were at the hospital just now. The doctors are looking for Sydney, too. They need to talk to her about her mother's condition."

"I'm afraid we can't help you. You could help us, though. Do Sydney and Jennifer have another sister?"

The aunt's already flushed face darkened to a shade more purple than red.

"This is not the time for that discussion," she said, and spun on her spiked heels and left.

Harriet came back to the sofa and sat down beside James.

"She's a real piece of work. I wonder what she meant when she said this isn't the time for that discussion."

Mavis came out of the bathroom and took her seat across from Harriet.

"Do you think she was really looking for Sydney?"

"What do you mean?" Harriet asked her.

"I mean, that woman is still on the suspect list, if you ask me. She benefits financially if her sister dies, she may get more if the two daughters are out of the picture, and that says motive to me. What if she's been slipping something into her sister's IV at the hospital to insure she doesn't wake up, and then did something to Sydney? This visit may have been her attempt to find out what we know."

"What does that have to do with Lauren?" Connie asked.

"She may have just been in the way," Mavis murmured, echoing Harriet's thoughts.

✂ --- ✂ --- ✂

Another hour passed with no news from Settle. Robin went back to her hotel to try to get some rest. Mavis had ordered carafes of coffee and tea, and those remaining sipped in silence. Harriet sat beside James, his arm draped over her shoulders. Remembering, she turned to speak to him directly.

"Before Aunt Jane interrupted, you were looking up birth and death records. Did you find anything?"

"I found Jennifer. Let me check for Jennilee." He tapped characters into his phone. "Huh," he said more to himself than her.

"What?"

"There's a 'Jennilee S. Johnson' in the birth records."

Connie sat erect in her chair.

"Is there a death record?"

James checked.

"No. Not here, anyway."

Mavis set her coffee mug down with a thunk.

"Check Sydney."

James bent over his phone as he typed the query into the database.

"Nothing."

Harriet stood and walked over to the tall windows. It was dark outside, with only the lights at the empty cruise-ship berth lighting the night sky.

"Let's call Bruce and see if he'll let us go look in Sydney's room."

James joined her by the window.

"What are you thinking?"

"I'm not sure, but I'd like to have a look at the wig and those 'prosthetic garments'."

She picked up the house phone and called the security office. Tyrone answered and explained that Bruce was grabbing a nap in one of the staff rooms.

"Could you let us into Sydney's room?" she asked. "Our friend is missing and so, it seems now, is Sydney."

"We're aware," Tyrone said, sounding annoyed. "Her battle-ax of an aunt was down here earlier."

"Will you let us into the room?"

He was quiet for a long moment. Then: "Well, Bruce did tell me to cooperate with you people because of the help you gave us earlier today. You'd have to promise not to touch anything."

"We can do that," Harriet told him.

"I'll be up in a minute."

She turned to the others and grinned.

"We're in."

Chapter 24

rue to his word, Tyrone tapped on Mavis's door in less than five minutes. He pulled a pair of latex gloves from his pocket as they walked the short distance to Sydney's room. He pulled them on his large hands in front of the door.

"Just to be clear, we're not doing anything illegal here. The hotel has the right to enter a room when they believe the resident inside could be in trouble."

He opened the door and stood aside as Harriet, Mavis and James entered. Connie was waiting in the room in case Lauren called or came back.

As was the case in their rooms, Sydney's closet was off the entry hallway, and four people crowded the space to the point the door couldn't be opened. Harriet and James pushed past Tyrone farther into the room but where they could still see into the closet.

"Would you open the closet?" she said. "I'm interested in that wig you found, and the 'prosthetics'."

"What are you thinking?" James asked.

Tyrone opened the closet door, and Mavis gasped.

"Oh, my gosh."

James moved closer.

"What?"

Harriet pointed.

"Tyrone, grab the edge of that thing and hold it out."

The big man did as he was instructed. Harriet leaned back against the entry wall.

"We've had it all wrong. Right from the beginning. Show me the wig."

199

A large suitcase sat on its wheeled end. Tyrone slid the zipper across the top and down the side, making enough of an opening he could reach inside with his gloved hand and pull the wig out.

"Curly," Harriet stated the obvious. "Not straight like Lauren's but wavy, like Jennifer's. And look." She pointed at a second wig, shorter and darker, at and an orange top. "James, this is why you thought you saw me go into Jen's room before she was murdered. Sydney must have seen what I bought at Tina's and gotten the same thing."

"Weren't you all at the shop at the same time?" he asked.

Harriet dug into her memory.

"Sydney left before we did, and then we talked with Boyce, the manager, for a while, and then we waited for the hotel car to come pick us up and circle the block. So, she had some time to work with."

Mavis tapped her chin with her finger.

"She probably dressed like Harriet and then watched from her room, which is just down from her sister's. If she heard anyone coming, she could have come out and done her charade, implicating Harriet. If no one came, no harm, no foul; she'd just find another method to implicate Harriet. But James came along, and she was set."

"It's been Sydney all along," Harriet said. She pointed to one of the flesh-colored undergarments. "That is a fat suit. From the looks of it, she has several. There aren't twins, just two sisters who look a lot alike. One came here to get married, and the other to insure it never happened."

James rubbed his hand across his chin.

"So, Sydney is actually Jennilee S-for-Sydney Johnson?"

"I think it was Sydney who hit me," Harriet continued. "She removed her fat suit, donned the blond wig and whacked me. We all, including me, assumed it was Jennifer, because I'd only seen her those few seconds the previous night. She wore her sister's clothes, and with the wig on, she looked just like her."

Mavis screwed her face up in thought.

"So, that means she attacked her own mother?"

Harriet blew out a breath.

"And possibly tried to do her in at the hospital. I'll bet you anything she's why Mama took a turn for the worst."

Tyrone stuffed the wig back into the suitcase and zipped it up.

"Are you thinking she attacked herself?"

Harriet thought about it.

"I think she could have. None of her injuries were very serious, and compared to what had happened to her sister and mother, that never made any sense. Why would an attacker kill her sister, nearly kill her mother, and then leave *her* tied up with superficial wounds?"

"We need to call the police," James said.

Tyrone shook his head.

"I'll wake Bruce up and tell him, but I think we should wait until morning to call the detectives. I mean, what can we really tell them? They already know about the fat suits. You may have drawn some different conclusions about them, but nothing that helps us find your friend or Sydney Johnson. All this does is increase the likelihood Sydney is with your friend."

"I disagree," James said, moving back past Tyrone so he could face him. "If Sydney has done something to Lauren, she could be leaving the area as we speak. The longer we wait, the farther away she's going to be."

Tyrone's face was flushed and full of indecision.

"This is my first chance at working security. I can't blow it."

Harriet stepped past both men into the hall.

"You do get that Lauren's life is in danger, right?" she demanded, hands on hips as she turned to the young security man. "She could be bleeding out somewhere right now." Her voice got louder. "You understand that, right? If you hesitate, it could mean Lauren's life."

Tyrone looked around as if hoping someone else would going to appear to make the decision for him.

"Okay," he said finally, shoulders slumping, "I'll wake Bruce up and then call the police."

Harriet suddenly realized one of their group was missing.

"Where's Mavis?" she asked James.

"I don't know. I didn't see her leave, but I was focused on you and Tyrone.

They quickly established she wasn't there.

"I'm going to go see if she went back to her room," Harriet turned, and almost ran over Mavis.

"We were just looking for you."

A grim smile creased the older woman's face.

"I could see you weren't getting anywhere with your young man in there, so I went back to my room and called downstairs and insisted they wake Bruce up. I also called the police station. They said they would call Detective Settle."

She led the way back into her room, and everyone sat around the coffee table. Bruce arrived a few minutes later, followed by a tired-looking woman from the lobby cafe carrying a fresh tray with cookies and a new carafe of coffee. She set it on the table and left.

"What have you found?" he asked.

Harriet explained their discoveries on the internet and in Sydney's closet.

"So, I think Sydney has been playing a long game. I think she dyed her hair black some time ago, and then began wearing a fat suit to make it seem like she'd put on weight. That allowed her to look distinctly different from her sister when she wanted to, but she retained the ability for her to imitate Jennifer at will."

"And that's what you think she did when you were attacked? You think it was actually Sydney who hit you? Why would she do that?"

"I should think that would be obvious," Mavis snapped. "She wanted to set up a motive for Harriet to kill her sister."

"And her mother," Connie added.

Bruce ran a hand through his hair, staring at the floor and looking thoughtful.

"I don't know. That sounds pretty elaborate. I mean, we're talking regular people here."

"Do you have a better idea?" James demanded. "Our friend is missing, and no one is coming up with anything else."

Bruce was saved from having to answer by the arrival of Detectives Settle and Grier.

"Don't you people sleep?" Grier asked as he stormed past Bruce into the middle of the room. His customary short-sleeved white shirt, tie and khaki slacks had been replaced with a faded polo shirt and cargo shorts. He went to the coffee, picked up a cookie from the tray, and took a bite. "And what's with all the cookies?"

Bruce's face reddened, but he didn't say anything.

Harriet stood up.

"We are in a strange town, and our good friend is missing. It's a little hard for us to just put on our jammies and go to bed when we don't know where she is or what's happened to her."

Grier put his hands in his pockets and rocked back on his heels, blowing his breath out as he studied their expressions.

"What've you got?" he said finally.

"Before she disappeared," Harriet began, "Lauren was researching the Johnson family. Something bothered her about the information she found —there seemed to be another sister. Because of her IT consulting work, Lauren has access to websites the rest of us don't. She told us she thought she had it figured out, but she wanted to check one more thing."

"Go on," Grier encouraged her. "So far, I'm not hearing why I need to be here in the middle of the night."

Harriet paced to the door and back.

"After you left today, we went back through Lauren's browsing history. Then we went up to Sydney's room to look at the prosthetics."

Grier raised an eyebrow and glared at Bruce, but the security man just shrugged.

"We realized we'd been looking hard for Jennifer's apparent third sister, but we hadn't checked Sydney out. We did, and discovered she has no birth, marriage or death record, at least not in the Social Security index. That led us to wonder: What if Sydney is a fiction? I mean, there's the whole J-name thing—Judy has daughters named Jennifer and Jennilee and then names the third one Sydney?"

Connie straightened up to her full five-foot height.

"And they are all blond...except for Sydney.

Mavis selected a cookie.

"I don't think she was adopted," she said. "There's been nothing in any of the pictures or documents we've looked at that would indicate anything of the sort. And those 'prosthetics', as you call them, are nothing more than fat suits.

"We think she changed her look and got people used to looking at her all fat and shlumpy so she could turn herself into Jennifer whenever she wanted," she continued.

Harriet came back to the sitting area.

"Like we told you earlier, Sydney was on the ghost tour with us when Lauren was looking up stuff about the Johnson family. We'd just finished our first stop when Sydney decided she didn't feel well enough to continue.

"She left to return to the hotel—or so we thought. We went to the medical school and then moved on to Hendley Row. We know Lauren made it that far, but then she disappeared into thin air. We went looking for Sydney because we thought maybe Lauren had figured out what was going on and came back here to tell her. But what if she confronted Sydney on the tour and got kidnapped—or worse?"

"Would your friend have left you to come back to the hotel without saying anything?" Grier asked.

Harriet looked at Mavis and Connie, who shook their heads.

"I don't think so," she said slowly.

"But you're not sure?"

Settle took a cookie, bit into it and chewed thoughtfully.

"Can you have someone check and see if the Johnsons had a car," he said to Bruce. "And, if yes, is it still here?"

Bruce went to the nightstand and picked up the phone to call the front desk.

"If Sydney's responsible for your friend's disappearance, it seems more likely she ambushed her at the Hendley Market or somewhere around there. It would be hard to do that at the hotel. You might be able to overpower someone in a room, but then you'd have to do something with the…" Settle hesitated. "…with the person, and that would be difficult with as many people as there are around at any given time." He turned to Bruce again. "You did question the hotel staff, right?"

"No one saw either woman tonight, alone or together." The phone rang, and he picked it up, listened and hung it up again. "The Johnson's car is parked in the hotel lot, and no one has asked for it to be brought out in several days."

Grier rubbed his forehead, looking like a man who was trying to avoid telling them what he really thought was going on.

Chapter 25

Settle sighed.

"If you have any ideas, I'm all ears. We searched the Hendley Market, the construction area, and we had officers conduct a door-to-door through the condo building. No one has seen anything."

Harriet resumed her seat beside James, clenching and unclenching her fingers. She could tell from the demeanor of the detectives they weren't hopeful, and the thought scared her to death. She'd never really had a best friend until Lauren. Of course, she'd been close to her husband Steve and considered him her best friend, but having a girlfriend was different, and she wasn't ready to have hers taken away from her.

James reached over and took possession of her hands.

"You want to go back to Hendley Market, don't you?"

"I do. We have absolutely no evidence she ever left there. I know I heard her phone. She's in there somewhere. And if she's not, there has to be something that will tell us what happened to her."

"*Can* we go back and look again?" James asked.

The detective leaned back in his chair, looked at his watch and sighed.

"Why not. We're all up anyway. We still can't go anywhere we couldn't go earlier, though."

Mavis got up and grabbed her purse.

"Lauren is very resourceful. If she's there, she'll find a way to let us know."

"I'll call for a car for you," Bruce said, picking up the phone.

✄ --- ✄ --- ✄

Grier and Settle were on the sidewalk in front of the Hendley Market when the hotel limo pulled up. Grier spread his arms and turned in a slow circle.

"Okay, here we are. Looks pretty much like it did the last time we were here."

Harriet walked over to the entrance.

"Can we get in here?"

Settle pulled a keyring out of his pocket.

"Let's see, the construction manager gave me a couple of keys."

He selected one and used it to open the door to the area the ghost tour had passed through.

"Can you open the door into that protected space in front of the teak wall?" she asked.

It took two tries before the lock opened, and he was able to open the crude plywood door.

"Lauren," Connie yelled, startling everyone.

They all listened.

"Do you have a whistle?" Harriet asked Grier.

He laughed.

"You watch too much TV."

Mavis reached into her purse and shuffled the contents around. She brought out a shiny nickel-plated brass London Bobby's whistle.

"Here," she said and handed it to Harriet. Then, she and Connie covered their ears as Harriet blasted on it. She listened for a count of thirty and blew it again. Still no answer.

She blasted a third time, and Detective Grier put his hand up.

"If you do that one more time, we're all going to be so deaf we wouldn't be able to hear if your friend was making any noise, which she isn't."

James leaned his ear against the teak paneling and held his index finger to his lips in a shushing gesture. The group quieted once again.

"Do you hear something?" Harriet whispered.

He nodded.

"I think I hear tapping."

Settle joined him at the wall, pressing his ear to the wood panel.

"Do you hear it?" James asked him when they'd straightened up.

"Blast the whistle again," Settle told Harriet, and he and James put their ears to the wall again.

This time, the tapping was audible—just barely—to the rest of the group. James moved away from the wall and guided Harriet to the spot where he'd been standing. She pressed her ear to the wall.

"The tapping seems purposeful," she said as she listened. "I think I heard 'S-O-S'."

Settle repositioned his ear and listened more.

"I think she may be using Morse code."

"Does anyone understand Morse code?" Harriet asked.

Mavis took back her whistle and dropped it into her purse.

"I can recognize a few words."

Grier pushed forward in the narrow space.

"That's okay, I did twenty years in the Navy. I got this."

He positioned himself carefully and eased his ear up against the wall, drumming the fingers of his right hand on his thigh as he listened. Then, he pulled his ring of keys from his pocket and rapped on the teak panel. He listened and then tapped again. This time, he listened longer before he straightened and stepped away.

"She's in there," he said.

"Oh, thank God!" Mavis exclaimed.

"What did she say?" Harriet asked.

He placed his hands flat on the wall and pushed.

"She said there's a hidden door in this wall, but she doesn't know where the latch is. Everyone take a section and press until we find it."

They lined up in front of the teak wall, spacing themselves along its length. Harriet pressed the edges of her panel and then the middle. Nothing moved. James did the same with the same result. Mavis and Connie pushed and poked, slowly covering their spaces.

Harriet turned sideways to lean her ear to the panel; she lost her balance and fell shoulder-first against it.

The one to her right silently swung open.

"Lauren?"

"It's about time," Lauren complained, her voice weak.

Harriet leaned into the opening, but James held her arm to stop her.

"Don't go in there till we get some light."

Detective Grier squeezed past Connie and Mavis and wedged himself between James and Harriet. He pulled a penlight from his pocket, but the beam was too weak to reveal much. What it did show was a dark gaping hole his light couldn't penetrate, with no stairs or ladder to allow them down into the abyss.

"Mike," he called. "Get a bigger light and call for fire and a bus."

Settle returned in a minute with a large flashlight.

"Are you okay?" Harriet asked when Grier shined the light into pit, revealing Lauren and Sydney at the bottom of a deep narrow chamber. She gasped—there was a dark bloodstain on Lauren's arm.

Lauren sighed.

"It's been fun chatting and all, but could you get me out of here?"

Grier leaned over.

"I'm Detective Grier—"

"You're a little hard to forget," she interrupted.

His face reddened.

"Sorry about all that. We've called for the fire department and the paramedics. Can you tell me where you're injured and what Ms. Johnson's condition is?"

Lauren turned her head slowly like it was painful to move. Her legs were tangled up with Sydney's. She took a deep breath, which seemed to pain her.

"We both fell down here during a struggle. She stabbed me in my arm, and I think I might have broken my collarbone in the fall." She glanced at Sydney. "I think she might have a broken leg."

"Has she been unconscious the whole time?" Grier asked.

"No, I just got tired of listening to her."

Grier and Settle looked at each other with raised eyebrows.

Harriet heard the firetruck siren, and she and James joined Connie and Mavis in the hallway.

"How is she?" Connie asked.

"She says she thinks she may have broken her collarbone, but her sarcasm is intact, so I think she'll be okay."

Detective Settle moved them out to the street so the firemen could bring in equipment to extract the two women. It took ten minutes for the construction manager to join them at the site and another fifteen for him and the firemen to remove the false wall so they could set up a tripod with a block-and-tackle and sling to haul them out.

Grier joined them when the firemen started lowering a paramedic into the shaft.

"You people could go back to the hotel where it's more comfortable. It's going to take them a while to get your friend out, and then she'll be taken to the hospital."

James glared at him.

"Save it. These three aren't going anywhere until Lauren is in the ambulance."

Grier shook his head.

"I had to try." He looked at Harriet. "She's is lucky to have a friend like you. A lot of people would have given up hours ago."

"That's not how we operate in Foggy Point," Mavis informed him, raising her chin proudly. "We look after our own."

They all turned as a paramedic wheeled the stretcher inside, where two firemen were raising a rescue basket with Lauren strapped snuggly inside.

They transferred her to it and wheeled it back out to. The ambulance took off, sirens blazing, and a second backed into the vacated spot.

Harriet headed for the hotel car, which was still parked at the curb; James hurried after her, and Mavis and Connie followed suit.

"Hey, isn't anyone going to wait for Ms. Johnson?" Grier asked.

Harriet shook her head without looking back.

Chapter 26

Anyone want tea or coffee?" James asked after the first hour had passed with no news. "There's a machine down the hall. I think they have hot chocolate, too."

Harriet gave him a weary smile.

"No, but thanks for offering."

She leaned her head against his shoulder and dozed. Another hour later, Dr. Hatcher came into the waiting room. He saw Harriet and came over, scraping his blue hair cover off in a practiced move.

She and James stood up, and she held her breath.

"Your friend is going to be fine."

Harriet slumped back against James, and he put his hands on her arms to steady her. She appreciated that he was there when she needed support but didn't treat her like some hothouse flower who couldn't take care of herself.

"She's upstairs in recovery. She has a nasty knife wound on her arm that had to be surgically repaired; and her collarbone is broken, probably in the fall down the shaft. When she comes out of recovery, they'll strap up her arm and shoulder to keep that immobilized and for support. She was dehydrated on top of all that, so we'll be pushing fluids for a while also."

"When can we see her?" Harriet asked.

He looked at his watch.

"You're looking at two or three hours, minimum, but probably more. If I were you, I'd go to the hotel, grab a couple of hours rest and come back. Your friend will be given painkillers that will likely knock her out, so she won't know if you're here or not."

"How's Sydney Johnson?" Harriet asked, trying to look concerned. It had occurred to her that unless the woman was unconscious, she could still pose a threat to Lauren.

Hatcher paused for a moment before speaking.

"I don't know what's going on, but the armed guard outside her room suggests this wasn't an accident."

Harriet held up her hand.

"Is that paper Ms. Johnson signed the other night when I came here with her still in effect? The one that said you can talk to me?"

"Technically, I guess it is. But, it's pretty clear your relationship has changed since then."

"But I'm still on her list, right?"

He smiled and shook his head.

"I guess you are."

"We don't really know what happened tonight, but I do know that Sydney still doesn't have much family." She'd heard Grier call Sydney's aunt at the hotel, but as of yet neither she nor the cousins had appeared. "Who knows when her relatives will show up? So, for now, we're all she has.

"I'm not suggesting I should make any life or death decisions for her. I just want to know her condition." Harriet was so furious at Sydney for attacking Lauren she hadn't really let it sink in that Sydney was the one who had attacked her, too. And, truth be told, she was angry at herself for letting the woman dupe her so thoroughly that she'd sat in this same emergency room, worrying while Sydney had her self-inflicted wounds treated."

Hatcher sighed.

"Ms. Johnson was the more seriously injured of the two. She appears to have been severely beaten and then broke her leg in two places in the fall down the shaft. I'm not sure how an air-filter mask saturated in ether came to be in the shaft, but your friend Lauren managed to sedate Ms. Johnson with it. It was a blessing, really, given how badly her leg was broken."

"Lauren's thoughtful like that," Harriet told him, struggling hard not to smile. She looked over at Mavis and Connie to see if they had anything to add, but Mavis, who was also having trouble with her expression, gave a small shake of her head. "I guess we'll take your advice and go back to the hotel."

"Leave you cell number at the desk, and if anything changes, we'll call you, but I don't think that will happen."

He looked around the waiting room, but no Johnsons had appeared. Without saying another word, he turned and went back through the double doors into the ER.

Harriet woke with a start. For a moment, she didn't know where she was. James reached over and took her hand.

"Hey,"

She sat up and looked around.

"I was sleeping so hard I didn't know where I was for a minute."

"Falling asleep fully dressed and lying sideways across the bed probably didn't help much."

She smiled at him.

"I guess we were tired."

"You had a pretty stressful time here even before we stayed up all night worrying about Lauren. You've got to be pretty exhausted right about now." He got up and took the coffeemaker carafe to the bathroom sink. "I remember coming back here, and sitting down together on the side of the bed, and that was it until I woke up just before you did."

"I remember kissing you goodnight before I planned to put on my jammies." She looked down at her clothes. "I guess I didn't make it that far."

He poured the carafe of water into the tank.

"Coffee will be ready in a minute or two. That'll help."

"What time is it?"

He glanced at his watch.

"Eight a.m."

Harriet stood up and shrugged out of her cardigan.

"We've got to get back to the hospital."

James came over and put his arms around her.

"Take a deep breath."

She did and relaxed, leaning into him.

"Lauren is in good hands, and I'm sure they're giving her pain meds that will keep her too drowsy to care if we're there or not."

"Still. I want to be there."

He rubbed his hands in circles on her back.

"You will be. After you have a cup of coffee and a nice hot shower. You'll feel much better and be in better shape to support your friend."

She looked into his face and smiled as she wrapped her arms around him. He tilted his head down and kissed her. She kissed him back and pressed her body into his. He cupped her bottom in his hands and groaned.

"You're killing me here."

She grinned as she stepped back and grabbed a handful of his teeshirt, pulling him back to her for one last playful kiss before shoving him backwards onto the bed.

"And I'm not sorry about that," she said. She spun on her heel and went to the coffee pot, poured two cups and brought them back to where James lay, propped on his elbows.

"We *are* going to have to talk, you know," he said, his voice suddenly serious.

She sank onto the bed beside him and sighed.

"Are you anxious to divorce me?"

His beautiful eyes held hers.

"Are you anxious to be divorced?"

It was a question neither one of them was willing to answer.

Harriet sipped her coffee.

"I'm going to take my shower now," she said, but didn't get up.

"I'm after you," he said. He took her cup and set it with his on the nightstand before pulling her into his arms.

Lauren was sitting up in bed and sipping a milkshake through a straw when Harriet and James finally found the room she'd been taken to.

"How are you feeling?" Harriet asked.

"Is Sydney in chains?"

Harriet scooted the guest chair closer to the bed and sat down.

"She was under police guard when we last saw her."

James stood behind her.

"The doctor said she was in worse shape than you are, so I don't think she's going anywhere anytime soon," he advised.

Lauren sipped her drink.

"I have to be honest, I thought I was a goner."

James smiled at her.

"We were a little worried about that, ourselves. But Harriet wouldn't give up. She made the police come back to that market until we found you."

Lauren looked at Harriet, all trace of humor gone from her face.

"I was counting on that. I knew Harriet wouldn't stop looking until you at least found my cold, dead body."

Harriet smirked.

"That's a little dramatic, don't you think?"

Lauren laughed.

"Maybe just a little, but honestly, I had a few dark thoughts while I was wedged in the bottom of that shaft, my arm bleeding and having to sit on that cow." She held up her milkshake. "I yelled so loud I damaged something in my throat."

Mavis and Connie arrived, trailed by a nurse.

"The doctor would like to limit your visitors, but these two ladies said it was urgent they see you."

"Tell the doctor it's critical to my recovery that I see all four of these people at once."

The nurse rolled her eyes.

"Five minutes, then two of you have to leave."

Mavis put her hand over her heart as if reciting the Pledge of Allegiance.

"I promise we'll be out in five minutes."

The nurse glanced at her watch and turned to leave.

"I'm going to hold you to it," she said over her shoulder as she went out the door.

Mavis dropped her hand.

"Okay, quick. We want the whole story before Nurse Ratched gets back."

Harriet got up and let Mavis sit next to the bed, and James pulled a second chair from across the room for Connie. Connie patted Lauren's good arm.

"Only tell us if you feel up to it."

Mavis glared at her.

"We're wasting time."

"All right, already," Lauren said and took one more sip of her milkshake before setting it on the tray table in front of her. She winced when the motion pulled on her collarbone.

"As you know, I was going over the searches I'd already done on my tablet, trying to figure out what we were missing. I kept going back to the pictures of the two little blond girls. There seemed to be a sister we didn't know about. Eventually, I discovered the other little girl was named Jennilee Johnson, and that she was born before Jennifer, so not a twin. Then I tried to figure out where Sydney fit in the picture.

"I dug deeper and discovered that Sydney was the odd sister out. Both Jens had birthdates and Social Security numbers. Sydney didn't seem to exist until I figured out that 'Sydney' was, in fact, Jennilee's middle name. She started going by it while she was away at boarding school.

"I was hanging out in front of the market waiting for Harriet to get there when the door to the construction area opened, and Sydney called out to me. At that point, I'd only figured out who was who, not the whole impersonation thing."

She grimaced as she adjusted the shoulder strap on her arm brace.

"Anyway, Sydney called out, I went to the door, and things blew up in my face. You may recall the picture we saw of her in her college martial arts picture. She has a purple belt in karate. That means she's a pretty serious fighter."

Harriet began to grin as she realized where Lauren's story was going. Lauren looked at her and grinned back.

"Yes, Sydney made the mistake of thinking no one but her does martial arts." She looked at James. "What she didn't know, but these three do, is that I have a black belt in kung fu. Anyway, she came at me, and as I was fighting her off, I realized two things—she had a dust mask soaked in something that smelled like ether, and she was wielding a really nasty knife.

"I figured out real quick she was going to try to do something bad to me, and it made me mad. She already had a second inner door in the construction area open..." She paused. "Keep in mind this all happened in probably less than a minute, and she was dragging me toward that second door the whole time.

"Anyway, I just about had her under control when she stabbed me in the arm. I staggered back and grabbed her wrist with my other hand to isolate the knife. Meanwhile, she used the change in momentum to throw us both backward, attempting to smash me into the wall and butt me with the back of her head. We fell into the teak wall that the plywood must have been protecting.

"As you now know, we tripped the lock that opened the hidden panel door to what was probably a place escaping slaves hid or more likely given we're in Galveston, a place that pirates or their booty or both were hidden. It probably had a rope ladder back in the day. We twisted as we went through the opening, and Sydney went in hot with me landing on top of her."

"*Diós mio*," Connie said. "I'm so glad you survived."

Lauren sighed and then squirmed, as if she couldn't get comfortable.

"Do you need me to call the nurse?" Harriet asked.

"Not yet," she said and picked up her chocolate shake. "Only after we were down there and she was probably going into shock, did she start blathering on about her master plan," she continued after a sip. "Of course, *she* was the injured party. Mama didn't like her as much as Jenn. Mama wasn't fair, and a bunch of other stuff I couldn't make sense of. Apparently, Daddy liked Syd or Jennilee or whoever she is. He thought she could do no wrong. But then he died, and Mama made the marriage arrangements that would end up giving a lot of the money Syd was planning on spending to her future niece or nephew.

"She played the long game—dyed her hair, started wearing progressively larger fat suits, pretended to be physically unfit." She looked over at Harriet. "And apparently, when she stormed in and hit you, it was based on which chair you were in at which table. She'd rehearsed in the empty room before we arrived. She knew how far into the room and which table to approach in order to not let anyone get a clear look at her face. If it's any consolation, she felt bad when you turned out to be such a nice person."

Mavis pulled a wrinkled tissue from her pocket and dabbed at her nose.

"We should have suspected her when she showed us her quilt piece."

Harriet raised an eyebrow.

"And why is that?"

"Think about it. What was Jennifer's favorite color?"

Harriet thought for a moment.

"She seemed to wear pink a lot."

Mavis nodded.

"She wore pink, her wedding colors were pink, everything about her was pink."

"Ahh," Harriet said when she figured it out. "The double wedding ring quilt Sydney was making for her should have been pink, not gray and green."

"Bingo," Mavis said. "Syd did the double wedding ring quilt blocks in her own colors."

"Time's up," said the nurse as she bustled back into the room. "Lauren needs to take her pain meds, and then she'll be napping." She started taking Lauren's vitals. "I'm not trying to be mean here, but she really does need to rest. She's been through quite an ordeal. Her throat is raw from hollering for help, and she lost a lot of blood from her knife wound."

"When would be a good time to come back?" Connie asked.

"If you could give her two or three hours at least, that would be good."

Mavis stood up and gently patted Lauren's good arm.

"We'll be back after lunch," she said and turned to go.

Robin was waiting in the hall when they came out.

"How is she?"

"Pretty beat up," Mavis replied. "Nothing she won't get over, but she's a bit of a mess right now."

"I came by earlier, but she was gone for a scan so I went by the police department to see what was going on. Specifically reminding them that now that we know it was Sydney who broke Harriet's eye, we would be willing to press charges against her for that assault."

"What did they say?" Harriet asked her.

"They're going to keep that in reserve in case they need it. With Jenn's murder, her mother's attack and the attack on Lauren, they have no shortage of charges against her."

James took Harriet's hand.

216

"Anyone want to go out to breakfast?"

Connie smiled.

"That sounds wonderful."

"I've heard The Sunflower Bakery and Cafe is pretty good," he told them. "Several of my cooking class buddies have been and said it's terrific."

Harriet squeezed his hand.

"Good enough for me."

"Where is it?" Robin asked.

"Fourteenth Street."

"I've got my rental car, and we can all fit if the three in the back seat don't mind being a little cozy."

Mavis put her purse strap over her shoulder.

"Sounds good."

✂ --- ✂ --- ✂

James folded his napkin and set it on the table beside his empty plate.

"Well, that was good."

Harriet smiled, something she seemed to do a lot when James was around.

"High praise coming from a chef."

Robin picked up her cup of tea and took a sip.

"It's hard to believe Sydney not only thought up such a diabolical plan but almost pulled it off."

Mavis took a deep breath and let it out slowly.

"Lucky for Lauren she had Harriet insisting she had to be at that market."

Connie ate her last bite of toast and wiped her hands on her napkin.

"I'm going to need a vacation to recover from my vacation."

They were waiting for their check when Bruce came in and was directed to a table across the room. He saw them and changed course, pulling up a chair and sitting down.

"How's your friend doing?" he asked Harriet.

"She's still in the hospital, but I think she'll be okay."

Mavis set her cup down on the table.

"I'm curious. Whatever happened with the maid who was stealing jewelry?"

"Another reason Harriet will have a free room at our hotel any time she comes to town," Bruce said with a smile. "It turns out the whole Comeaux clan was involved in a scheme that involved switching out gems in jewelry that people bought on one of the cruise ships and replacing them with glass. One of the kids worked on the ship, so they knew what was pur-

217

chased. Several of the family work at the hotel, so they had access to reservation lists. Odette could access the rooms to swap the real for the fake jewelry. They'd probably still be stealing jewelry if Harriet hadn't caught Odette in the act."

Harriet blushed.

"It was pure chance."

"She was very nervous about being forced by the family to steal. Her older sister had gotten married and quit working at the hotel, so Odette had to take her place. She wasn't very good at it, and as fate would have it, when we were questioning her she tried to bargain with the fact that Sydney had caught her in the act days earlier and forced her to give her a master key. Syd was going in and out of everyone's rooms at will, including her mother's, which is how she was able to her."

"Wow," Harriet said.

Bruce stood up.

"I better eat and get back to the hotel. As you can imagine, we're pretty busy with all this. I'm serious about the hotel giving you a free room. They are very grateful."

"Thanks," Harriet said. She was sure at some point in the future it would seem like a good deal. Right now, she wanted to collect her friends and get on a plane going far from here. She kept that thought to herself, though, and just smiled at Bruce as he turned to leave.

"Speaking of hotel rooms, we need to go back to ours and call the airport to re-book our flights and the front desk to see if we can stay at least one more night."

Mavis didn't waste another minute acting on that plan.

"Let's get at it then."

Chapter 27

Harriet and James were waiting in the hotel lobby when Connie and Mavis came off the elevator ahead of a bellman pushing a brass luggage cart carrying their suitcases.

"I would never wish harm on Lauren," Connie said. "But I'm really glad we had the opportunity to stay a couple of extra days while she was in the hospital."

Mavis smiled.

"I agree. We wouldn't have had the chance to take the horsedrawn carriage around town learning about the local history."

James slid his hand into his jeans pocket, pulled out two hotel keys and set them on the front counter.

"Don't forget all the food, too. We got to visit…" he looked at Harriet. "…two or was it three new restaurants?"

"All I know is I'm going to have to go on a serious lettuce and water diet when we get back."

Mavis laughed.

"You can bet your aunt will be all over that. And this time you won't be the only one on her radar."

A dark-shirted bell man came in from the street.

"Your car is here," he said and held the keys out toward James.

Harriet stood between Mavis and Connie and put her arms around their shoulders.

"Notice how they assume if there's a man in the group, he's going to be the driver?"

"I heard that," James said from the top of the lobby steps.

"It's true," she said.

He held the keys out on his open palm.

"I'm happy to be the passenger if you want to drive."

She laughed.

"You can drive. I think you have to drive. Lauren needs to be in the passenger seat because of her bulky brace and three people have to ride in the back seat. Size wise I think it's better me than you."

Bruce came out from the office hallway carrying two fluffy bed pillows.

"These are for Lauren for the car ride."

Harriet took the pillows.

"Thanks, I'm sure she'll appreciate them. And thank you for all the help you gave us."

"We should be thanking you, between the jewelry theft ring and the near disaster with the two guys at the memorial service. And while the hotel didn't have anything to do with the woman attacking you, we do feel bad that it happened on our property."

Bruce gestured to the bellman who was waiting by the door at the bottom of the entry steps. The man came up and carried their suitcases from the luggage trolley, down the stairs and out to the open trunk of their rental car.

✂ --- ✂ --- ✂

The flight back to Seattle was blessedly uneventful. Lauren was able to upgrade to first class at the gate. Mavis had insisted they call for a wheelchair to navigate the airport in Houston, and the airline automatically did the same when they arrived at Sea-Tac.

Harriet, James, Connie, Mavis and finally Robin gathered in the aisle and seats around Lauren as the last of their fellow travelers gathered their bags and made their way up the jetway.

Harriet sat down in the seat next to Lauren.

"You doing okay?"

"I will be in a few more hours when I'm home, in my own bed."

"I hope your vision doesn't include being home alone. I talked to my aunt this morning and she's got the rest of the Threads lined up to provide private nursing for you. And Jorge is busy cooking meals to put in your freezer."

Lauren looked up and then closed her eyes.

"Great."

"Hey, I tried to tell her she needed to talk to you first."

Lauren opened her eyes.

"She knew I'd say no. Speaking of homecomings, which home are you going to?"

James looked at Harriet.

They both started to speak at the same time and then fell silent.

Robin moved past Connie and Mavis to stand in the aisle beside Harriet.

"Now that Sydney's in custody and you aren't a murder suspect, you and James can go back to living your lives as if none of this ever happened. Since this wasn't ever a real marriage, I can file your annulment papers tomorrow and it will all be over in a matter of weeks."

Harriet and James looked at each other for a long minute. Mavis got up and stood in the aisle facing Harriet.

"Define 'real marriage'," Harriet finally said.

Robin opened her mouth to speak but noticed the flush creeping up Harriet's neck and stopped. She glanced at James and saw his face was also burning red.

Lauren giggled.

"Scratch the annulment," she choked out through her laughter.

Robin cleared her throat.

"It may take a little longer, but you can still get divorced. If that's what you want."

Mavis reached out and patted Harriet's shoulder.

"You don't have to decide anything right away." She glared at Lauren. "You know where to find Robin if you need her."

An airline employee brought a wheelchair to the plane's door.

"Are you ready, ma'am?"

✂ --- ✂ --- ✂

Harriet felt like they were in a royal procession with Lauren in her wheelchair leading the way trailed by Connie and Mavis, carrying her pillows and James and Harriet following with their own and the two women's carry-on bags and Robin bringing up the rear with her own and Lauren's.

"What's going on ahead?" Harriet asked James as their group slowed to a halt just past the security exit.

He raised up on his toes to see what was going on.

"Oh, boy," he said.

Before Harriet could ask anything else, Aunt Beth pushed through the group and grabbed her into a bear hug.

"Are you okay?

"I can't breathe," she gasped.

221

"Sorry, I'm just so glad you're okay." She held Harriet at arms-length. "Your eye looks puffy. Can you see okay?"

Jorge put his hand on Beth's shoulder.

"Give the girl a chance to catch her breath."

Beth looked at him and smiled. He handed her the bouquet he'd been carrying. A silver, helium-filled Mylar balloon with the word *Congratulations* written across it bobbed on a string attached to the flower bundle.

"These are for you two," she said and smiled at James.

His eyes widened.

"Don't worry, I know you're not married in the traditional sense, but you got married under such stressful circumstances I thought we could have a little fun with it so you'd have at least one good memory when this is all just a fading memory."

Harriet and James looked at each other and laughed.

When they looked up, they realized DeAnn, Carla and Jenny were clustered around Lauren and Connie's husband was standing between her and Mavis, Carla's daughter Wendy in his arms.

Jorge took Mavis's bag from Harriet.

"They've all been worried about you while you were gone. I tried to tell them they should wait until you got home. But they couldn't wait. Your aunt was worried about you of course, but everyone wanted to be sure Lauren was all right."

"I'm fine and as you can see, Lauren is a little worse for the wear, but no permanent damage has been done."

Jorge turned to Beth, who was giving Lauren the once over.

"Let's go get everyone's baggage and get these weary travelers home."

They all headed for the baggage area, and DeAnn fell into step with James and Harriet.

"Congratulations, you two."

Harriet sighed.

"Don't start, please."

DeAnn laughed.

"Sorry, I couldn't resist. I mean, you two are the last people I would expect to marry anyone, much less each other." She stopped when she realized they weren't laughing and looked from one to the other. "Oh," she said. "If I spoke out of turn. I'm sorry."

"Don't worry, I'm just tired," Harriet said. "We've been through a lot this week."

They walked on in silence. James slowed and when the rest of the group was in front of them, he slid his arm around her waist and after a quick glance to be sure no one was looking, he leaned in and kissed her gently on the lips.

"Don't worry, we'll get this figured out. We don't have to do anything today."

They walked on hip to hip, until they reached their baggage carousel. James was about to lean in for another kiss when a voice called out from the next carousel over.

A tall dark figure with silky shoulder-length black hair and ice-blue eyes stood staring at Harriet and James.

"Harriet?" Aiden Jalbert said, and glanced at the balloon bobbing over her head. "What's going on?"

END

About The Author

After working nearly 30 years in the high tech industry, where her writing consisted of performance reviews, process specs and a scintillating proprietary tome on electronics assembly, **ARLENE SACHITANO** wrote her first mystery novel, *Chip and Die*.

Quilt As Desired, the first mystery featuring long-arm quilter Harriet Truman and the Loose Threads quilting group was published in the fall of 2003 and was followed by eight more adventures; *Double Wedding Death* is the tenth in the highly-successful series.

When not writing, Arlene is on the board of directors of the Harriet Vane Chapter of Sisters in Crime as well as the Latimer Quilt and Textile Center in Tillamook. She teaches knitting at Latimer and, of course, is a quilter. She's been married to Jack for more than thirty years, and they split their time between Tillamook and Multnomah Village in Portland.

Arlene and Jack have three lovely children and three brilliant grandchildren. She also has two wonderful friends named Susan. She is aided in her writing endeavors by her canine companion Navarre.

About The Artist

APRIL MARTINEZ was born in the Philippines and raised in San Diego, California, daughter to a US Navy chef and a US postal worker. Dissatisfied that she couldn't make use of her creative tendencies, she started working as an imaging specialist for a big book and magazine publishing house in Irvine learned the trade of graphic design. From that point on, she worked as a graphic designer and webmaster while doing freelance art and illustration at night. April lives with her cat in Orange County, California.

There's no place like home...

Dassas Cormier returns to Marshall's Bayou in the spring of 1924 to find that his old friend Red Doucet has been murdered. Grace, the only woman Dass has ever loved, is also back in Marshall's Bayou, and she wants him to look for her missing husband. He's surprised when his search leads to another murder. Are the two murders linked? More important, is Grace involved?

Chapter 1

Marshall's Bayou, Louisiana
September 26, 1924

I never thought I'd look forward to returning to Marshall's Bayou. Nothing ever happened there. Even when the rest of the world was listening to jazz and racing around in motorcars, I knew I'd find everything at home just as it had been the day I left.

Leaning over the side of the boat, watching the black water slip by, that thought was somehow comforting. I was twenty-four with the bitter taste of duty fresh in my mouth—swearing I'd never return—when I left the marsh right at the end of the war. Burying two brothers has a way of making things bitter. Especially when I was the one who wanted to go, and I was the one left behind.

Yet, five years later, I returned home, not as Dassas Cormier, conquering hero, saver of damsels, civilization and decency. No. I returned as Dassas, failed cowboy, failed roughneck and, most recently, failed lawman. I rode the mail boat with my tail between my legs.

If there had been some way to return in the middle of the night I would have. But there wasn't. Determined not to look like a thief slinking in, I climbed up and balanced on the side of the boat as it approached the waiting group, then I hopped onto the ancient dock and tied the rope to the cleat as if I didn't have a care in the world. I even tipped my hat and flashed my best smile at Widow Clawson and her daughter, Celia.

I must admit, Celia had changed for the better. The last time I'd seen her, she had been a towheaded kid dragging a tattered doll by the hair. Now she was a blossoming young lady with curves a little too full to be stylish. She batted her eyelashes in response to my attention.

"Dassas Cormier, you dirty dog! Get your ass over here and let me look at you." The dock shook under Harley Herbert's weight as he marched toward me. Realizing he'd spoken a bit too loudly, he reddened and muttered an apology to the ladies for his language before grabbing my shoulder and hauling me into Theriot's.

Theriot's dance hall was dark and dusty, as if abandoned; but Buddy Theriot leaned on the bar, a rag draped over his substantial shoulder, and Isaac Broussard sat on a stool, smiling as usual. If not for a few gray hairs on the two of them, I would have sworn I had stepped back into an afternoon in 1918. The huge mirror behind the bar with the reclining woman etched into the center was still intact. It had always been considered a capital offense to break that mirror, no matter how serious the fight.

"My word, I can't believe it. The travelin' boy is back," Buddy said. "You too good to drink with us now?"

"Of course, he ain't," Harley answered. "Whiskey's on me."

"Whiskey?" I asked, glancing around. Theriot's wasn't as well-hidden as most speakeasies.

"Sure," Harley said. "Who's going to stop us? There ain't no law around here no more."

"What happened to Red?" I asked.

"Dead," Buddy said, shaking his head slowly. "Shot and left to die out in the marsh."

My stomach clenched at the news.

"When?"

"About two weeks ago."

"Who did it?"

"An escaped convict from Texas."

"They caught him?"

"No, but he robbed the bank in Orange four days before Red was killed." Buddy sighed. "Now we can't find a soul who's willing to wear the badge."

The thought of Red's death hit me hard. I had fond memories of the burly redhead who'd been the only law in Marshall's Bayou since before I was born. He'd helped me out of a scrape or two and even taken me under his wing when I was a kid.

"I don't suppose you'd be interested?" Buddy eyed me strangely.

"*Bien sûr,*" Isaac said. "You have the experience."

I shrugged. "I'll think about it."

My three drinking partners exchanged meaningful glances as Buddy filled a shot glass and placed it in front of me.

Now, I had no intention of ever wearing a badge in Marshall's Bayou. Or anywhere else, for that matter. But I was a firm believer in keeping all options open as long as possible. That was the only reason I didn't turn the offer down flat.

I raised my glass and downed the contents. Whatever it was they called whiskey was liquid fire in my throat. I cringed, trying not to gasp.

"What did you make this out of," I croaked, "sugar cane?"

Harley slapped my back, nearly sending me to the floor. "Hell, no! We keep the sugar cane gin for important guests. I call this the cow piss special. Nice color, no?"

His comment sent everyone into a fit of hysteria—they were a few shots ahead of me. It felt good to laugh with old friends.

I tried not to think about Red Doucet.

We talked about Isaac's family and Buddy's business. The group showed me the trapdoor behind the bar that would be used to dump the stash if the law ever appeared. I wasn't sure the trapdoor actually worked, but it was good in theory.

Several drinks later, my courage sufficiently boosted, I decided to start on the final leg of my journey. I was sent off with a round of cheers.

It was hard for me to remember the marsh with any fondness when I was away from it. I'd think about the long, hot nights with mosquitoes buzzing in my ears and the miserable, sticky days of cutting hay. Sweat glued the hay to my neck and arms, and every movement worked the dried stalks a little farther into my skin. It was wretched work.

So why, then, was it all so beautiful? Maybe it was the alcohol, I didn't know. Whatever it was, I felt like I was seeing the marsh for the first time.

The trail from the dock followed the bayou then turned east for a quarter-mile. A flock of red-winged blackbirds led the way, clinging to the taller blades of marsh grass while waiting for me to catch up. Heavy clouds had rolled in from the Gulf, sending waves of shade along the trail to cool the air; and the long, low call of a gator broke through the insect noise. The short grass was greener than emeralds, and the thick, salty air filled my lungs. By the time I stepped into the yard, I was smiling.

I stopped, dropped my bag to the ground and studied the house. What was different? The pecan and fig trees were a little bigger, and the paint was fresh, but there was something else. It took a few moments to realize it was the roses that made the picture perfect. Mama's roses, so long forgotten, bloomed again along the side of the house. It had to be Becky's touch.

"Daddy! Someone's here!" The voice belonged to my nephew, Frank. He had been a child when I left. I was stunned to find him a young man already.

I grabbed my bag and continued toward the house.

"Well, I'll be. Dass!" Becky hurried down the steps and threw her arms around my neck. She was the same slender woman I remembered—motherhood certainly hadn't ruined her figure or dampened her spirit. I'd always envied my brother.

"I can't believe Al didn't tell me you were coming." She held my arms and looked up at me.

"It's not his fault," I said. "He didn't know."

"Then why on earth didn't you write us? We'd have been at the dock to meet you."

"I didn't know I was coming myself until I started out. If you don't have room…"

"Don't be a goose," Becky said. "We always have room for you and you know it." She nodded to the young man who stood on the top step with his hands in his pockets. "Frank, come down here. You remember your Uncle Dassas."

Frank shook my hand and tried not to stare. He had his mother's black eyes, a head full of the Cormier brown curls and a firm handshake.

"It's good to see you, Frank," I said. "I won't mention how much you've grown since I saw you last."

"Yes, sir." Turning, he took my bag.

"And this," Becky said, pulling a smaller child out from behind Frank, "is your niece, Chloe. Say hello, Chloe."

"Hi." The child was a third the size of her brother, and a perfect replica of her mother. She had been born shortly after I'd left.

"Hi, there, Chloe." I touched her rosy cheek, and she smiled at me. Her smile warmed my heart.

"Any more?" I asked.

Becky grinned and grabbed my hand to lead me inside.

"Only one." In the front room, she lifted a toddler from the floor and handed him to me. "This is Fred."

The boy had hair as orange as any I'd ever seen. He grinned as he tried to pinch off my nose.

"Well, now, that's a sight and a half."

I turned to find Alcide standing in the doorway, fists on his hips. When I tried to shake his hand, my brother grabbed my shoulders and hugged me, careful not to flatten his son between us.

"It's sure good to see you," Alcide said. "Why in tarnation haven't you written?"

I felt bad enough for my lack of correspondence; there was no excuse. "Al…"

"Oh, what difference does it make now?" Becky asked. "I'll put the coffee on. You two sit at the table."

Alcide was the brother closest to me in age, and the only one left alive. He'd made it back from overseas without visible injuries, but there were scars, nonetheless. He moved slower than he had before the war, and there was a sadness in his eyes. He led the way to the dining room.

As soon as we were alone, Alcide leaned forward with his elbows on the table.

"Dass, are you in some kind of trouble?" When I frowned, he said, "It doesn't matter if you are. I just want you to know you can always stay here."

I shook my head. "Thanks, Al, but I'm not in trouble. At least, not the kind you're talking about."

"What, then?"

"It's nothing," I said. "Really. Just some things I have to sort out."

He nodded. "I'm here if you need me."

"Thanks."

Becky's coffee was even better than I remembered. We sat and talked well into the night.

The morning air the next day was thick and sweet.

"You know you don't have to do this." Becky handed me a bucket and held the bottom of the ladder.

I pinched and twisted the figs loose, careful not to tear the tender skin. Milk from the ends coated the gloves she'd insisted I wear. I'd forgotten how much figs used to make me itch.

"I know," I said.

She pointed to the fruit I couldn't see, and I picked it while a persistent fly circled my face. When we had one side of the tree stripped, I handed the bucket down and then followed it. We started anew on the opposite side.

"Dass."

"Yeah?"

"What's it like?"

I maneuvered around a large branch and glanced down at the woman. She leaned on the ladder and stared dreamily at the sky.

"What?" I asked.

"New Orleans. What's it like living in a big city like that?"

"Oh, it has its advantages, I suppose. The restaurants are open late, and there's always a show in town somewhere." I thought about Cherry, whose show drew men from all over the city, and smiled to myself. "But it has its disadvantages, too."

"Like what?"

I sighed and placed an unusually large fig gently in the bucket.

"When you get that many people together in one place, some of them are bound to be bad. There's just no way around it."

My comment was met with silence for a while.

"What happened, Dass?"

"Where?"

"In New Orleans. To you."

I steeled myself against the fresh wave of pain and continued to work.

"It's a long story, Becky. There must be something better to talk about on such a nice day."

"I suppose," she said.

"How are things going for you and Alcide?"

"Good. We lost some cattle to the drought last year, but it rained buckets this summer. I think we'll do well in the spring sale."

"And Al? How's he doing?"

"Better. He still never sleeps all the way through the night, but he doesn't have the nightmares like he used to. I guess it just takes time. I do wish he'd talk to me sometimes."

"I don't know," I said. "Maybe talking about it makes it kind of real again."

"Maybe."

There was no maybe about it. I knew it for a fact.

"Where are all the kids from school these days?" I asked. "Is anyone left in the marsh?"

"Well," she said, "DeeDee is still here. She and Antonio are on their fourth child. Will Strickler is working with his father. Their herd is the biggest down here. And of course, Grace married Billy White…"

Grace Trahan—the subject of every fantasy I'd had as a youth. Her golden eyes held wisdom far beyond her years, and her long, black curls fell seductively around her shoulders and breasts. To tell the truth, she'd never really left my dreams. I sure as hell couldn't imagine her married to Billy White.

"Dass?"

"Huh?"

"Anyone in particular you want to know about?" She looked at me with concern, kind enough not to mention my childhood crush on Grace. Becky was the only person alive who knew about it.

"Oh, no. Just curious."

"Well, I know Mae always had an interest in you."

"Me and every other guy in the parish."

Becky slapped my leg playfully as I started down the ladder.

"Oh, Dass, you shouldn't talk like that. Especially about Mae. After all, she married Daniel Griffin, the new Methodist minister."

I stepped to the ground.

"Wait, wait, wait. Are we talking about Mae Strickler?"

Becky nodded.

Mae had always been the wildest girl in the marsh. Good-hearted, but wild.

"What happened? Did she suddenly start believing in hell?"

"Dass! You're terrible."

I grabbed my heart. "You wound me to the core."

She grinned and shook her head.

I tried to imagine what my life would have been like if I hadn't left home. Would I have ever had the guts to tell Grace how I felt about her? Probably not. Maybe I would have married Mae and had a couple of kids. Or maybe I would have ended up a crazy old man who wandered the marsh and hunted gators. Whatever the case, my life would have been very different.

I never would've shot Dolores Minster.

A shiver ran up my spine.

"Dass? Are you all right?"

"You bet your boots, sis. Which tree you want to clean next?"

She studied my eyes a moment then pointed out the next over-laden tree. I closed the ladder and balanced the middle rung on my shoulder.

It wasn't until the second night descended that I finally relaxed.

"Here." Alcide pulled the cork from a fifth of whiskey and handed the bottle to me. "This isn't the junk they serve up at Theriot's."

"Becky doesn't mind if you sit around and drink with me?" I asked.

His whiskered face widened into a smile I could barely see in the moonlight.

"Becky's a good woman," he said. "She knows me better than I know myself." Love glittered in his voice like gold dust. "She said she's been saving this bottle for just such an occasion."

I took a sip and leaned back in the old wooden chair, recalling the day Alcide had told me he wanted to ask Becky to the spring dance. I actually did the asking. Alcide just stood there and shook like a leaf—a dumb leaf. When Becky said yes, I thought my brother would faint.

That night was the first time I saw Alcide drink. And he told me, in something of a drunken stupor, that he planned to marry Becky. I think I made some remark about him being a big, clumsy oaf, and that she'd just felt sorry for him. I was jealous as hell.

That night and the one before his wedding were the only times I saw Alcide drink before he left for France. He was the serious one of us—the rock, we used to call him. Becky was a lucky girl.

"What else does your wife say?" I took another swig and handed the bottle back.

"She thinks something bad happened to you."

"Damn, she's one smart cookie."

"That she is," he said, "but it doesn't take brains to see it, Dass. It's in your eyes."

Sitting on the dark porch with my only brother, I felt as safe as was humanly possible. Still, I knew that if I closed my eyes at that very moment, I'd see Dolores Minster's face. I'd hear the terrible noise I wanted so badly to forget.

"I shot a woman."

In the long moments of hesitation, my chest tightened.

Finally, he asked, "Was she a criminal or something?"

"No," I said. "It was a mistake. I killed a woman, Al. Just an innocent girl who happened to be in the wrong place at the wrong time. How in the hell am I supposed to live with that?"

"You just do," he said quietly.

I thought about the horrors my brother must have seen. But it was war —he was a soldier.

"It's not the same," I said, trying to bite back the anger.

"Death is death, Dassas. They were all innocent, all those men who died in those bloody damned trenches. They were all in the wrong place at the wrong time."

I looked over, surprised by the tears that ran down his cheeks. Staring at the moon through the screen, he handed me the bottle.

"You just do," he whispered.

I thought about Red. Even Marshall's Bayou was stained with death.

Later that night, I lay in my old room. The salty Gulf breeze eased across my bed and the songs of insects and reptiles filled the night. It wasn't until I closed my eyes that I saw the darkened doorway and felt the gun in my hand. I squeezed the trigger—just slightly—and waited for the thief to emerge. My body shook and I held my breath. My stomach tightened into a knot...

There was nothing to do but let the dream run its course again and hope to live through it. Morning would eventually arrive.

"The breakfast was wonderful."

Becky beamed a smile at me as I handed her a stack of dishes. Alcide carried drinking glasses to the counter.

"You help me?" Chloe stood at my feet, holding an oversized apron closed behind her back.

I knelt, turned her around and tied a bow.

"Thank you," she said, her eyes wide.

"You're welcome."

She reminded me of Coralee, my baby sister. I hadn't seen Cora since she'd moved to North Dakota with her husband. I have to admit—as much of a terror as Cora could be, I missed her a little.

Alcide grabbed my shoulder, and we walked together into the sunroom.

"Dass, I'm sorry I have to leave so soon after you got here. If this hayseed is as good as Phil Mayhew says, I don't want to miss out on it. I'll be back Sunday night at the latest."

"Don't worry about it," I said. "I'm not going anywhere right away."

"I find that hard to believe." He lowered his voice. "But I'm really glad you're here. I always hate leaving Becky and the children alone. Especially now, with the shooting and all."

"Don't worry, Al. Just think of me as their guardian angel."

"Angel, huh? I have a heard time thinking of you that way."

I grinned.

Al clapped my shoulder then grabbed the bag that waited by the door. The family followed him out to his saddled horse. I waited on the steps and watched him tie the bag behind his saddle, kiss his offspring and then kiss Becky and hug her. Feeling like an intruder, I looked away.

We waved as Alcide turned down the road. Only his head and shoulders were visible for a while above the marsh grass, and then even they disappeared. Becky wiped her eyes on her sleeve as she walked past me carrying Fred. She smiled through her tears.

"I always blubber like a baby when he leaves."

When was the last time someone had cried for me? Probably not since I left Mama standing on those same steps the first time I went to the oil fields. I felt like I was missing out on something important as we went back inside.

"Becky, you need anything from the store?" I asked.

"Yes, please," she said. "Will you see if Mr. Brandon got the soap I ordered?"

"Will do. Frank, you want to walk with me?"

The boy looked wistfully at his mother.

"I've got chores," he said.

Becky wiped her eyes again and smiled at us.

"If you promise to do them as soon as you get back, you may go."

I thought the boy's face might break, for all the effort he put into not grinning too much. His eyes gave him away.

"Yes, ma'am. I promise."

We walked side-by-side in silence for the first half of the trip. Frank's lanky frame promised a tall man someday, just like his father. Now he had the clumsy look of a man-child. I remembered the awkwardness well.

"Daddy said you were a policeman in New Orleans," he said.

"Yes, I was."

"Did you have a badge and everything?"

"Yes."

He shoved his hands in his back pockets as he walked.

"Did you ever catch any bank robbers?"

"No."

He frowned at the trail in front of us.

"I bet there's lots of pretty girls in New Orleans," he said, watching my reaction out of the corner of his eye.

"Yep. Lots."

"I'm going there," he said, "as soon as I turn sixteen."

"You're just going to leave your folks? Who's going to help your dad drive the cattle? Or your mom weed the garden?"

My questions elicited quiet contemplation. Finally, as we approached the dock, he shrugged.

"Maybe I'll just go for a visit."

"I think that sounds like a good idea."

"Uncle Dassas, will you take me to New Orleans?"

"We'll see, Frank."

That time, he did grin. I held his shoulder as we walked up the stairs to the dock.

The door to Theriot's was already open.

"You want a root beer?" I asked.

"Mama doesn't let me go in there," he said quietly.

"You've never been inside Theriot's?"

He shook his head.

"Well, how about we keep this our secret?"

The boy nodded then fell in behind me.

"Dassas!" Harley Herbert's voice shook the walls. "Dry already?"

"I guess I'm not the only one," I said.

Harley laughed and pulled out the stool next to his.

I motioned over my shoulder.

"Ya'll know my nephew?"

Buddy nodded, and Harley shook hands with the boy.

"Buddy, how about a root beer for Frank?" I asked.

"Comin' right up," Buddy said. "And you want the house special?"

"It's a little early, don't you think?"

Harley shook his head. "Never too early for the good stuff."

I cringed at the glass Buddy slid in front of me. Not that it really mattered—I wasn't on duty or anything. Taking a deep breath, I downed the golden fire. It hit my stomach like a brick.

Frank drank from his foamy glass, his eyes trained on us. I remembered the first time Papa bought me a root beer at the same bar. I was considerably younger than Frank.

"Another?" Buddy asked.

"No. No thanks."

Harley slapped my back.

"You been away from the marsh too long, son."

"I guess so." I shook my head. "Tell me, who found Red?"

"I did," Buddy said.

"Where?"

"Up in the piney woods, near Mrs. Richard's. After I found him, I came back here and got Harley."

"You both saw him?"

They nodded.

"How many times was he shot?" I asked.

"Twice," Harley said. "Once in the back and once in the chest."

"What was he shot with?"

Harley huffed as he frowned in thought.

"Well, it wasn't no shotgun. My guess is a pistol or a small caliber rifle."

"What caliber?"

"Hell, I don't know. You'd have to go to Cameron and ask the sheriff. He ain't tellin' us nothing."

I nodded. "So, what was Red doing out there?"

"Who knows? Maybe he was chasing the convict."

"Was he on horseback?"

"I don't think so," Buddy said. "His old buckskin was still stabled."

"Anything unusual about the place where you found him?"

Harley and Buddy both shrugged.

"He was just lying there on the ground," Harley said.

"On the trail?"

"No. He was off the trail a ways, up in the bushes."

"You know," Buddy said, "there was one thing, now that I think about it."

"What?"

"There wasn't a whole lot of blood around. Not for a man who bled to death."

Harley nodded. "That's true. I hadn't given it no thought, but you're right."

Strange. Maybe the blood had seeped into the ground. Or maybe Red's body had been moved.

But why would his body have been moved? Unless where he was killed was important. What if he hadn't been shot by an escaped convict? That would mean the murderer was still on the loose and safe because no one was searching for him.

I tried not to be enticed by the thought of a mystery, but I couldn't help myself. Besides, someone had to know for certain what happened to Red. The old man deserved at least that.

Looking up from the bar, I found Buddy, Harley and Frank staring at me.

"Are you done?" I asked Frank.

"Yes, sir."

I pulled several coins from my pocket and tossed them onto the bar with a nod.

"Don't forget where we are," Buddy said.

Harley chuckled.

I took a deep breath of the warm marsh air and strolled along the dock to Brandon's Mercantile, the only other official business establishment in Marshall's Bayou. Frank walked through the door I held open.

The place hadn't changed any more than Theriot's had. Shelves were filled with goods and hardware. I ran my fingers down the length of a cane fishing pole and then continued on to the pile of crab nets. A long day of fishing sounded just about perfect.

Frank waited behind the woman who stood at the counter, studying the box of buttons. I stopped beside him.

"Then, I guess I'll just take two of the black ones," the woman said to Mr. Brandon. There was something about her voice that grabbed my attention. I stared at the back of the blue skirt that was gathered tightly around a small waist. Her shoulders were broad but slender, and her black hair was pinned into a severe bun on the back of her head. The woman suddenly turned and caught me with her golden eyes.

My heart thumped hard.

"Well, Dassas Cormier," she said, "I didn't know you were back."
I bowed slightly as I worked to steady my voice.
"Grace," I finally said.
She was every bit as beautiful as I remembered.

Murder in Marshall's Bayou (A Dassas Cormier Mystery)
By S. H. Baker
Historical Mystery
Published by Zumaya Enigma
ISBN: Paperback: 978-1-934841-76-1;
978-1-93614-448-8 (Kindle); 978-1-61271-187-4
(EPUB)
**Trade paperback, perfect bound; $14.99; 224
pp.**
Available from Amazon, Barnes & Noble Online,
Books-a-Million, and from cooperating indepen-
dent booksellers.
Ebook
Available from Amazon Kindle, NOOK, and the
Zumaya Publications online bookstore.